A man, wearing a purple-striped single-strand neckring, sat at a desk. He looked up from his writing briefly and said to Detter, "You go ahead," gesturing to a set of ebony doors, then, holding up a palm to me, "You wait."

As Detter walked forward, the doors swung open. A similar set of tarnished brass doors was revealed just beyond, before the black doors closed behind him. I sat down to wait, feeling like a customer at an expensive fortune-teller.

A moment later, a terrible harsh scream reverberated through the room, and a thunderous boom sounded. I jumped to my feet. The mage continued to write, ignoring the commotion. The screaming and pounding continued for a long time, and then there was a hideous silence, followed by a slamming of doors.

I was shaking with shock and fear, but the mage just said, "All right. Go ahead." He didn't look up. So I stood and passed through the black doors. They closed behind me . . .

Books published by The Ballantine Publishing Group
are available at quantity discounts on bulk purchases
for premium, educational, fund-raising, and special
sales use. For details, please call 1-800-733-3000.

NAMELESS MAGERY

Delia Marshall Turner

A Del Rey® Book
THE BALLANTINE PUBLISHING GROUP • NEW YORK

A Del Rey® Book
Published by The Ballantine Publishing Group
Copyright © 1998 by Delia Marshall Turner

http://www.randomhouse.com

Library of Congress Catalog Card Number: 97-95363

ISBN 0-345-42430-1

Manufactured in the United States of America

First Edition: July 1998

10 9 8 7 6 5 4 3 2 1

CHAPTER ONE

In Which I Don't Eat a Rat

It was winter. I was half-starved and so wet my armpits were starting to mildew. My father's finger bone hanging on a thin metal chain was the only thing left of my life—all seventeen years of it, but that was forever to me then—and it seemed my future was going to end shortly in a dismal pile of my own bones.

I knelt down in the slush of half-frozen mud. Stretching as far as I could to avoid leaving a scent, I spread my awkwardly constructed snare next to the hole in the tree. I placed the tiny lump of rotting meat that I'd kept back from the last meal in the center of the snare. Paying out the trip-line, I backed up on my knees through the mud until I was out of sight behind a bush. I settled myself to wait. The bush was leafless and gave no shelter from the relentless rain, but I was already so wet and cold it made no difference. Sooner or later the ratlike thing that lived in the tree would let its hunger overcome its caution and come out, and I would have something to eat for today.

I tried to meditate, but I couldn't separate my mind from the slithery feeling of the wetness between my skin and the tattered old robe I wore. Meditation was meant to be sung aloud, on a sunny day, with friends and family singing with you, and food set out warm and smelling good at the worship table. My Voices, muttering in the caverns at the back of my mind, had no prophecies to give and were reduced to nonsense, mostly speculations on the spiritual significance of the number four.

My nose was running, the eye I had injured the week before

was beginning to water again, my feet were falling asleep, and the rain felt like it was getting colder, but I didn't move. Food was too hard to get in the cold season, and I was hungry. At least the Enforcers' casual blows had finally taught me what my Guardian couldn't, how to keep quiet when it was necessary. The Living God never had to be cold or hungry or even in pain, except at the end of the year. The rain fell, and I waited, watched, and listened to the hiss and crash of water on the tree branches.

Later, some time after I lost sensation in the fingers holding the trip-line, I heard a sound that was not caused by the winter rains. Something big was crashing up the hill from the stream, something with four feet, that didn't care about the underbrush. I snatched the snare back to me with a quick motion and rolled it up. There had been no large animals in the forest in the year I had been hiding there. Were there things that ate flesh here? It was very heavy, whatever it was. The ground thumped beneath me to the heavy steps. I peered through the stems of the bush, crouched and ready to run if my numbed limbs would let me.

When the source of the noise surged through the underbrush on the other side of the clearing, it was the last thing I expected to see on this god-lost planet: an ordinary big bay horse with a whiskered nose and furry fetlocks, and a tall man riding on it. He was wet and grouchy with a dripping nose and sodden leathers, not looking where he was going and not particularly caring. He could have been an ordinary traveler in any backcountry on Mennenkaltenei, except for the wispy streaks of blue flame I could see trailing from his head and questing about him.

I almost stood, almost ran to intercept his horse as it plodded wearily by, almost shouted to him to stop and help me. I didn't. I held my breath and stayed crouched behind the bush, watching him go and cursing myself. How many times had I promised myself that if anybody found me I would grab them by the knees and beg them to adopt me? I had thought I would even welcome Enforcers, endure their dead cruelty for the sake of food and warmth and human company, however hateful that company had been. But I couldn't do it.

When the horse had passed behind the nearer trees, and the sound of its steps receded toward the top of the hill and the narrow path there, I stood painfully and followed after. I had to know where he was going. I had seen no people since I'd sacrilegiously escaped the Enforcers, stranding myself on this strange world. I looked up at the top of the hill, and saw distant flickers of the man's cold flame disappearing into the darkening sky, and found myself hurrying. I moved as silently as I could, though. If he turned out to be an enemy, I could always fade back into the forest. The woods were not always against me, only in winter, and spring might come again.

The walking horse and its weary rider were unaware of me as I stole along, always a few trees behind in the gathering dusk. I watched him as closely as I could. The horse, if shaggy, was well fed, unlike most servants of the Enforcers. The man was not dressed like an Enforcer, either. He had obviously been traveling for some time; his leathers were well worn and cracked in places, and the boots on his long legs were creased and coming apart at the seams. Though he kept his head down to keep the rain out of his eyes, his shoulders were strong. He was neither a starving ascetic nor an overfed parasite. He did not treat the horse badly. He never struck her in the hours that followed, and though she must have been terribly tired and cold, she kept on willingly.

After a time I followed them only by the blue wisps of light, the fire that only a few spirit-born Mennenkalts could see. Lle fluttered and flicked about his face, veining and forking, looping and whirling, never still, always seeking, but he paid ller no mind. If lle was so attached to him, he could only be an Adept himself. Why, then, was he dressed so? My mind was not working very well by now, what with pain and tiredness and water running down my face. I'd forgotten the Adepts were all dead.

Puzzling woodenly over the problem he posed, I nearly ran

into the back end of the horse when she came to a halt at a fork in the path. With a gasp of fear, I took a step backward, but the rider wheeled the horse around at the sound and, startled, stared at me in the light of his spirit-fire.

In that moment, before I lurched away, I saw his face clearly. Then I bolted off the path, through the whiplash switchings of the wet bushes, hearing a tired baritone chuckle behind me. I kept running for a long time, longer than I needed to, until the pain in my chest and my hoarse breathing forced me to stop. For the rest of the long cold night, as I crouched inside a rotten stump far from the path, I saw behind my closed eyes the straight nose, the wide arrogant mouth, the high cheekbones, and the dark lock of hair falling slantwise across a high fore-head. It would have been an attractive face, the first face I'd seen in two years, if the amused and astonished eyes had not glowed a ghastly, cold, phosphorescent green. I'd seen the like only once before, in the face of a possessed woman being ritu-ally exorcised. Toward dawn, exhausted and half-hallucinating, I fell asleep in a crouching position, braced against the rotting wood.

There were no birds in this winter-shriveled forest to sing the approach of morning, and what insects there were didn't buzz or whine, but crawled about their business silently. The weak winter sun, rising high enough to glance through the top of the hollow trunk, finally woke me from my dismal and un-easy slumber. When I opened my eyes, I could see the sad true sunlight, but my spirit sight drowned it out with a sulfurous, pulsating glow. Gentle languid streamers of luminescent yel-low, as insubstantial as a rainbow, were slowly circling my shelter, interweaving llerselves in a lattice as though to capture me in a cage of light. More yellow ropes of glowing plasm, in-substantial but lazily purposeful, wound toward me across bushes and around trees like intoxicated snakes.

I scrambled over the top of the stump and dangled myself down to the ground, sliding cautiously between the circling shell of light and the skin of the dead tree. With my back to the stump, sucking at a splinter in the heel of my hand, I considered the opalescent blaze inches from my face.

It was the wrong color for Enforcer fire. The hard sad dead fire the Enforcers used was a metallic blue like reflections in steel. On the Enforcer ship, they hauled themselves through space with claws of glittering cold spirit fire, spreading death in endless fractal patterns, and it had always been blue. So this was familiar ller, not Enforcer fire. I knew how to deal with ller, though I'd preferred not to since my improper, irregular theft of the lifeboat.

Clasping the finger bone dangling from my neck, I closed my eyes briefly, aimed my will, made my desire clear, then opened my eyes and raised my hands, saying, "May I pass?" As I gestured, the lattice of light unwove itself politely and curled away from me. I stepped composedly through the opening. I jumped and ran like a rabbit, spoiling the effect, when a startled voice cried out from somewhere very near me. As I ran, I heard footsteps behind me and a deep, exasperated voice shouting in a language I didn't know.

My rotting soles picked that particular time to finally rip free of my shoes, and I was running painfully, prancing almost, and flapping my robes like a chicken with the effort of keeping my balance, when I slammed face first into a tree I'd thought I was avoiding. I wasn't sure who I was for a second, and when I finally figured that out, my head hurt, and somebody was tying my thumbs together behind my back while I had my nose ground firmly into the tree. As soon as my thumbs were tied, my captor said something incomprehensible in an admirable voice, put his hands on my shoulders, swung me around, and firmly propelled me back the way we'd come. As I staggered ahead of him, guided by brisk but not unkind shoves, I reflected that there was nothing like complete calamity to take one's mind off the daily grind of starving to death in an inadequately rat-infested wilderness.

We came back to the trail, where the shaggy bay horse was calmly scratching her massive side against a young tree. My abductor, when I finally got a look at him, turned out to be the unexpected wraith of the night before, though his eyes were no longer glowing chartreuse. Now they were an ordinary gray. He seemed exhausted, dirty, irritated, and surprisingly normal. He confirmed that impression by flopping down on the ground with a heartfelt groan. I followed suit, my hands still bound, and we examined each other with suspicion.

Finally, he said something to me with an inquiring lilt, and when I didn't answer, he sighed and dug through his pockets, unearthing some solid and greasy bread, which he broke in half and shared with me. It was probably the best meal I'd ever had, hard and chewy and stale as it was, shoved in my mouth piece by piece with his grimy fingers. It had been a long time since I'd had bread of any kind.

Once we were fed, he bundled me unceremoniously onto the back of the horse, swung up in front of me, and continued his interrupted journey southeast on the half-cleared trail. It was a clear pale day in the last dregs of winter. The dead leaves on the forest floor were shabby gray, the hardy scaled beetles had shredded the weedy undergrowth that hung on from last fall, and the endless trees were purple, stark, and sad. But the sun, though pale, filtered through to the ground in delicate patterns, the horse's rolling motion was soothing, and the man's back before me was stolid and warm. Eventually, in spite of the burning in my bound arms, I fell asleep with my cheek between his shoulder blades.

I awoke with a jerk at noonday to find him sliding nimbly off the horse. He hoisted me down, untied my thumbs, spoke to me briefly in his incomprehensible language, and walked aside to relieve himself matter-of-factly against a tree. I stood there in my filthy and tattered robes, with my bony feet, absurdly adorned by the remnants of my shoes sticking gracelessly out at the bottom. My chopped-off hair was matted and greasy, and I felt a ridiculous pang of injured vanity. Even though I was supposed to be above such things, I'd always enjoyed young men's appreciation, but this creature obviously didn't even realize that I was female.

Actually, I hadn't had much occasion lately to think about my gender either, but in spite of the road dirt and worn leather clothing, he was a very attractive man, well put together and supple with enough heft on his bones to give a woman something to hold on to. I would have crooked my finger at him any day on Mennenkaltenei, and maybe even tumbled him if I was somebody else. He turned, lacing up his flies, saw me watching him like a skinny dog at a duck roast, and grinned one-sidedly, motioning me to sit down and relax. I had no more doubts now. Whatever this weary wayfarer might be, he was no Enforcer slug.

I learned over a dry noon meal that my abductor's name was Simon; I am, though I didn't tell him then, called Lisane, meaning "Nameless." It's more of a title than a name, but it's not an appropriate title anymore, since I vacated the office it describes. On Mennenkaltenei, if I was named at all, I was called Kaltenhelsterdeimennet, meaning roughly "did a pretty good job of picking her parents." The Enforcers never knew me by any name, but the mages nowadays call me the "damnable foreign witch," which should give an idea of how few real foreigners showed up before on this planet.

Over the next few days, I kept my mouth shut and never understood a word Simon said. He didn't tie me after the first day, seeming confident that I wouldn't try to get away.

Did he have more up his sleeve than the luminous, yellow, spirit-fire net and the eerie glowing green eyes? If not, he had no reason for confidence. I was more capable than most of playing that kind of trickery, though it was rankest heresy. I wasn't supposed to handle ller that way, but I was less rigid about matters of religion than I'd once been.

Simon showed he was, like me, a pragmatic practitioner of elemental manipulation when the first night of our joint travel he summoned some tendrils of air spirit with a spoken word and a flick of his finger to start a campfire. It seemed presumptuous to harness spiritual energy to cook dinner, but a lot more practical and not nearly as heretical as the Enforcers' way of killing ller to ram their warships through the universe.

I'd always known that lle was good for other things than worship service, anyway. When I'd been a cheeky ten-year-old on Mennenkaltenei, confident that no one would dare scold the Unnamed whelp of the Year-King, I'd called up some elemental energy on my own and found a way to put it to a more prosaic use than the usual ecstatic communal ritual. Before my sister's mother discovered me and, to my injured surprise, whacked me in the head for my perverse materialism, I had managed to conjure disembodied arms to steal fruit pies from the local harvest-wife.

Those elongated arms had shone eerily, just as Simon's conjurations, only half-visible to me as if shining with something other than light. My sister's mother couldn't see them at all, but she could see the pies floating, so she smacked me again and took me to my tutor, Jenneservet, for extra training. Jenneservet got the petty vandalism out of my system fast, but I tucked away the information that elemental energy was good for more mundane purposes than the glory of the spirit. It had come in handy when I'd escaped the Enforcer, though I still felt guilty about that.

Now I was glad of the fire at night, however it was started, and of the fat tree-rats and swamp-swimmers he caught and cooked over his fires during the next few evenings. I would sit picking the last shreds of meat off fragile bones in the warmth of the campfire, and he would sit with his long arms around his knees, contemplating me seriously. He was growing more and more puzzled by me. He'd obviously made some kind of assumption originally about who I was and where I'd come from, because he'd been more amused than dismayed by my sudden appearance in the middle of wilderness where there had been no other human for over a year. I'd given him pause when I broke free of his yellow spirit-net so swiftly, but he didn't stop to marvel at my skill, just took advantage of my clumsiness, whomped me, and cheerfully dragged me along on his trip.

Now, though, something was beginning to itch at him. For one thing, I wouldn't talk to him, and I obviously didn't take in a word he said. He tried all kinds of conversation on me, from lectures to questions, to creeping up on me and yelling, but nothing he did got through. Well, it did get through in one way; he had a lovely deep voice with an agreeable huskiness to it, and if he'd offered me barley sugar with that voice, I would have sat on his knee, or any other part of his body, immediately. He didn't offer, though, not that I could tell.

For another thing, I was dressed funny and I acted funny. He couldn't place the once orange draperies that were my legacy from the Enforcer lifeboat, and he couldn't fathom why, every break I got, I wandered off into the underbrush and squatted down with my robe spread out around me, staring into space. He was beginning to act as if he thought I had severe brain damage, and for myself I was beginning to wonder if this delectable creature had ever watched any woman pee, including his mother, from a distance of closer than a mile.

The only thing that kept me from opening my mouth and shattering his illusions was that I didn't know where he was taking me, and I didn't know if I was going to like his friends nearly as much as I did him. It went against my grain to mistrust him. On Mennenkaltenei, we welcomed strangers as much as friends. But when the Enforcers came along, and we welcomed them as amiably as any other tourist group, they disemboweled us. They killed the Year-King before the spring had even started, they incinerated my Mother, they murdered my sisters, they slew the Year-King's postulants, and they killed any Elders and Adepts they could identify. They would have killed me too if they'd known what I was, future llerKalten, earth's blood, and Mother's mouth to the whole planet. Jenneservet told me to lie to them when they came, but I never lie. I just didn't say anything. They shoved my tutor and me in with the rest of the hostages they took until that greasy dolt took a liking to me.

So now I sat enigmatically by the fire, keeping my counsel and picking my teeth while Simon puzzled away at the conundrum I posed. By day I rode behind him on the tree-legged horse, trying not to press my chest too firmly against Simon's back, although at my age and weight my feminine attributes there weren't too evident, and enjoyed the ride. Then one day we emerged from the forest to find ourselves at the foot of a steep precipice topped by an appalling erection of masonry and rock, as huge as a minor mountain, riddled with windows and bedizened with architectural embellishments like a hat with fruit.

Simon dropped the reins, raised his cupped hands, and shouted something up at the top of the cliff. From above, a disembodied voice intoned a substantial and sonorous incantation. Thick cords of half-visible spirit plasma writhed down to wrap around and beneath us. The horse, the man, and I began to float grandly up the cliff face. It was certainly an elevating spiritual experience, but I couldn't help thinking, as we rose amidst evanescent fields of force, that it was missing some kind of point to harness fire elements for a job that could be done just as well and more permanently with stout rope and some lumber. Or even, in a pinch, with some of those little tools it wasn't polite to use.

It was the most appalling building I'd ever seen, and it kept getting uglier the closer I got. Warty towers stuck up everywhere, balconies sprouted on blind walls, gargoyles belched rudely under and over and behind every arbitrary outgrowth of builder's whimsy, and none of the hundreds of windows were the same shape. Fat brown birds fluttered and squawked on the highest ledges, dropping the occasional bomb on the vast array of shabby laundry that draped various windowsills. I don't like big buildings on principle. They just put a lot of people in one big box and make them useless. You have to haul food in to feed them, pipe the sewage out, hire middlemen to deal with the rest of the world. Before you know it, you have to have money and accounting and bureaucracy, and you don't know what's real anymore. The only thing a big building is good for is a temple or a jail, in both cases because it keeps trouble-makers out of circulation. It turned out that this pile of building was both of those things, as well as an exclusive boys' school and one of the seats of planetary government.

Once we reached the top of the cliff, Simon sketched a salute to the stolid individual who'd apparently brought us up, and led the horse and me through a dismal dripping archway leading to a courtyard and stables. The horse stalls, at least, were well kept. Simon shouted out, and a wary teenage boy trot-ted out to take the horse. Without looking back at me, Simon headed briskly for a broad stair. I swung hastily off the horse and trotted after him, clutching my disintegrating robes. The seams were almost completely gone by now.

Simon was looking for somebody. He stopped and ques-tioned a heavy-browed boy of eight or so, who pointed, gave him brief directions, and shot me a poisonous look after Simon passed him. I smirked back. He spat venomously at my feet. I stuck closer to Simon after that.

After several more inquiries from equally surly male people under the age of seventeen, Simon finally tracked down his quarry, a gray-haired, broad-chested man in scarlet knee pants, who had cornered two twelve-year-olds at the end of a corridor and was cursing them with his hands on his hips. I wished I spoke the language, because he sounded brilliant, never re-peating himself once. His words leapt out like hammer blows, sharp and bright and perfectly placed. The two boys were backed up against the wall, still and expressionless, until he finished in a blaze of vituperation and turned his back on them. Then they split up and dashed past him on either side, yam-mering unrepentantly.

The gray-haired man ignored them, looking astonished and pleased to see Simon. They embraced each other and spoke for a moment, and then Simon turned and gestured me forward, gripping my shoulder sharply as I came to stand beside him. The man examined me with puzzled protruding blue eyes, and shook his head "no" to Simon. I wasn't sure what was happening, but from their expressions, they weren't sure either. Simon began to argue, the gray-headed one kept shaking his head, and finally Simon hauled me around to face him. He demanded something in a pleading tone, and since he was turning out to be a lot nicer than anybody else I'd seen so far, I nearly talked to him.

Before I could open my mouth, he blew his breath out in exasperation, stepped back from me, pointed at me, and shouted something dire. A hideous pink not-really-there blast of spirit-fire streamed slowly from his fingertip toward me. I wasn't about to hang around and find out if lle smelled as bad as lle looked, so I dropped and rolled under the stream, losing the rest of the rags of my robe in the process. The elongated blob of fire flowed around in a curve, following me. I panicked, rose to my knees, pointed my own finger at it, and yelled, "Aspect of ller! Lose this form and go back to where you came from!"

Now, that was an unpardonable contraction of a simple but elegant exorcism ritual I'd learned as a child, and in its extended form it was designed to reduce a curse to infinitely small particles of ectoplasm and send ller spiraling back in a flaming cloud to purify the soul of the misguided one who'd set the spell in the first place. The Adept who had taught it to me would have slapped me silly and made me perform it all over again if I'd tried to cut corners like that on Mennenkaltenei. Sloppy as it was, it worked, though not the way it was usually supposed to. The pink plasma snapped into a nervous glob, quivered in the air, and rushed back into Simon's fingertip. He jumped as if he'd been bitten, and snapped out something that made the glob disappear before it ate his finger.

Then the two of them just stood there gawking at me like cornered rabbits at a weasel. I looked down and realized I'd blown my cover in every possible way, down to and including my so-called clothes. I sat back on my naked scrawny haunches, laced my hands demurely in my lap, smiled at them innocently, and said, "Well, boys, great party so far. You want to dance now or shall we get something to eat?" When I spoke, they flinched. I'm lucky they didn't understand Wirdenish, because it turned out later their idea of a party with girls resembled my idea of guerrilla warfare. Of course, my idea of guerrilla warfare hadn't worked very well against the Enforcers. Sarcasm and sullenness have their limits as weapons when the opposition has flamethrowers and disruptors.

Simon, particularly, was staring at me in complete horror. I was certainly not in the best shape to be flaunting my body, a diet of roots and rats and very little of both having made me bumpy where I should have been bouncy, but I didn't think that called for such an appalled look.

The gray-haired man turned to Simon. Simon wrenched his gaze from my anatomy, and they conferred worriedly. With nothing else to occupy my attention, I noticed that Simon's friend wore a necklace made of two cords wrapped in a spiral, one black like his shirt and one the same cherry red as his knickers. Where he showed skin, it was thatched with thick gray hair, so the costume jewelry had a jarringly juvenile effect. Simon wore a coffee-brown choker that matched his leather and homespun just as neatly. His was less affected-looking, though.

They came to some decision and I found myself being rushed down the hall between them, Simon snatching the rags of my robe up from the floor and flinging them over my shoulders. I was getting hungry, and I hoped there was some food where we were going.

Up stairs and down ramps, around curving corridors and through connecting rooms, we scurried past the occasional slovenly boy, until we arrived at a set of ornately carved wooden doors. Gray-hair gabbled an incantation, the doors swung open of themselves, and we entered a dim, cool library. At the other end, a dark man, perhaps fifty years old, sat casually on a low stool reading a leather-bound book. He paid no attention to us, though we stood before him panting and fidgeting, until he finished the page he was reading.

Then he closed the book, sliding a silken marker neatly into it. He leaned gracefully and placed it where it belonged on the shelf. His square hands were strong, sure, and swift. Though he was tonsured, his neatly turned skull made me wonder why other men bothered having hair. He wore a neckring like the other two, though his had three cords that were black on black on black. The plain shirt and loose trousers on his pared-down body were black as wet winter trees at home. Then he looked up, looked at me, and all I could see were his black, glittering, fathomless eyes. He was a well of power, dark, deep, utterly controlled but with wildness in the depths.

He held me transfixed like that for a long moment. Then Simon at my side jerked my tattered covering away again. The dark man raised his eyebrows, turned up the corners of his generous mouth, and surveyed my naked body minutely, with amusement, before turning to Simon to ask him a question. Even his voice was black and smooth as funeral velvet. It made all my exposed skin tingle.

He listened at length to the explanations of my two companions, then sat gravely thinking, his knuckle to his lips. We were silent, waiting. The room creaked occasionally with footsteps from beyond the walls, and a breeze scurried in and scurried out. Then he dropped his fist, extended the fingers of his hand to me, and spoke one word. I heard only the beginning of the word, and then the room, all the books, the air, the sky outside, and the earth itself drowned him out, roaring, "Understand . . ." and I understood.

For at least a minute I had a working knowledge of the secret of the universe, of which I only remember that it was hilarious. Then enlightenment fled, but I had voices in my head, talking very fast and with great detail, even more insistent than my own Voices. I put my hands to my temples and bent over in pain.

Dimly, below the shrill gabble in my brain, I heard him saying, "No, she's real enough, even if she is female; and she's very strong, or what I just did would have killed her. I'm afraid she'll be quite vivid when she's healthy. Look at those green eyes and the black hair, and I believe the skin would be particularly fine if it wasn't so grubby." He hesitated. "No, there's no help for it, and she's strong enough to defend herself. Put her with the older students. If she survives for a year, Council will figure out what to do with her then. She's your responsibility, boy," he added to Simon. "You will have to teach her as well as teaching the student you've already been assigned. I don't want to see her; I don't even want to hear about her again until Council judges her." He turned away from us, looking out the window as if we no longer existed.

Simon and the gray-head said, "Sir," gravely and in unison, and led me, still naked and doubled over, my head spinning, out of the room. Simon paused outside the door to fling those wretched rags over me again, and I looked dizzily under my arm to find the man in black looking back at me past the slowly closing door. That was how I first met Kaihan, King and Wizard, Eldest and Master.

CHAPTER TWO

In Which I Don't Learn the Rules

It seems odd to me now that I didn't realize I now spoke their language. I understood everything Simon and his friend said as they steered me to the senior Student rooms, but I was so confused and sick with migraine, and the new tongue was so much part of me now, that I couldn't take it in until I lay tucked into a small bed in a narrow cold room. All I remember of their talk was that Simon was upset and aggrieved, his friend thought the dark man senile, and they argued over whether I could possibly be attractive. It didn't help that the mages don't have any word for their own language—either you can talk or you can't talk, as far as they're concerned. So now I could "talk," and it seemed as if Wirdenish was an imaginary language. My head was soggy as a swamp inside my skull and alive with chittering creatures. My Voices were sulking.

How much of thought came from words! "Lle," for instance. Everything I called "ller" was "magic" to these people. Have you any idea how blind, malicious, and dangerous the universe looks when everything is caused by a thing called magic? No wonder they summoned the spirit to do their mechanical work, and lit campfires with elemental plasm. It was all self-defense, mastery of the wilderness, putting things in order. Very admirable, really. At the same time, in another language, it was blind materialistic pigheaded atheism.

I lay, sick, tired, and limp, wishing I could sleep. Every stray thought I had ran bang into incongruity and split into fountains of jarring contradiction. "Sick and tired," for instance, sounded like "defenseless and defeated." I couldn't find any words in my new language that would make it sound all right to relax. Everything had hard edges and ominous overtones. "Sleep" defined in my new language had more in common with a dangerous ship voyage than a safe haven.

The tiny white-plastered room had a very high ceiling. Near the top was an open stone-framed window shaped like an arrowhead. Late winter afternoon sun cast an arrow-shape of light crazily across the wall and ceiling. A dim blotch of shadow fluttered into the sunny shape, and I saw that one of the plump brown birds had come to perch on the sill. It preened each wing feather carefully, extending and resettling its pinions with a shake as it worked. Finally, it shifted its claws, puffed its chest out with a wriggle, and dove its brown-eyed ball of a head beneath a wing, matter-of-factly and with finality. I followed its example by curling into a ball and hiding my head beneath the thin coverlet, carefully not thinking in words, just holding the picture of the sleeping bird in my mind.

When I opened my eyes, the patch of sun and the bird were gone, and the sky was a pale cold rose color. The coverlet was wound about me and the room was morning chilled. I was so hungry I felt as if my guts had been scooped out and thrown away, but the inside of my head was quiet now. A dark blue cotton shirt and drawstring pants were flung over the end of the bed. They were baggy but long enough. I would have to gain some weight before they looked like anything but a couple of sacks on a pole. Clothed but barefooted on the cold floor, I tried the door and peered out cautiously. It opened onto a big common room full of shabby leather divans and armchairs, low heavy tables, and half-empty bookshelves, with closed doors spaced along the walls. No people, though. It must have been just after dawn.

I padded out, closing the door silently behind me and marking its location. Closer up, the furniture was furred with dust in its corners and the wood was interlaced with roughly carved names and crude pictures. A blooming purple iris grew from the leather back of one of the chairs, its leaves pinched and torn, and from the center of a table sprouted a fist making a rude gesture. Someone had wound a wilted sprig of parsley around the upthrust finger, giving it a festive air. The scattered books on the shelves were torn and beaten up. I took one down. It fell open to a dryly illustrated technical discussion dealing with extracting groundwater from arid ground by supernatural means. Several hands had scribbled irrelevant messages in the margin. I shut it back up and laid it on the dusty shelf. From the combination of dust, vandalism, and disorder around me, it seemed I was in some kind of boarding school. The students must be sleeping behind the doors that surrounded me.

I could smell porridge cooking somewhere in the distance past the archway at the end of the common room. The hollow space inside me expanded further, and I stole out with my nose lifted, searching.

The kitchen, when I found it, was a vast cavern designed to feed an army. Only a corner of it was in use, by a puffy-eyed gaggle of juvenile cooks, supervised by a lanky young man with a purple necklace, arms folded, who looked profoundly bored and remarkably dissipated. When he saw me, he looked even more so, and flapped a languid hand at a line of carts, each loaded with a vat of gray porridge, chipped earthenware bowls, and wooden spoons. I took a cart and trundled it out as if I knew what I was doing. It shook and swayed and rumbled, and my stomach rumbled louder, so after I was out of earshot I stopped, served myself a bowl, and gulped that and a second one down scalding hot.

It was lucky I did, because as newest student in the senior hall I would have had to fight for my food. The moment I shoved the cart back into the common room, doors flung open with a series of crashes and a horde of half-clothed young men raced out, elbowing each other to get at the food. I stood by the door watching them warily, and they paid me no mind until each was firmly settled in a chair with his precious breakfast. One long-nosed lad was left forlornly scraping and licking the vat.

Then a grizzled veteran of perhaps seventeen, sporting a precocious and inadequate beard, looked up from his next-to-last spoonful and spotted me.

"Ho! New boy!" he shouted. The others watched me sidewise and continued to eat. I didn't correct him, and he repeated, "New boy! I'm talking to you. Get your hindquarters over here." I decided not to. He slammed his bowl down, stood up, and shouted, "*Now,* pie-faced mongrel!" Little sparks began to pop into existence around his head, so I guessed what was going to come next. I shook my head at him gently, bending my knees so I'd be ready to jump or roll if he threw some mechanistic conjuration at me. It seemed to be a habit with these people.

His eyes watered with anticipation. The whole room was watching us openly now, grinning with malice. Sure enough, he clapped his graceless hands together, and when he drew them apart there was an orange-sized glimmer of spirit wavering between them, which slowly flowed through the air at me like a frog swimming upstream. It was the silliest thing I'd seen in a while. I straightened my legs back up, put my hands on my hips, and addressed the floating spell directly. "Lle zhattern begtevogen hals bekmelter," I said. How odd. Wirdenish as a second language. The spell stopped in midair and flattened slowly as if it had hit a wall. "Kop mesmikken rhee ver, loselt," I said firmly. Lle snapped gladly into a pea-sized ball, zoomed back to the bearded boy, and the next thing the unlovely worm knew, the hairs were pulling themselves out of his chin one by one. It was handy I could still speak Wirdenish, because the language of my new home didn't have the proper declension for speaking to ller fire directly—the practitioners call ller "it" or sometimes "you," but lle doesn't listen real hard to that. I don't blame ller.

There was dead silence in the room, except for the strangled grunts from the one being unbearded. The grins had melted away. I looked around. There were fifteen closemouthed, hard-eyed, half-naked juvenile criminal types staring at me. I figured if I ran for it they could bring me down easily, so the only hope for it was to show no fear. I walked, as calmly as I could, through them toward my room. I had to pass particularly close to one blond blue-eyed angel with a sculpted pink-nippled chest who lay across his armchair with his eyes narrowed thoughtfully. The rosy tip of his tongue showed between his rounded lips, his delectable hand caressed his smooth belly, and he looked capable of any number of disgusting things. As I passed by him, he said languidly, "You have an odd voice, child, though you're pretty enough. Are you younger than you look, or are you by some unfortunate accident missing something between your legs?"

I looked at him, puzzled for a moment, and then realized he also thought me a boy, and was trying to be insulting. I'd never met so many males over the age of three who couldn't tell a woman when they saw her. I wasn't that skinny. "You are all sadly lacking in experience," I said to the room in general. I walked haughtily past him, went into my room, shut the door, and climbed back into bed. I could still feel the weight of that sinister angel's gaze between my shoulder blades, but two bowls of breakfast went a long way toward easing the burden.

At mid-morning Simon slammed the door open, yanked me out of bed, and hustled me off. It turned out that I had to go to lessons every day, as did all the rest of the half-baked monsters who called themselves students, and Simon was my teacher. He wasn't anywhere near as nice when he was playing teacher. He could also turn a better spell than I'd thought, as I learned after he stuck me to the ceiling for an hour for arguing with him. I usually spent the mornings with him, and every afternoon I had to work like the rest, in my case digging up the fields that lay beyond the monstrous conglomeration of towers. The building, I found, stood not on the edge of a cliff but on a towering mesa that stood in complete geologic impossibility in the center of the rolling forest.

Except for the field foreman, who only spoke when I made a mistake, nobody besides Simon talked to me much. Simon was busy catching me up on the basics I'd missed by showing up at school ten years over-age. The pimply noodlebrains who grudgingly shared the senior student hall with me had come to the school as young children, though most not as young as I was when I had my name taken away, and had spent the intervening years mastering magic. I didn't think it had done them much good, but I tried to keep my opinion to myself. That's something I'm not very good at.

According to Simon, the practice of magic followed complicated rules, which had to be followed rigidly, and which he vainly tried to teach me. There was a graded scale of difficulty in spells, ranging from simple illusion, which any student could master, to the creation of new self-reproducing life, which was barely possible but explicitly forbidden. He was disappointed to find that I couldn't do illusions at all, because I couldn't see them as illusions. They just looked like oddly shaped balls of spirit-fire to me. I'd always been able to see the spiritual elements, being godling born and bred. Most Mennenkalts have to work blind, by feel, smell, hearing, or guesswork. Simon would create some glamorous apparition or another, and I would stare at it blankly and guess until he dissolved it in disgust. I said, "All I can see is magic."

He couldn't believe for a long time that I saw it. Finally, suspiciously, he said, "What does it look like?"

I said, "Well, when I first saw you, you had snakes of blue fire flicking around your head. And your eyes glowed green, too. It's why I ran away from you."

He was puzzled for a while, and then he remembered. "I was using a locator spell because I didn't want to get lost, and a spell for night-sight because it was getting dark. No wonder you looked so terrified. I thought at first it was because you were a student on your ring-Quest who had been abandoned by your guide, and you were frightened because you thought you'd be punished. Then, when you wouldn't speak, I thought you might be a renegade mage." He considered, looking troubled. "Perhaps you are one. No, if Master Kaihan didn't bring it up . . ."

"What's a renegade?"

"It's probably better not to discuss it." And that was that.

As for the so-called forbidden task of making living creatures, both physical and spiritual, I had done that myself many times before, both alone and with worship groups. All you had to do was explain what you wanted clearly enough, and lle was happy to please, though you had to be willing to live with the results and maintain the proper reverence.

Simon didn't like it when I tried to explain my attitude toward what he called magic and I called ller. It made him nervous and edgy. When he glued me to the ceiling, it was because I told him I wasn't going to act like some solemn technician. I said, "Magic likes you to enjoy yourself and be creative. Where's the fun in following procedures and rules?"

He said, "That's a good way to get yourself or somebody else killed. Magic is very dangerous." I hated it when he talked like that, as if he were the Year-King and I were some farmgirl caught praying to the crops all alone.

"Yes, I'll bet it's dangerous, the way you manipulative bugsuckers treat it. I'd be dangerous, too, if someone tried to shove me around like a machine all the time."

"Stop trying to make magic human. It's not human. It's pure energy, and it can fry you."

"It surely isn't human, you've got that right. But it's not just energy. It's . . . you don't have the word. Listen, it's important to respect magic, but you have to love it too, because it deserves that from you." In retrospect, I suppose I sounded like an Adept dressing down a shamefaced smith. He didn't like that tone of voice any better from me than I liked it from him.

He snapped, "Woman, your so-called mind is an emotional morass. You'll have to learn to fear and mistrust magic, or it will eat you alive. Let me give you a mild demonstration."

I found myself bobbing up to the ceiling, my gravity reversed. I lay looking up at him, or maybe he was hanging by his feet from the floor. He continued, "Think about this until I decide to let you down. Every last student is here because the first thing he did when his Power awoke was hurt somebody. Uncontrolled magic can cause terrible damage, and the whole purpose of our brotherhood is to control magic and keep it out of the grasp of individuals. I won't even go into what a fully developed renegade mage can do when there are so many examples close to hand. There are boys in your own hall who have killed their whole families with magic. One destroyed an entire village of people when he was only five." He turned on his heel grandly and left the room, presumably leaving me to meditate on my foolishness. I rearranged the magic so I hung more comfortably, and settled myself for a short nap.

So these miserable children had all awakened to uncontrolled Power, and had hurt someone with it. Little ones have tempers, just like grown-ups, but they don't know how to handle getting angry. It went a long way toward explaining why every child in this bollixed barn of a building looked hostile or hunted. Why had nobody stopped them before they hurt someone? It's easy enough, if adult Adepts are in the community, to pick out which babies have Power and train them properly.

I had an idea which lad had blitzed a village. The blue-eyed blond creature was very dangerous. He had no scruples, and he knew when force was the wrong approach and when it was the right one. The other boys in the hall where I lived feared him and avoided him.

They feared and avoided me as well, especially when they realized I was female. It seemed I was impossible. They didn't believe women could have Power. In my turn, I didn't believe it was possible, what with the elementary rules of genetics I wasn't supposed to know, that males could be born with Power and females without it. Whether or not they believed in me, they left me alone during the day, but at night they practiced every nasty trick they knew and a few they weren't sure of yet. Every night before I went to bed I checked my room and set a ward spell on the door, and every morning I defused an assortment of trivial and painful traps they'd set. They only got me once, though, and it wasn't with sorcery. Fat Ommo and Benoit, the newly beardless one, balanced a bucket of water on the ledge over my door, tied with a rope to the knob, and when I came out it poured all over me. I shrieked loudly and then laughed myself silly, sitting on the floor with the bucket in my lap and water everywhere. The whole lot of them were confused and offended by my laughter, which was a shame. The direct simplicity of the trick was so refreshing after the torturous manipulations of their earlier efforts, I almost liked the boys then.

The blue-eyed boy always sat watching, expressionless, his elegant legs flung over the arm of his chair, cleaning his nails with a slim knife. He was prettier than a male animal should be, with rose-petal cheeks, long blond lashes, and wheels always turning inside his sleek head.

The end of the first week, Blue-eyes walked right up to me and introduced himself. Everybody by then knew I was a woman. "Mistress Green-eyes," he said, "allow me to introduce myself. My name is Deteras Anhand, and I must apologize for speaking so boorishly before." He held out his hand, and pearly teeth glinted graciously. He reminded me of my sister's uncle Willemheed, who was all please-and-thank-you until, whoops, he had his fist up your ass.

I ignored the hand and said shortly, "Deteras Anhand, I am Lisane." I felt like a bumptious rube next to this glossy creature.

"Call me Detter, sweetness," he said gently, bringing his hand closer. I swayed away from it and barely avoided being hit with a poisonous lump of spell that had been behind his fingers. It had scarlet tentacles and a mouth, and if I hadn't ducked behind the hapless long-nosed youth it would have gotten me. Long-nose, whose name was Peselin, got all glassy-eyed when it hit him, and tried to embrace Detter intimately.

Detter had to fend him off while canceling the spell, and I sat on top of a chair and chuckled.

Detter gave me a mature and reproving look, and sauntered serenely to the other end of the common room. A war had begun, and I knew my enemy.

The other boys only wanted to humiliate and hurt me, partly because it was what they did to each other and partly for my offense of being female and stronger than they. Detter did not do me the compliment of hating or fearing me. He saw me as a thing, a potential possession, a handy tool he wanted to add to his collection, and quite a collection it was. In addition to a corps of pale, frightened children who ran all his errands, he had a string of well-formed underclassmen who took turns attending to his physical needs. They left his room at odd hours, blank-eyed, rumpled, and sometimes bruised. He avoided such entanglements with the senior students mostly, I think, because they were at the late stage of adolescence when they were coarse and half-finished, neither boys nor men. I certainly found them unattractive enough.

Detter's conjurations against me were subtle, well crafted, and just infrequent enough to take me by surprise. They usually involved mental rather than physical assaults, which meant according to Simon's scale of difficulty that he was skilled and accomplished.

One afternoon in summer, for instance, as I weeded in the sun-baked glare of the potato bed, I suddenly looked forward to spending the evening manicuring Detter's toes. I straightened up to stretch my back, rubbed my ribs as well, and ruminated on the real elegance of his delicate feet. Funny I'd overlooked that before. I wondered how they tasted. I thought of sticking my tongue between his toes and cleaning out the crevices. I felt a mounting impatience to get started. The field foreman saw me gazing idly into the drifting clouds and said sarcastically, "You see potatoes in the sky that need weeding, Lisane?"

"No, just feet," I answered absentmindedly. That didn't sound right, so I tried again in Wirdenish, "sheppenborter," which sounded even stupider. The spell was already inside my head, so it took me fifteen minutes to coax it out while I pretended to dig. Detter didn't even look disappointed when I showed no interest in his nether extremities that night, so I put a rot spell on his dinner. He threw it up on my favorite chair.

I asked Simon about him at lesson the next morning. Simon said only, "Avoid him."

"But Simon, I can't avoid him. He's determined to control me somehow, and he's a really good magician."

"Lisane, get it straight. He is, like everyone else here, a mage, but he is not yet a Magician. He is only a student. He may never become a Magician, if there is any justice."

"I can't keep track of the ranks. Why is it so important to you to have titles?"

"They are not mere birth-titles," he said impatiently as if inherited rank were the lowest of the low. "They are earned titles, and earned with great pain and trial. A student is only a young mage who is learning how to practice magic. A Magician has had to learn when magic is not appropriate, and how to ignore his own desires. Detter has not learned that, and he may never learn that. By all means defend yourself against him, but don't make the mistake of taking him too seriously."

"Don't take him too seriously? But he's incredibly powerful and subtle. He's better than any other student I know. If he's not going to make it, where does that leave the rest of them? They're unbelievably incompetent, and they're almost as malicious as he is."

"We are not here to discuss your classmates. We are here to pound some elementary knowledge into your thick skull. Stop trying to distract me." Simon took his job seriously, and anything I said that didn't fit was a distraction.

Our mornings together were pleasant, though much of what he was teaching me seemed arbitrary and upside down. Simon would sit with me at the table in his study, impatiently going over and over the rules and regulations governing correct magical behavior, his clear gray eyes crackling with intensity. He was always shoving his shining dark hair back when it fell stubbornly over his forehead. When I got bored with our studies, I would tune out his voice and admire his body, imagining myself crawling over the paper-strewn table between us to straddle his lap and shove his head between my breasts. I had no excuse, except he was the only soul in the place who talked to me. He always caught me out just when the daydream was getting good, I guess because my expression gave me away.

"Lisane," he'd bark, and I'd jump guiltily. "Pay attention, rot you, this is important," and he'd go through the whole rigmarole again. As far as I was concerned, he had his priorities reversed. I'd have loved to show him what was really important, if he hadn't been such a blind dunderheaded lump of a pedagogue, and if I weren't a professional virgin princess. In spite of his handsomeness, though, I supposed he was probably what every other male in this monastic prison seemed to be, a flaming gravedigger. He was certainly very careful to avoid touching me, though it seemed more like caution than distaste.

If you take a bunch of little boys away from their mothers, shut them in the middle of wilderness with a lot of nasty bigger boys, and make them grow up that way, that's what you get. It's fine for little boys to play fiddle-the-latch-hooks in between playing priest and kiss-the-muffin with little girls, but for almost-grown men to spend *all* their time in that activity struck me as a waste of good material. Not to mention what it would do to the fertility after spring rites, though I supposed they didn't have them here.

Summer passed slowly, and fall, and then the winter rains hammered the fields flat again. Somewhere in there, I turned eighteen and grew two inches taller. I acquired hips, finally, something I'd given up hoping for. I sparred with Ommo and Peselin, Benoit and Pick, and the other vermin in my quarters, establishing a sullen truce of sorts. Detter's legs got longer, but his skin was still as creamy as a baby's, and the hexes he threw at me grew more viciously subtle. Three of the older boys disappeared one by one, and were replaced by truculent but swiftly subdued junior students.

In early winter, we had our only excitement. The older neck-ringed men who ran the place started talking in furtive twos and threes, falling silent when the students came near, though I overheard the words "animals" and "were-beasts." Then for several days they disappeared on an expedition, leaving only the younger men to supervise us. When the expedition returned, the students found out somehow and we were all waiting on the broad stair to watch their arrival.

It was a miserable group that levitated to the plateau. The men with rings were wet, grimy, tired, and sour, but they had an unringed prisoner with them who must have been even unhappier. He was blindfolded and gagged, his hands and feet were bound with cloth and wire, and he was in a sling carried by four men who seemed intent on not touching him.

The gray-haired man I met on my first day brought up the rear of the procession. I only recognized him because of the scarlet knee-pants. His hair was still gray, but now it covered every visible patch of skin in a thick pelt like a dog's. His upper lip was furry and split down the center, black whiskers jutted out from his muzzle, and the teeth that showed on either side of his long pink tongue were yellow and pointed. The end of his nose was black and shiny, and he was looking away from everybody's eyes.

"I wish I was a renegade. I'd give anything to be able to make the old geezers dance to my tune. Even if they caught me in the end," breathed Benoit to me. Then he realized I wasn't the person he'd thought he was talking to, and he moved away hastily.

From the entrance they went straight to Kaihan's chambers, and didn't come out for the rest of the day. When they came out, their prisoner wasn't with them, Gray-hair was back to normal, and nothing was said. That was it for the excitement.

Gray-hair had a new student a week or two later, one who didn't live with the other students. He was an older man who looked as if he'd been badly beaten; he was undoubtedly the renegade, and he followed Gray-hair around like a bewildered shadow.

Nobody explained it to me. Nobody except Simon ever really talked to me anyway, and the older neck-ringed men who ran the place looked right through me as if I didn't exist. It still all seemed better than trapping rats in the forest.

Simon's lessons grew more intense, as if he were racing against time. He kept discovering another important gap in my information, getting more upset each time.

One dreary late winter day, with rain and wind spraying sidewise through his study window, I asked him, "Simon, what are those necklaces you and the other men wear? The students don't have them. Do they stand for something, or are they just decoration?"

His face fell, and his hair fell too, into his eyes as usual. "You don't know? Haven't I told you that?" he demanded.

I shook my head dumbly. He took a deep breath and shoved the books away from him. He leaned forward, hooking his thumbs under his brown neckring to show it to me.

"This is a badge of rank, and also a permanent warning. It was placed on me when I became a Magician, and it cannot be removed except at my death, even if I should acquire the rank of Sorcerer, when another would be added."

"So you *are* a Magician, then. I wondered," I interrupted.

He drew his imperious brows together and demanded, "How can you not know that? Don't you even listen when your classmates talk?"

"They don't talk much when I'm around. They treat me like a contagious disease."

He blew his lips out frustratedly. "Oh, all right. A single ring is a Magician, of whatever grade. A double ring is a Sorcerer. A triple ring is a Wizard. We don't completely understand the significance of the colors, but they have something to do with individual skills and ability."

"How do you get them? Who puts them on? Who makes them?" I said. "And why don't you understand the colors?"

Simon let the ring drop back on his collarbones. It looked as if it were made of some kind of semiprecious stone or translucent ceramic. "You'll find out if you ever need to know," he said dismissively. I hate it when people do that. They've been doing it to me all my life.

I tried another avenue. "So the skin-headed old goat in black you took me to when you brought me here must be a Wizard. He has a triple ring."

Simon slapped his hands down on the table with a sharp crack. I jumped. "You will speak with respect," he said. He seemed truly angry now, not just stuffy. "He is Master, and he did you a great favor by allowing you to live at all. He is older and wiser than any mage in the world, and he could crush you and me both, or the entire school for that matter, with only a single word."

I knew it was a mistake, but I said anyway, "So he's in charge here. Does he have a name? Or do you just call him 'Sir' or 'Oh, Great Bald of Head'?" I really wanted to know. That sinuous dark man in the quiet library kept creeping into my thoughts and dreams at odd moments, and I wanted to hang a label on him.

But Simon said only, "This lesson is over. I'm tired of this. No other teacher has to deal with two students at once. I don't know if I can stand to face my other student this afternoon. You are both making it incredibly hard for me as well as for yourselves." He did look tired, and despairing. I knew I gave him a hard time, and he was so earnest and well meaning. I left him massaging his forehead.

The next time we met he drilled me dryly on the different types of transmutation, refusing to be sidetracked. A week later the rains finally broke, and the buds began to swell open on the trees that clung on the plateau. I had been in the school for a year, and Mennenkaltenei seemed even farther away, something I had dreamed. But then of course I always take my dreams seriously.

CHAPTER THREE

In Which I Don't
Behave Myself Correctly

I was sitting on a windowsill in the lazy spring sunlight, half a mile above the world, making kissing noises to a doubtful brown bird and trying to coax it to me with the rest of my supper from the night before. My room was temporarily uninhabitable; Detter had somehow infested its walls with slimy chittering bugs that started to eat me when I went to sleep. I'd been too tired to deal with it last night, so I'd found a useless tower room toward the top of the building and bundled there. I had spring fever. I decided not to go to Simon's study that morning. Simon had been unbearable this week, nervous, tense, and angry.

Something was bothering him. I had asked him, but he wouldn't tell me what it was, just cursed me sharply for prying. "If you'd just do your own work instead of poking your pointy nose into my business," he said, "my life would be a whole lot simpler." Later on, over a minor matter of setting his chair on fire when I'd meant to light the candles, he called me a moronic bitch, and said if I didn't blow my incompetent self up before the week was out he'd have to kill me himself to keep the world safe. When I left him, he was slumped red-eyed at his table, his hair rumpled and greasy. He looked as if he was about to cry. So let him mope, I thought, let him snivel until he dissolved, see if I cared. My nose was not pointy, just pleasantly assertive.

The shabby brown bird cocked its head at me and scrabbled a few steps closer to my hand. Like everything else about this place, it was a little worse for wear, missing a few feathers and a chunk of its beak. It chirped at me scratchily, and when I didn't stir it pecked the bread from my hand, getting some into its mouth while the rest fell swirling down the side of the building. It fluttered its wings, hopped back to the other side of the window, and chirped again, a dull, dirty sound.

I heard voices calling from below, indistinctly. My own Voices were saying something scratchy and unpleasant about duty, honor, and powers of two in the back of my head. I tucked my legs back into the corner of the window, hoping nobody would find me. The last time I'd been caught playing hooky, the gray-haired gent in the crimson knee-pants—Memmipeg, the school Warden—had given me a command performance with his wretched renegade student as sole audience. He was as good at verbal abuse as I'd suspected, but it was hard to listen appreciatively when I was the one being called a slatternly, dawdling, second-rate, pig-humping streetwalker.

A flicking blue search spell trolled up the outside wall toward me. Some mage, probably Simon, was looking for me. I told it halfheartedly, "Lle benteren eckesterverter," but lle merely dimmed politely and kept coming. Oh well, so much for my holiday.

The tower room door behind me crashed open and, sure enough, Simon came stomping through, all dressed up in brown satin robes and curl-toed slippers, and mad as a polecat. He reached out the window and pulled me in by my hair. I admit I did scream, something I normally disapprove of, but he just gritted his teeth and kept pulling. I crashed to my back on the floor and barely got my feet under me as he charged out the door, his fist entwined in my hair. He kept banging me into the walls, and I was busy grabbing at his hand so I fell over a lot. He went up some spiral stairs that way, and I managed to trip him halfway. We both fell down the stairs, tangled up, but at least he had to let go of my hair to keep from sliding through the banister. I jerked my leg out from between his chest and an unforgiving chiseled stone step, and kicked him. He grabbed my ankle and we both slid through the banister, falling heavily to the landing below. I got to my hands and knees and stood up, my chest heaving, but he just lay there on his back, groaning over and over, "Why today? Why of all days today?" He had a deep cut on his chin from the steps, and his finery was block-printed all over with dust and stair grime. I nudged him with my toe cautiously and said, "What's today? Why the fancy dress?"

He rolled a wild eye at me. "What's today? Why, nothing at all. Completely unimportant, you misbegotten slut." He dragged himself up, trying to slap the dust off his robe. "Who cares whether you live or die? Why should I be so sentimental? I don't want to drag you with me half the way around the world anyway, you monstrous abortion. I'll have enough trouble as it is if my other student survives." He gave up dusting himself and headed for the stairs again, not looking back. I trailed after him, asking, "What's going on, Simon? What do you mean, whether I live or die? You never tell me anything, Simon, how am I supposed to know you needed me today? Hey, Simon . . ." up the stairs and through a passageway, up some broader stairs and across a grand hall, until finally he came to a stop at the bottom of a ramp leading to a pair of enormous ebony doors. He kept his back to me as I trotted up, still nagging, and he said, "Just shut up for *one minute*, Lisane."

I waited, nearly bursting, shifting from one bare foot to the other. Finally, he turned around and faced me. He was absolutely hollow-eyed with rage barely kept in check. It frightened even me.

"Listen to me for once," he said. "Lisane, the Master made me keep you here and train you, sky's blood knows why, but not without conditions. You've had as much schooling as I can force into your head in a year, and my other student is as finished as he'll ever be. So school's Council summoned you both and me as well this morning, to pass judgment on us all. The worst that can happen to me is that I'll have to stay here another year with a new student. My other student should be killed outright if the Council has any sense at all, and it would be small loss. But you, you're the only woman with Power this Council has ever seen, and you seem to be horribly strong. It doesn't matter how innocent you are. If they don't think you're safe, they'll kill you today without a second thought. I don't know why that bothers me, but it does," he finished forlornly. His forelock fell into his eyes again, and he brushed it back impatiently, leaving a smear of dust on his forehead.

"Simon, if you'd told me before," I started, and Simon said, roughly, "I was not allowed to," so I fell silent again, my eyes smarting. I had been under sentence of death one way or another all my life, so I wasn't as disturbed as I suppose I should have been, but I was sorry to see Simon so distraught.

"We'd better go in now," he said gruffly. I said, "Wait a minute," and wiped the smear off his face with my sleeve. He looked angry, tore himself from me, and went up the ramp. I threw a little dust-catcher spell after him hastily, so at least his pretty clothes would look all right.

We reached the doors. Though they were two stories high, they swung open silently at Simon's touch, revealing a shallow anteroom ending in slightly smaller doors of inlaid enamel. Detter, my nemesis, was standing there before the inner doors, his peach-fuzz face flushed unhealthily. He saw me, but I wasn't important. He said to Simon, "They didn't do it. They didn't kill me. I'm going with you, after all." His lovely pink lips twisted up in a dreadful victorious grimace. "I knew they were going to kill me in the end, and I didn't care. But they didn't do it." Between his clenched and grinning teeth his breath came in an audible hiss, and his glassy blue eyes were triumphant.

Simon embraced me and pushed me toward the inner doors, saying hastily, "Whatever you do, tell the truth. The chamber is spelled to destroy you if you lie." I backed toward the door, watching as Simon turned exhaustedly to face the grinning figure of my enemy.

I emerged, unsteady on my feet as I turned around, into a

great high-ceilinged chamber like an amphitheater, where fifty mages glared flintily down at me from the benches. I must have looked like a scared stray cat as I padded on bare feet to the center of the floor, but their expressions didn't soften. I was still wearing the blue cotton pajamas I'd lived in and worked in for a year, now far too short in the legs. My scraped ankle was bleeding and matted with dust. My hair felt half torn out and was probably standing on end. Simon had probably wanted me perfectly clean and properly dressed for this event.

I stood in the center and surveyed them all, swiveling around. They were a grim bunch. They looked as worthless as the Enforcers and a lot healthier. Every neckring was at least a double, and there were seven triples, including the choker on the neck of the Master. He sat in the center of the curve on a black granite throne that swept from the alabaster stone steps in chiseled sweeps as if it had grown there like a giant tulip. The Master was leaning forward, his chin resting on his hand. The other hand was splayed neatly on his thigh. I was willing to bet he knew exactly where every cell in his body was and what it was doing. He was dressed entirely in deep dull black, and the throne framed him with granite sparkles that matched his living eyes. I hadn't seen him for a year, yet he was exactly as I remembered him. And I had remembered him often.

A voice came from one side, making me jump. I'd already forgotten anybody but the Master was in the room with me. "You are late. Is there a reason?" The voice came from a young man, or maybe not so young once I saw his eyes, who was wearing green and maroon and holding a carved ebony staff.

"Not a good one," I said, but my voice wasn't there. I cleared my throat and said, "Not a good one, sir." He waited, but I didn't have anything to add.

Green-and-maroon consulted a sheet of paper. He had a dark toothbrush mustache and a mobile upper lip, so the mustache jumped up and down as he spoke. "Your teacher, Magician Simon, says you are opinionated, egotistical, stubborn, and argumentative. You are unable or unwilling to perform the simplest of spells, while you perform complex and dangerous ones with no caution whatever. You are at odds with the entire senior student hall, you are utterly undiplomatic in all situations, you repeatedly question authority, and it is your teacher's opinion that you have frequent hallucinations." He looked up. "Have you anything to add to your list of defects?"

Well, thank you, Simon. I never hallucinate. Everything I see and hear is quite real, thank you. The rest of it sounded about right. I just shook my head no.

He looked at the paper again and his mustache started jumping again. "He also says you are honest, terrifyingly bright, hardworking, considerate when it occurs to you, and passionately idealistic. If given an alternative, you prefer not to use magic at all, even if it means physical labor or pain to you, despite your remarkable command of the Power of magic. Again, have you anything you wish to add to your list of assets?"

That list was even more insulting than the defects. Idealistic? Me? I consider myself coldhearted and pragmatic. I just shook my head again. No use contradicting these people. The mages were shifting in their seats and muttering to each other.

Green-and-maroon put the paper down, pounded the staff on the floor with a startling crack, and intoned, "Colleagues of the Council, your attention, please. The candidate stands before you. From the preliminary investigation two things must be considered. First, she is the first woman to come before this Council and is therefore unpredictable. Second, her origin is unclear, and some have suggested she is not naturally born, but a trap, an abomination constructed by a renegade wizard seeking to disrupt the Order. The candidate is free to be questioned." He waited, and there was silence for a moment. My heart was thumping. My palms were sweating. How odd. If I let go my control for a second, I felt as if my rigid muscles would shove me squawking and twitching into the ceiling. Somewhere in there since I'd sauntered into the chamber, I had become terrified.

Finally, a lean mage in an ornate tunic hunched forward and

addressed me, with a tired and condescending air. "I understand you were found starving in the forest by young Simon. How did you come to be there?"

Now they ask, I thought bemusedly. No one had even wanted to know until now. "Self-absorbed" doesn't begin to describe this bunch.

"My . . . my . . . boat . . . landed there a year before. I was running away from enemies, and I ended up on this world by accident." That sounded just great. The mages stirred and grumbled.

The lean one said, disbelievingly, "Your *boat* landed in the *woods*? What is that supposed to mean? And what do you mean by 'on this world'? Did you live in the clouds, then, or behind the sun?"

Oh, great balls of geneventner dung. He wanted me of all people to explain astronautics and cosmology, in a language that didn't even have those impolite concepts. "Sir. It was a kind of a sky boat, a boat that flies between the stars. And, umm, the Sun is a star like the ones you see in the night sky. I came from a world like this one, whose sun is a different star." This came out very confused and self-contradictory in their language, and I blushed furiously at actually admitting that the Lisane could know of such ideas. They discussed it between them heatedly, except for the Master, who still sat poised, unmoving, on his massive throne. He was exquisite. I still remember how he looked.

My interrogator started to say something further, but the Master broke his trance and interrupted. His voice projected through the babble like a battering ram. "You were running from enemies. Who were they?"

I had to think for a moment, to translate it into his language. "They were called Enforcers."

"Why were they your enemies? Had you done something to harm them?"

I was outraged. "They came to my world, a good place, full of love and life, and they killed us. They killed my family, they destroyed every other ruler or priest, they took us as hostages and dumped useless, bewildered strangers on our planet. The only reason I was not killed with my family was that I was so young they did not know my Power." I stood up straight and proud to address the Master, as IlerKalten would have. I've been told I looked like a monkey standing on its hind legs and babbling, but if I didn't look as good as I thought, at least I wasn't paralyzed with fear anymore. The Master looked relaxed and genuinely interested, unlike his fellows, who chuckled sarcastically and looked aside at each other.

I continued, "They are utterly evil. They hate themselves and all other human beings. They hate life itself, and they believe their way is a truth all others must obey even if it means the end of life. They don't believe in what you call 'magic,' though they wield and consume it with powerful machines."

"This is fantastic nonsense, Kaihan," said a plump grumpy Sorcerer in ice-blue and white to the Master. "Let's get it over with and have lunch."

The Master ignored him and asked, "This was one of their ships that you landed in the wood?"

"Oh, no, that was just a little lifeboat, a raft kind of thing. One of the Enforcer ships is as big as this building." The mages began to laugh, a nasty jeering roar.

Master Kaihan said low, cutting through the noise, "Silence," and they froze, affronted but cautious. "Something very strong and strange certainly occurred in the wilderness west of here two years ago. Student, what happened to your 'little boat' after you landed in the forest?"

"I set it on fire, sir. I didn't want the Enforcers to find it or me. The fire was hotter than I expected, and it burnt up a good deal of the trees. I barely escaped." I still felt guilty about asking spirit-fire to consume the boat, though I should have gotten over that after a year with the mages.

"There was such a fire, hot and fierce," he said.

"Kaihan, what are you trying to prove? This abomination is obviously making it up as it goes along. It has no history to tell.

It's circumventing the truth spell somehow," said a triple-ringed Wizard with ferocious red eyebrows.

Kaihan said gently to me, as if the man hadn't spoken, "You mentioned machines. These Enforcers control magic, you say?"

I nodded. "They use it, and in using it, they destroy it."

"How powerful are they? Could they defeat a mage of full Power, say?"

I nodded again, vehemently. "From what I've seen, they could defeat a thousand such, Master. My world was full of wielders of magic, yet the Enforcers shriveled our spells like tissue in a bonfire." He looked me in the eyes a long moment, and parted his lips as if to ask something further, then leaned back instead, placing his arms on the throne's sides and relinquishing his command of the floor.

The others tore into my story promptly and sarcastically. I rapidly became too angry with them to behave myself. The debate raged on, my judges enjoying my torture too much to kill me just yet. I half believed by the end that Mennenkaltenei was a figment of my imagination and the Enforcers a nightmare. I was red in the face, spluttering incoherently, when Kaihan came back to life, negligently waving the others back. They fell silent, settling complacently in anticipation. I supposed it was judgment time, and I'd half decided the fools had no jurisdiction over me after all. It could have been very ugly.

"Supplicant," said Kaihan. "This building has been erected over millennia by small individual acts of magic. Would you consent to add to it?"

The mages leapt to their feet in unison, turning to Kaihan and shrieking with rage. What with neck-cords standing out, fists waving, and raised voices, I couldn't make anything out. I put my hands over my ears. Kaihan raised a finger and said the same thing over and over until enough of them ran out of breath for his voice to be heard: "Humor me. What harm can it do? The Beast will eat her if my judgment is poor."

Green-and-maroon snarled, "She's here as a student, and a

strange one at that, not a full-fledged Sorcerer asking for final search. Are you finally losing your mind? It is our job to prevent monsters like this from entering the world." Kaihan smiled at him warmly, as if he were murmuring endearments.

I was still furious and I didn't care anymore what I said in front of these idiots. I interrupted, my high voice falling thinly in the still echoing hall. "Excuse me, Master, but this building needs another addition like a fish needs hair. It's already the ugliest mess I've ever seen." They all goggled at me as if I had blown flame out my ears, but Kaihan laughed, the skin tightening about his eyes.

"I agree," he said, "but you must do something if you wish to leave here. Would you care to rearrange the whole thing, wipe the slate clean?" There was an intake of breath from the outraged men around us.

I thought about it, but shook my head. "I could make it look good, but somebody would be bound to come along after me and stick another lousy turret in the middle of the wall." To the accompaniment of hostile jibes from the benches and solemn advice from my Voices, I looked around the room, trying to think something up. I raised my eyes to the windows that ringed the top of the wall, and saw a pair of fluttering brown forms perched on a sill. I smiled, and said, "I've got it. It's not a change in the architecture, but it will change the building permanently."

"Then go ahead," he said.

It was going to be a complicated and difficult piece of work, since so many parts were involved and each part must give permission. I braced my legs apart on the floor, stretched my arms, and called as much of ller as I could get from the room. A mage fell off his bench as a spell-mended leg failed. It wasn't enough of ller, so I called harder, and flaming swoops of spirit poured into the room from the sky and earth—chartreuse, cinnamon, crimson, every color I knew and others I couldn't name. The room filled, and filled again, until I couldn't see anything but coruscating swirls. I spoke and shaped ller, until a deep hum began to rise in volume and tone. When it sounded like a crystal mountain struck by storms, I asked the roomful of ller to do me this small favor. Abruptly the room was empty again except for mages.

They looked old and shaken, even Kaihan, whose head lay back canted against the high back of the granite throne, his eyes blinking. I felt just fine, the best I'd felt in weeks.

"It's done," I said. "It's only a small change, but it should cheer things up."

"Show me," said Kaihan with a rasp in his voice. I looked up toward the fluttering forms still perched in the window, and chirped, calling one to me. The bird came gladly now, no longer brown, but a graceful glide of brilliant color. It perched on my finger lightly, cocking its crested head at me. Its emerald eye gleamed, the iridescent feathers with the cerise tips fluttered, and the long trailing royal blue tail switched and flipped like a silken cord. I looked up at Kaihan and said, "All those ugly brown birds are like this now, and so will be their children and their children's children. Forever." The bird opened its throat and a glorious music like golden hammers on hanging chimes struck out in the still air. Its mate sounded from the high window, weaving a duet of exquisite sadness and joy that finally fell to silence like a promise. I lifted my hand, and the bird flew back up and out, into the midday sky, starting to sing again. I could hear echoes, other songs, in the distance. I was pretty pleased with myself. I'd done a good job. My Voices murmured appreciatively.

"Oh, yes," I said. "They taste terrible. In case the students get any bright ideas."

Kaihan looked around him. The others avoided his eyes. "It is solely the Master's right and responsibility to declare a Supplicant ready for Final Search. I do so now." He added to me, "May the Beast be merciful to you—and may you be merciful to the Beast."

I didn't know what that meant. Kaihan said to me, "Go on, girl, get out of here," and I turned to leave. He called after me,

"Tell Simon to come back this afternoon," over a mounting babble of strenuous objections from my erstwhile judges. That was my second meeting with Kaihan.

When I came back through the curtains, Detter was no longer there, and Simon was stretched out on the floor with his arm over his eyes. "So Detter's your mysterious other student, hmm?" I said. He flung his arm out wildly and jerked upright, his eyes bulging at me. "I think I just got the Master in trouble. What's a final search, Simon? And what's a beast?" He was suddenly all over me, clutching me to his chest and pounding my back. I tried to keep talking, but my face was buried in his chest and he was quivering, whether with laughter or tears I couldn't tell. I forced my chin up to look at him. "So what happens now?" I said.

He looked down at me with bright eyes and kissed my nose. Then he backed away from me as if I had attacked him, looking upset and shy. It was a shame. He had a nice, firm body, just as I remembered from our time in the forest.

I never went back to the senior student hall. I had nothing left in my room, anyway. Simon led me down to the ground-floor caverns where the stables and storerooms lay. He refused to answer any of my questions, saying only, "You don't have any choice in the matter. You don't need to know anything, just do what I tell you." He rapidly regained his normal color and his maddening air of avuncular condescension. I followed his broad shoulders down the stairs, talking to the stiff back of his head and dancing with impatience. We walked through the stable, the horses nodding their heads at us from the musky dark, and passed through the dim tackle room into a large clean room filled with lockers, chests of drawers, and wardrobes. Detter was standing before an open cabinet, a large jumbled pile of clothes and tools lying on a blanket spread out behind him. Simon looked annoyed at that, his mouth compressed to a thin line, but he didn't say anything to Detter, just introduced me to the contents of the room.

Everything a traveler could desire was there, light and heavy clothing, fishing rods, cookstoves, climbing tools, spears, swords, and tents. Simon told me, "You may take anything you think you might need for a long, arduous journey through all kinds of country and every extreme of weather. You will be traveling *on foot*," he said, but Detter didn't take the hint, just threw another gewgaw on his pile.

I went over to the knife drawer as Simon left the room, saying he would return in a couple of hours. I knew just what I needed, having spent a year in the woods dreaming of such a wish list. First, a knife, light but strong, not too short. I found one at the back with a roughened bone handle and a tempered straight blade, sharp and true but sturdy. Then a leather harness. It had clips in front for the knife scabbard, for small game, and for the medium-sized waterskin I chose after checking the seams. The harness had strong hooks at the shoulders for an oiled fabric backpack, not too large. Detter was admiring a curved ornamental sword that flashed and glimmered in the lamplight, but finally decided against it, thank goodness.

I moved to the drawers of woven goods. A woolen blanket, an oiled rain cape, a light cotton all-over robe with a hood and a face mask. They all folded neatly into small bundles and went into the pack. Detter added a carved wooden staff to the jumbled heap on the floor.

I agonized over a slender, beautifully twisted fifty-foot length of linen rope, and finally added it to the pack, which left room for gloves, a small iron cookpot, a spoon, and a bowl. Detter was rummaging through a trunkful of tents.

Now for clothing. It didn't take long for me to find some cotton knickers, a long-sleeved undershirt, a soft hat, and a capacious high-buttoned dark green wool shirt with sleeves that could be rolled up. Trousers were a different matter. I really did have hips now, and either the waistband stood out from my belly like a rain gutter or the pants were so snug in the thighs I couldn't raise them high enough to button the fly. I finally settled with a grimace on a serviceable but worn brown wool pair, sized somewhere in between. I shoved five pairs of socks into the crevices of the pack, and tried on boots for nearly an hour until I found a heavy pair that fit without pinching or sliding.

Detter, expressionless, had found a mirror in the corner, and was modeling a series of embroidered cloaks that made him look like an elvish prince. Never in my life would I be as beautiful as he was, I thought, and the thought made me feel obscurely pleased. I avoided the mirror myself, out of habit, though I supposed there was no real reason anymore not to look.

Finally, I was set. I bit my lower lip and glanced at Detter under my lashes. He was oblivious to me, lost in his vanity, so I quickly shucked off all my broken-down ill-fitting student clothes and slid quickly into the new ones. I tried on the harness, adjusted it, clipped on the knife and waterskin, and slung the pack on my harness hooks. I bounced up and down, testing, and breathed a sigh of relief. It was light, well balanced.

I took the pack off and sat on the floor with my arms around my knees. Detter sorted through his pile, trying to decide. He couldn't seem to abandon anything, though he hadn't picked anything that wasn't either useless, heavy, or more easily made on the trail. It was obvious he'd never even been on a day's hike.

It was puzzling. The way these students were raised you would have thought their masters were trying to make sure they were as unpleasant, incompetent, miserable, and self-destructive as possible. What earthly use could they be to themselves or anyone else that way?

I was beginning to understand that Mennenkaltenei had been a fool's paradise, but there had been much good in the way I was brought up. As an infant, I was dirty, into everything, taken everywhere. My milk-mother gave me suck until I couldn't spare the time from my play. When I was two, it was clear how closely I lived with Iler, so I was Chosen by IlerKalten, even though IlerKalten was also my true mother. The priest called a blessing on me that protected me from my Power until I was five, when I was considered wise enough to take on some

responsibility for my gift. When I was not running and learning worship with the other children, I was being trained in my
life's work. I was loved, indulged, trained, protected, and dis-
ciplined by every adult I knew, though every Mennenkalt child
was raised so to some degree.

I *was* treated differently, for I was the future fount of the
spirit as well as the Power-blessed daughter of the Mother and
a Year-King. A Year-King so adored that at the end of his reign
they saved his finger bones from the spring feast and made
them into pendants for his babies. It was an idolatrous act, not
polite at all, but I cherished my token, the worn bone still dangling between my breasts. I slid my hand into my shirt and
fondled it now, dreaming idly. It was the only thing that made
my life before the Enforcers real, and it had given me courage
to escape them.

The room faded out as I drifted into my favorite well-worn
fantasy. I had been initiated as Mother after all, and I stood before the Celebrants, facing the newly crowned, naked Year-
King, his hands red with his predecessor's blood, and the joy
and fury of the Living God glowing in his face. I raised my
hands gracefully to the catch of my golden cape. My head was
raised proudly, and as the heavy fabric slithered down my body
the assembled throng began to cry out gladly in one ecstatic
voice. . . .

"Wake up, girl, we have to get moving," said Simon, standing in the doorway, and to Detter, "What is this cretinous ex-
plosion of garbage supposed to be?"

I hauled my mind reluctantly back to the gear-littered room.
Detter's face was as calm as ever as he stood up. He did not answer. He did not seem to care when Simon kicked his heap
apart with a scornful toe. He acquired a restrained and superior
smile as Simon grabbed plain and useful things from the drawers and threw them at him. Graciously, Detter condescended to
pack according to Simon's orders, as though he were the master and Simon an amusing, bumptious pet. If I had not seen his
performance that morning, I would have been content to hate

him. Now I also feared him. His pride and desire for victory at any cost would have made him a worthy enemy were he not consumed entirely by the effort of denying his terror. A man who will not permit himself even the thought of cowardice is a vicious and unworthy opponent.

Simon made me dump out my pack. He grunted approvingly. I put it back together, even better this time.

"You know the rules," he said to Detter, who nodded, bored. To me, he said, "No matter what status Kaihan gave you, I am in charge. I am your guide. You are my apprentices, and you travel where I lead. These are the rules. From now until I tell you otherwise, no spells, no conjurations, no use of magic whatsoever under any and all circumstances, or I will destroy you utterly. Obey me in all things, or I will kill you without a second thought." He paused, and said, "And since I have been cursed with two incredible monsters instead of the usual single incompetent fool, my first order is that you both leave each other strictly alone. No fighting, no sniping. Don't even talk to each other. Understand?"

I nodded mutely, but Detter didn't budge. Simon flicked out a hand and struck him in the mouth. "I said, do you understand?" Something shone incongruously in Detter's heavenly blue eyes, and he breathed, "Yes." It looked like I was in for a lot of fun.

"We are leaving *now*," said Simon. Picking up his own pack where it lay outside the door, he strode out. We headed for the edge of the plateau, but this time there was no bay mare, and we didn't take the magical express elevator. We walked down a goat-sized path the whole interminable way. The sun was already half set when we reached the bottom. Detter had already tripped me twice.

CHAPTER FOUR

In Which I Don't
Kill Either of Them

Three battered travelers stood peering from under a massive copper-tinted tree, looking out at a voluptuous green prairie with faint blue mountains beyond it. Nearly a month after we started, we had finally come out of the forest. Simon looked wonderful, lean and regal, his eyes creased at the corners. I had not fared so well. My worn trousers were loose on me and torn at the knee, and my arms and hands were scratched. I had an especially long scabbed stripe running diagonally down my face; Detter had released a bent-back thorn branch as I walked behind him on an overgrown path. Walking behind him was only slightly safer than walking in front of him.

Detter was the worst off of the three. He had been unused to exercise, relying on his sophisticated use of Power so much, and he had lost too much weight on the trip. His face was badly roughened and wind-burned. His hands were scorched, bruised, scarred, and chapped. Worst of all, he walked with exaggerated care, hobbling, for his feet were a mass of oozing, infected blisters. Every night Simon made him boil water and cleanse his feet. Afterward Detter sat, hands clenched at his sides, and stared expressionlessly at the flames until it was time to sleep. He was almost too miserable to torment me, but he managed somehow. He had not cast a single spell I could see since we left the school, but he was ingenious and persistent with his petty cruelties nonetheless.

He had tripped me, pelted me with rotten fruit, led me through briar patches, mud holes, and spiderwebs, and burnt me with stray coals. He had poured water on me (by accident), urinated on my blanket (by accident), dropped my food in the dirt (again by accident). He never spoke to me. He never spoke of me. He never acknowledged my existence. It was like traveling with an enormous eight-year-old boy in a permanent snit.

Simon was remote, pleasant, considerate, but firm to both of us. I no longer found him attractive in the least. I didn't even like him. I hated him. I hoped he would fall headfirst down a hole and die. Then I would kill Detter. After that I would sit down and cry for a week. I was very tired.

The flat plain lay before us now, full of rushing grasses. The sky was overcast but blinding white, the air was dry and smelled like singed bread, and it was hot. Simon said, unhitching his thumbs from his pack straps, "Midday's a bad time to travel across the plain in summer. Let's rest here awhile."

It was pleasant under the tree. I waited until Detter sat down, then sat far enough away from him. Simon squatted at the edge of the shade, chewing a grass stalk and peering at the dim mountains. "There's a good pass between those two peaks," he said, pointing. "We should be able to reach it in less than a week if we walk fast."

Out of the corner of my eye I saw Detter's face grow pinched. He could barely walk now. Fast walking in hot sun would kill him. I sucked my teeth, listening to the quiet Voices in the back of my head, which were making sense for a change. Detter kept silent, of course. He would walk through a desert on the bloody stumps of his ankles with a bored smirk on his face if the alternative was any kind of surrender. I would be happy if the fool died, but the Voices were firm.

"Simon," I said. Simon grunted inattentively. I threw a clod of earth at him and he looked at me, startled. I said, "Explain something to me. If a person wants to kill himself and you help him do it, does that make you an altruist or a murderer?" Simon narrowed his eyes with scorn and turned away again. That was all I felt moved to say, so after a while I lay back and stared up at the inky leaves.

I woke from a doze to find everybody in the same place, though Detter had removed his boots. I couldn't tell where the sun was in the hazy white sky. I turned to my side and went back to sleep. Simon woke me in the late afternoon, saying, "Go catch us something for dinner." I rolled to my feet still groggy and sweating, and stumbled off. When I returned at dusk with two fat birds, he had gathered wood and dug a deep fire pit. Detter still sat under the tree, not looking at anything, his suppurating feet sticking out before him.

This trip was apparently something every student mage had to endure before he became a Magician, and Simon, to become Sorcerer as he wished, must take his students on the journey he'd already once taken himself. What was the point? If they wanted mages to learn how to behave themselves in the real world, they should raise them in the real world, not walled away in that elevated dungeon they called a school. If the point was to kill us off, they should have done it before we left. My Voices disagreed with me, and also pointed something out about prime numbers I hadn't known before. I supposed they were bored. They never used to be interested in numbers.

Though Simon never actually said we were waiting for Detter's feet to heal, we stayed there four more days. When we started out again across the plain, we only traveled for half a day at a time. Detter's feet slowly got better. He didn't even speak to Simon anymore, he didn't play any more tricks on me, he just walked, mechanically, until it was time to stop.

Walking on the plain was deceptively easy. You simply swung your legs forward from the hip, parting the blades below with the foot and above with the hands. But after a time, our clothes were covered with burrs and clinging, bloodsucking insects, our pockets and folds were full of seeds and chaff, our hands burned from the constant strokes of the sharp edges of the blades. Our eyes swelled and watered with the pollen and the sun. Our backs began to hurt from the goose-step gait, mine in particular since I was shortest. When we finally gave up for the day, we would sit in a circle below the tops of the grass, sneezing and picking off parasites. At night, the wind blew across the surface of the grass, and the land hissed and sighed above us where we lay in a calm still pocket beneath the wind waves.

I finally got Simon to talk to me a bit, by asking why there were no large wild animals.

"Large wild animals? You mean like lost cows or sheep?" he chuckled.

"No, big cats, lizards, wild dogs. Meat eaters. In wild country like this I'd expect to meet up with some dangerous animals."

He was scornful, disbelieving. "Those are things to frighten children with, dragons and such. There are no large animals that are not tame."

"Maybe not here, but where I come from they're common. Master Kaihan mentioned a beast. Isn't that some sort of wild animal?"

"The Beast is dangerous enough, but he's not an animal at all." I could hear the capital letter in his voice.

"What is he, then?"

"Different things to different people." He changed the subject. "Kaihan did say you came from a different world. It seems that must be true. Is this very strange country to you?"

"Not so strange. All worlds have forests, plains, and mountains. I'm used to seeing more people, though. And why was the school stuck way in the middle of a dense forest on top of a rock, miles away from anywhere?"

Simon said, "There was a time when there were small kingdoms dividing up the whole center of the Lesser Shore—that's the continent we're on now—but a few centuries ago, the Sassevin Council, the ruling council, moved all the people to the coasts, created the forest around the school, and thrust up the plateau beneath it."

"Why? What were they afraid would happen to the students?"

"*To* the students? Nothing. They were afraid *of* the students."

"Oh, come on. Frightened of a handful of incompetent brats?"

Simon said, reprovingly, "You know nothing of the past, and you continue to underestimate the danger of magic. Your ignorance will end up destroying you." So pompous already at his age.

"Simon, my ignorance is enormous. If you like, I'll shut up. But how can I know anything of the past? I'm from another world with another history."

He remained silent. But next morning, as we waded hip deep in the wild grasses, Detter trudging doggedly behind us, Simon began to talk as if telling a fairy tale.

"In the childhood of the world," he said, "when every father's son was heir to a kingdom, magic rolled across the land in waves like an invisible ocean. To plow a field, the farmer had only to speak, and the earth turned itself over and sprouted grain. To sire only sons, the farmer had only to speak, and his wife's womb was filled with healthy life. A child's laugh made the sky rain flowers, and flowers rained down day and night. All men were mages then, and the life was sweet and golden.

"Yet rich as each man was, there were always some who wished more wealth. Misers gathered magic to themselves as a jackdaw gathers river stones, and to less purpose. They envied one another, and quarreled, and drew apart, each to his own land, the better to guard his store of magic.

"There came a time when, to cast a simple spell, a lesser man must go and beg his fellow to release some from his stores, for magic no longer flowed free, but sat in stagnant pools, puddled around this greedy one or that. As one man grew richer and more powerful, hundreds were bereft of power, and had to till the land by the poor strength of their arms. Savage wars of spells broke out. Neighbor no longer welcomed neighbor, and one hand was raised against another.

"Humanity was now two kinds, those without Power and their masters, who feared losing it. Children starved, and no one cared. The farmers in the valley feared the herders in the hills, the horsemen in the plains fought the hunters in the forest. Each man spoke only the words of his master, and no two masters shared their words. Chaos ruled, and brutal fear, and the blasted land became scorched and barren. Across the wreckage of the world, the mages fought sorcerous battles, conjuring demons and dragons and djinns. Only the innocent died, in numbers too great to be told, while the evil ones lived and thrived. Darkness fell across the world, broken only by wavering witchlight and the blaze of burning mountains. To our twilight was added the blight of vengeful invaders from the sky, the people of the sunset, who seared us with their terrible judgment.

"Then from nowhere came a stranger with no name, the first true mage, who wandered the world in its days of desperation. He sought joy and pleasure, tenderness and love, yet found only filth and fear. After untold years, the mage with no name rested on lost Mount Erichelah in the heart of the Greater Shore, and decided to leave this world and, leaving, mend what was broken.

"He stretched up his arms and drew down magic from the stars, where none before him had been able to reach, until the mountain itself began to loosen from its roots and float in the air. With Erichelah bearing him, he drifted into the heavens, paying with his earthly life for the Power he must wield. As he entered the night behind the blazing stars, he called down his curse on the world, and the world changed forever and for good. Each man turned in wonder to another, and spoke, and was understood, for all spoke the same words now. Where Erichelah had lain, Sassevin city of mages now rose, and at its heart was the Beast in his Room. The Beast called out, with the voice that commands, to each master of magic from all parts of the world. Each mage in turn must face the Beast alone, to prove beast himself and die, or true man and live, but as slave to those he would have ruled. And as the sign of slavery, the Beast bound those who lived with a collar, and sent them out to wander all their long lives, landless, alone, and unloved."

Simon fell silent, looking solemn. I had managed not to laugh. What a grim and self-important fable. Where were the gods and spirits for these people? Where did women figure in their stories? And how bizarre to even think of owning magic.

I said, "So your ancient ancestors are supposed to have screwed things up and you're still paying for it thousands of years later? That doesn't seem fair. You shouldn't take on so much guilt and pain for something you didn't do."

Simon said harshly, "Oh, something we didn't do? Do you really believe I would spend my life doing penance for someone else's crimes? You must think me a virtuous fool. Thank you very much, but I must disappoint you. I have committed cold and bloody murder like every other mage, and you'd better get it through that piece of moldy cheese you call a head." He pushed ahead of me coldly, soon leaving me far behind as I struggled through the grass.

Some time later, a cool and elegant voice wafted from just behind me, saying, "I am curious. Please enlighten me. Have you never tried to kill anybody or are you just being deliberately naive?" I was so surprised, I felt like my entire chest had just tried to shove itself up my throat. I hadn't really expected Detter ever to speak again, and certainly not to me.

I said warily, "I hit somebody once as hard as I could with a piece of pipe, but that was self-defense. He was trying to rape me."

"No, no," he said reasonably, coming up even with me. "Have you never used your Power to destroy someone? You are as inhibited now as priggish Simon is, but surely when you were a child you must have been angry enough to kill? Come now, be honest."

I felt like I was talking to a ghost, though the sun cast a real enough shadow behind him. Detter was wading along through the grass beside me, swinging his arms, as if we were continuing an ongoing chat instead of having our first conversation ever.

"Detter, I've been mad enough to murder as recently as last

week, but if I did, I'd do it with a rock or knife, something with some heft, not with magic. It wouldn't be any fun if I couldn't do it with my own hands. I was the same way when I was little. Besides, if I'd tried anything, the closest grown-up would have spanked me raw and told my mother."

"What could your mother do to stop you? You have Power, you could make her do your will as well," he said. "Or is it just that you are female, and thus more submissive to authority?" He seemed to be genuinely trying to understand, so I didn't belt him just then.

"When have you seen me ever submitting to authority? Dog eggs, Detter, my mother was bigger and meaner and stronger than—than Master Kaihan. She had more Power than anybody I've ever met. I did what she told me."

"Your mother had Power, and yet bore a child?"

"Well, sure. Fifteen children. And every one of them by a man of great Power himself. It was her job, kind of. Weren't your parents mages?"

He said remotely, as if commenting on the terrain, "My parents were ordinary, normal. When I was five years old, I set my mother on fire like a torch with my very first spell, and I watched her burn, because I was tired of her beating me." His blue eyes were calm. "Then I did the same to my father, because he tried to hit me, and my sisters because they were screaming and it hurt my ears. And after that, I set everybody else in my village on fire because I thought they would tell on me, and then I sat down and waited to die myself. When the mages came to get me I was nearly dead of starvation and thirst."

We walked in silence together a few minutes. Moths and jumping insects leapt out of the stalks we thrust aside.

I said, "I think you did die. You've been dead a long time. Why don't you lie down, have a nice funeral, and get it over with?"

"I thank the gracious lady for her kind advice. It's good of you to condescend," he said with no perceptible sign of offense, but he too forged ahead of me, to my great gratitude. My two companions were even leakier in their upper stories than I'd dared believe.

I turned and looked back, with no great hope of escape. A wavering trail, smudged and bruised, blurred back across the surface of the high grass toward the horizon, disappearing in the middle distance. In another day there would be no sign we had passed this way.

After three weeks we were across the grasslands and hiking in the foothills below the sedate mountains. Up close the range was a worn and ancient one, eroded and rounded, great organic swells of rock mostly covered with greenery.

Detter kept popping up at my side periodically to chat of death and deviltry. Simon said nothing after all to stop our conversations, probably relieved we were keeping each other busy. Simon was growing more and more silent, staring into the distance when he walked and when he rested. He looked happy, and I left him alone, but I wasn't sure I could stand being Detter's confidante.

Detter told me candidly of all the petty tortures he had practiced and of prolonged revenges he'd taken for minor slights, seeming neither to gloat nor to confess. When I could bear it no more, I would say something cold and cutting. He would call me a hypocrite and wander away, relaxed, leaving me shuddering. Was this some elaborate punishment? Had he found my weak spot and concentrated his efforts there to break me down? Or was this all he knew to talk about if he wanted to converse? I couldn't tell. There were times I wished I could match him bloody tale for bloody tale. I felt so innocent and naive.

Yet one time, as we wound among low flowers in a valley between two ridges, I managed to shock him. He was rambling on about his sexual practices with the junior students, in elaborate and unpleasant detail, and I was passing my thumb absentmindedly over and over the well-worn bit of bone hanging from my neck.

Detter, seeing I wasn't paying attention, lost interest in his tale of power, terror, and petty cruelty. "What's that you're fiddling with?" he said. "Let me see it."

"It's just a little worry-stone," I said casually, folding my hand over it to hide it.

"Nonsense. You get an expression on your face like you're seeing things when you touch it. What is it, a magic talisman? That's breaking the rules."

"It's not a talisman. There's no spirit in it at all. It's a keepsake, that's all. It reminds me of home." He had me on the defensive, and he was starting to get that considering expression that meant he was seeing a weak spot. I was surprised to find it *was* a weak spot with me, just where I'd thought I had only strength and comfort. I opened my hand and looked at it, gray and porous and grubby on my palm. I lifted the chain over my head and handed it to him, which was not what he'd expected.

I said, "It's a human bone, the tip of a finger. My father's finger. Someone gave it to me when I was a baby, after his death."

Detter's eyes widened. I had finally managed to startle him. "How ghoulish. So part of him didn't get buried."

"Oh, none of him got buried. He was IlerMennet, the Year-King; he was special. We cooked him and ate him and burned the leftovers. Well, I didn't really eat any, I was too young for meat yet."

Detter's lips were pulled back in an involuntary grimace of disgust, or possibly pleasure. "Was he alive when he was cooked?" He stared at the bone in fascination.

"Oh, no, no, no." What a horrifying thought. "His successor, the new Year-King, slit his throat first. *Then* we cooked him."

"What had the man done that you had to execute him in such a gruesome way?"

I was puzzled and a bit taken aback by Detter's reaction. "He was the Year-King. He ruled the world for a year, he chose a successor, the new King killed him, and we ate him. That was his job. There wasn't anything gruesome about it."

"Why would anybody take a 'job' that was going to last only a year and end with death?"

"That's like asking why be born if you're only going to die eventually. It was a short but glorious life, and a lot of men wanted it."

Detter's blue eyes blazed from his sun-reddened, road-weathered face. "What good is a glorious life if it's cut short?"

"It's better than a miserable life that lasts forever."

He seemed to take that personally. He flung the pendant back at me and strode ahead, looking like a straw-headed scarecrow. He wasn't such a limpid porcelain youth anymore, not after going without a hat all that time.

I considered the bone again for a few moments, turning it over and over again in my hands. Then I tossed it into the underbrush, leaving it and the past behind. It was the best thing I could have done, and I regretted it immediately. Detter didn't talk to me again for a long while, to my great pleasure.

We made it through the pass easily, not even needing my rope. On the way down, we came across a mountain spring and followed it from its source until we came to a twenty-foot waterfall with a turbulent pool beneath, the first water deeper than a puddle we'd seen in weeks. Simon and Detter immediately started stripping their clothes off by the pool to do their laundry and wash themselves. I retreated swiftly up the bank to the top of the waterfall and took my own bath. I lay down face-up in the shallow rapids and let the water run cold slithery fingers through my hair and over my skin for a long time, until my breasts, my face, and the tops of my thighs were the only parts of my body that weren't numb and shriveled. I didn't feel completely clean even then, but I had to get out.

I sat on a flat rock in the hot sun, waiting for my clothes to dry. Idly I peered over the top of the fall, to see Detter and Simon lying naked near each other, dozing on a rock shelf.

They looked funny, with tanned faces and pale bodies, and they looked beautiful, too. Detter was pink and white, with golden hair only at his groin, and his muscles were firm, round, and young. Simon's skin was more opaque, richly furred, and he was all nerves, tendons, and bones. Like all naked men, they looked surprisingly vulnerable, soft, and delicate. I leaned back so I couldn't see them anymore. They were very irritating people.

I felt languid, relaxed, and clean in the sun. I lay on my back and closed my eyes, seeing only a red glow, and thought sleepily about the paradoxical nature of desire. If I'd never cared for Detter, I could at least appreciate him as an art object. I couldn't imagine coupling with him, even though he obviously could imagine coupling with me. Simon, on the other hand, I could have desired and admired. He had the fervency of the young Postulants who encircled my mother. But like them he seemed to be retreating further and further from his own humanity, seeking solace in his rules and ideals and the voyage itself. Unlike them, he had no hope of redemption by Possession. Perhaps he was just going to get grayer and grayer until he turned into mist.

I tried to summon up my favorite dream of the Year-King, but since I'd thrown my pendant away there was no longer any passion there for me. I had seen nothing but indifferent males on this benighted world, and I was beginning to feel like some genderless lump of flesh, but the sun felt good on my chilled skin so I didn't care. I dozed off.

I was in that library. My Enforcer rags had peeled from me like an onion skin, and Master Kiahan's bleak, humorous eyes were flickering over every inch of me like invisible tongues. The smooth skin of his head rippled as he began to smile, and he looked up again at my face. My skin was tingling again. He leaned back, and I sauntered closer to him. I saw a woman reflected in his eyes as I approached, and I did not know who she was. On the sides of his head, close-cropped salt-and-pepper hair glinted subtly in the light as he moved. What did his head feel like? Was the skin as smooth and warm as it looked? How did that chiseled, considerate mouth taste? I was standing bent over him, my hands framing but not touching his face, and his face was full as a clear glass brimming with the dark-flavored liquid of eager desire. But who was that woman I saw in his eyes?

I awoke with a foul taste in my mouth. My clothes were dry, my companions were calling me, and we moved on. I was annoyed with my dream all the rest of the day. It hadn't felt like a false dream, but I didn't accept it. Jenneservet had raised me better than that, that I should think lustfully about old men with Power.

Two weeks later, we encountered a real road, with horse carts traveling it, and hitched a ride with an obliging farmer all the way to the port city of Deistel Dom, capital and royal seat of the country of Emsadorn. All Simon would tell us was that we would be visiting someone there.

On this road, I finally saw some other women. Though they dressed, spoke, and acted differently from the men, and seemed not to associate with them, at least they were identifiably members of the same species. Though I stared at everyone we passed on the road, none stared back at me when I could see them. It was as if I should not exist, and they were politely ignoring me.

My first view of the city was uninspiring. We were entering the gate nearest the market, at dawn. The air smelled of rotting garbage, the stones of the street were slippery and dark, and the warehouse buildings were patched and tumbledown. The farmer dropped us off when he came to his broker's station, and Simon led us around the back of the building and up a steep narrow street. As we walked, the sun rose above the low buildings and clear light shone on the scarred walls, vagrant dewdrops sparkling on scattered weeds. By the time we reached the castle park at the height and heart of the city, the sun was high and hot, the streets were dry, and the citizens were in full display. Detter was gawking as much as I at the bright costumes and the bewildering variety of goods for sale. After all, he had spent most of his life imprisoned in the school. He must be nearly as naive as I about the outside world, though that didn't seem possible.

Simon knew his way and spared no attention to sight-seeing. He said, "Follow me closely and do not speak," and led us to the entrance gate, where several well-fed soldiers lounged. One of them stood up as Simon approached, and the others eyed us lazily.

Simon said, as he approached, "Good day. My name is Magician Simon, and I am guide to these two, student mages both. The King issued me an invitation—" He stopped, perplexed. The guard was grinning and waving him through.

"—the King's old apprentice," said one of the loungers aside to another. Simon's ears were turning red as he led us in. The soldiers eyed us all frankly, but with goodwill. Simon was walking too fast, and I stumbled to catch up. It was nice to see Simon being human again, even if I didn't know what the joke was.

We arrived at a grand entrance completely overgrown by a vine with drowsy-smelling white flowers. A spectacular color guard stood ranged on either side of it, with crimson and orange diagonal striped uniforms and glossy steel pikes. Simon stopped before them, looking, with his wayward black hair, brown neckring, and dusty brown clothes, like a pirate compared to the gaudy soldiers. He began, "My name is Simon—"

And the lead guard interrupted, "—to the life! Welcome, sir! I'll tell His Majesty." Simon rolled his eyes resignedly and the entire guard laughed in a friendly way, beckoning us into the entrance hall.

A few minutes later an enormous man barreled into the hall, trailing ginger-colored spirit-fire like the wake of a boat, and slammed Simon against the wall, kissing him full on the lips. Simon squirmed helplessly and shoved at him. He was taller than Simon and would have made two of him.

He pulled his head back and laughed at my crimson-faced teacher delightedly. "You solemn, pompous duckling! So you're still alive, are you? You look just the same, only stuffier." He released Simon, whose mouth was twisted wryly, and turned to us, saying, "Introduce me to these darling playthings. A matched set, I see, boy and girl, how handy." He was massively fat, with a large head, florid and jovial, but he judged us both shrewdly while Simon introduced us. He was the King himself, of course, and his name was Jens, and we were to call him by it. He wore a double saffron neckring half-concealed by the magnificent ruff around his neck. I made a mental note to ask Simon how it was that a mage could be a king—from the fable he'd told me on the road I'd thought mages were sworn to renounce possessions and power.

Jens was particularly interested in Detter, prowling around the boy while Detter tried to pretend he was made of ice. The King turned to Simon, and said, "Bet you've been utterly polite and correct with this animal. Looks like he's been driven right to the edge. Lucky he hasn't murdered you in your sleep, you sanctimonious prig. May I borrow him for a few days?"

Simon raised his eyebrows and gave him the faintest of nods, whereupon Jens slapped Detter on the side of his head with a meaty hand, so hard that Detter fell to his knees. "Come on, boy, let's get you cleaned up. Don't want my sheets getting dirty," he said, and he dragged Detter out of the room by the back of his shirt.

I looked at Simon, half-appalled and half-tickled, and Simon said, "Detter will have the time of his life. Don't worry." His mouth was still twisted ruefully and his eyes were sparkling with amused embarrassment. "Jens is full Sorcerer, and a match for Detter on his worst day. He was my guide when I was student, and my master when I was apprentice. In case you hadn't guessed." Simon looked much younger with his cheeks flushed like that.

Now a young woman of infinite unreality and fragility floated into the hall with a rustle of full skirts. "The King instructed me to see to your wardrobe for the reception this afternoon," she said brightly to me. "Come this way, please." I trailed after her dubiously, feeling like a hoyden in my worn boots and dusty trousers. Simon stood behind in the hall, rocking on his heels and whistling.

CHAPTER FIVE

In Which I Don't
Take Care of My Clothes

I was standing at bay behind a chair, wearing only a few ludicrous scraps of silk. The three laughing women who were encircling me had already managed to force me into slippery stockings that were clipped to a bizarre contraption slung around my hips, and beguiled me into donning a breastband and a worthless pair of knickers that clung snakily to my various crevices and swells. But the condescending and amused ladies who had me cornered in the dressing room were not going to make me wear the thing they were brandishing. It was made of sticks and wire and whipcord, it was ugly and painful-looking, and it was designed for someone whose internal organs were distributed differently from mine.

"Oh, come, child," said one of them entreatingly. "Don't you want to look like a woman? I promise this will do wonders for you. Just try it. Come on."

"I *am* a woman. I don't have to try to look like one. Don't come near me with that thing. If I even tried to wear it, I'd throw up and then I'd pass out." While my attention was on her, the other two darted at me from the sides, trying to wrap the thing around me and lace it up. I sat down on the floor, pulled my knees up and my head down, and resisted the attack. They were laughing, but I had given up trying to keep my sense of humor. It seemed to me that I was getting the same kind of treatment as Detter, though it was less obvious.

"What is going on in here?" A stout young woman in her twenties with flaming red hair swept into the room in a spectacular purple gown. She obviously wasn't wearing any sticks or wire under her dress, because she rippled and bounced as she moved.

One of the woman wrestling with me, red in the face with amusement and effort, said, "She's some kind of a female student mage, visiting for the reception with her guide. She was wearing man's clothing and looked a sight. Jens told us to dress her up and make her look presentable for the reception."

I still had my jaw set and my arms wrapped around me. The redhead, her hands on her hips, said to me, "You don't want to wear the corset?" I shook my head grimly. "Will you let them dress you up if you don't have to wear the corset?" I nodded. I was being spoken to as if I were a three-year-old having a tantrum. The redhead said to my erstwhile adversaries, "Go ask Mistress Jessie for the loan of her green gown. It will fit her just fine without the corset." They left the room laughing and I relaxed cautiously.

The redhead still stood there, chubby hands on ample hips, looking at me appraisingly. "So you're a woman mage. Why didn't you just cast a spell on the girls instead of letting them pick on you like that? Or are you just a high-flown herb-wife?"

I grinned up at her. She had blue eyes and freckles, and she looked wonderful. "I'm a mage, but I'm on my student Quest. That means I'm not allowed to use magic at all. I'm Lisane. Who are you?"

"My name's Annesil. Come on—if Jens insists on having you dressed up, we'd better get going. The reception starts in half an hour." Annesil helped me into some petticoats, found some low shoes for me, and started brushing my hair. The dress arrived, a cool mint green with white piping and lace, and it took all four giggling women to slide it over me while I awkwardly tried to help them. I wasn't used to fitted clothes, and I wasn't sure I was going to be able to move once I got the dress on, but I was pleasantly surprised. They sat me down, threw a drape over me, and trimmed and arranged my hair. Except for Annesil, they made me feel like the unfortunate beggar girl in the fairy tale, being made up to play the doomed princess—or like a cat being dressed up in doll clothes. They thought it was terribly funny.

Finally, they finished. Annesil said, "Go take a look at yourself before you go downstairs." She pointed to a standing full-length mirror.

"I never look in mirrors," I said uncomfortably, slightly revolted at the idea but not wanting to offend. To my horror, Annesil took me by the shoulders and shoved me forcibly over to the mirror. I tried to close my eyes, but she tipped my chin up, and suddenly I thought, Why not?

I opened my eyes and saw a tall black-haired young woman with flushed cheeks and cool green eyes, whose black eyebrows tilted sardonically. Her wedge-shaped face was lightly tanned, but her arms were milk white. In the mint green dress her high soft breasts, wide shoulders, and firm waist were displayed with shocking audacity and exaggerated femininity. If I were to meet her in the street I would hide from her. She looked like my mother, and like the woman reflected in Kaihan's eyes in my dream. My heart ached for her. She seemed to be all display and no defense.

Annesil hooked her arm through mine, drew me away from the mirror, and we set off down the stairs, her confederates chattering along behind us.

She said, "Honey, we're going to be the only two real women down there. The rest of them are all sealed up like sausages in their corsets." I felt dizzy, and held on to her arm like a lifeline, though she had been the one who had done this to me.

We rounded a corner and everyone looked up, a whole ballroom full of dressed-up aristocrats of every shape and size, all turning their heads to look at me. Or no, they were looking at her.

Annesil felt my arm tighten in panic, leaned to my ear and muttered, "Sorry. Forgot to tell you. I'm the Queen." I started to laugh. I couldn't help it. She said, "Oh, good. I do like you.

Let's get something to eat," as we paraded grandly down the rest of the sweeping stairs.

We came upon Jens and Detter halfway through the crowd. Detter was much cleaner, was dressed all in white, and looked as confused as I felt. Jens had his arm linked through Detter's and was whispering in his ear. Annesil waltzed up to Jens from behind, tickled him under the armpits, and danced away when he made a grab for her, nearly knocking Detter over again in the process. She coyly let him catch and caress her intimately, while Detter looked offended and fascinated. When Jens let Annesil go, she said, "Have you been officially introduced to Lisane?"

The enormous man looked at me, looked at me again, and roared, "Stop me! I can't help myself! I must have her!" waving his arms like windmills. It was funny, appalling, and almost serious.

Detter, taken aback, was also staring at me as if I had grown a tail and scales. He said, looking me up and down insultingly, "I hardly know you without your trousers on." I made a face at them both and slipped back into the crowd, aiming for the refreshment table I'd seen from the stairs. I felt silly and wild, bold and frightened, not like myself at all and nothing like a Mennenkalt Mother. Did I really have green eyes? I wanted to run upstairs again and check the mirror. The noise and crush of the red-faced, cheerful crowd was overwhelming. Someone's hand ran over my backside as I forced my way through, and I could feel eyes looking at me.

Annesil joined me at the table. She seemed to have adopted me for the afternoon. We ate some of everything, and Annesil watched as I inexpertly fended off several propositions both verbal and nonverbal. She thought it was funny, but she didn't have to put up with it herself, as no one seemed to dare flirt with the King's wife. After I managed to thoroughly insult one waggishly gallant old man, she said, "Don't you get any practice at this?"

I said, helplessly, "Back home no one would have dared, and since I left home no one has noticed I was female."

She looked puzzled, and was about to say something, but trumpets sounded a fanfare across the room. The people around us turned and began to shuffle in one direction, and Annesil said, "Oh, kitchen slops. I have to go be gracious. See you later." She sailed off in another direction, rippling and bouncing majestically.

It seemed everybody was drifting into line. I squeezed between a young and spotty scholar and a painted lady of an older vintage, and wondered what was going on. I saw Simon wandering alongside the line, looking for somebody. Maybe he knew. As he came up, he looked right through me and kept walking until I grabbed his arm and hissed, "Simon!"

He started violently and stared at me, his mouth open.

"Are you all right?" I said testily, forgetting for the moment how I was dressed. He did look simple gaping like that.

"Yesss. I'm fine. Yes," he said awkwardly. "Lisane, listen, when you get to him, don't curtsey like the rest. Kneel down on both knees, and stay down until he tells you to rise."

"Get to whom? The King?"

"No, no. Curtsey to the King, that's fine, just watch out because he's likely to tickle you. Lisane, you look wonderful," he said, sounding like no Simon I'd ever known. His eyes drifted downward. "I didn't recognize you."

I said, "Kindly remove your nose from my cleavage," more sharply than I'd intended.

He recoiled, said, "Sorry," and went back up the line. I still didn't know who it was I was supposed to kneel to. I couldn't get any clues from the conversation of the people in line near me. All I heard was things like "historic occasion," and "once in a lifetime," which could have described anything from snow in the summer to a naked gulay band playing ducks-and-buckets.

The line wobbled forward solemnly, and finally the scholar ahead of me was bowing formally to the honored guest standing beside the King and Queen. An honored guest whom I already knew. An elegant, amused, clear-eyed dark man in black with a triple neckring, standing like a column of smoke in the gaudy fire of the crowd.

Then I was standing before him in my turn, frozen for a moment looking at his face before he recognized me, and I sank slowly down to my knees, watching his expression change and thinking, oh my, oh dear, I don't want to know that. I stayed on my knees with my head down, my skirts spread around me, until I felt a warm dry hand gently lifting my chin.

Kaihan's face was expressionless again, and he said, "You may rise, Student Lisane. Well met on the path." I was now curtseying to Annesil, who looked at me with round eyes, saying, "And I thought I was the big shot around here. You know the Master?" I sidled past her, my face hot. Jens grabbed me and tried to kiss my neck when I curtseyed to him. I escaped and went back up the stairs at the other end of the ballroom, and sat down on a step around the corner out of sight.

My heart was pounding. I was out of control, too silly, too wild. It was this damned dress, it wasn't me. I would go back upstairs and find my clothes, go back to being invisible and unimportant. That black-haired, green-eyed woman I'd seen in the mirror was dangerous for me when she was dressed like this. I was riding a runaway donkey in heat, and there was no safety here.

Simon's reaction had been bad enough. He had looked stunned and confused. Kaihan had been just the other way around. As he recognized me, in that moment before I knelt to him, his eyes had narrowed, his nostrils flared, and his lips had parted. He looked like a predator about to spring, like the avid, lustful man in my dream that day above the waterfall. Now I knew the dream hadn't come from nowhere, and I was even more afraid. It had indeed been a true dream, and I didn't know what it meant. I needed some kind of protection from myself.

Someone was sitting down on the step beside me. I looked

up, and it was Simon. He said, "Sorry about my rudeness earlier."

"Simon," I said, "what is Master Kaihan doing here? He took me completely by surprise." I wished Simon weren't sitting quite so near to me.

Simon stared. "Don't you know? Didn't anyone tell you?"

"May your brains be fried, Simon, get this straight. Nobody tells me anything, ever. I am eternally and unremittingly ignorant. I ask you questions because I hope you will answer them, not because I like to make myself and you crazy." I took a slow breath. "What is Kaihan doing here?"

Simon still wasn't paying proper attention to the question, but he answered. "The Master of the Sassevin Council, the leader of the prime council of the order of mages, died in a freak dueling accident. Kaihan was named to take his place and is traveling there now. Since he had to pass through Deistel Dom, he paid a state visit. It's pretty rare for any Master of Sassevin Council to travel outside Sassevin, so every bootlicker in the country is here to smell his shoe leather. All right? Enough information, ignoramus?"

"Yes, thank you, wisest of teachers," I said demurely. Apparently the Master of Sassevin Council ranked with dead kings and disasters of nature as a sight that must be seen. Simon was looking intense and purposeful. He had a peculiar smile on his face. He slid his arm around my waist and, leaning over, kissed me firmly. Half of me suddenly wanted to drag him off to bed and the other half wanted to run screaming from the castle. Both urges being equal, I spent the next hour behaving disgracefully, teasing Simon and then biting his head off while he followed me around through the jovial crowd.

We ended up out on a balcony. I didn't know what to say to him, so I leaned on the balustrade, staring out into the late afternoon sunlight. Simon stood behind me, his hands on my shoulders. He said, dropping his hands to my hips and turning me indecently to face him, "Lisane, I don't know what to do. I don't know what you want. I'm helpless. Tell me to leave you

alone, or let me make love to you, but please don't torture me."
He looked terribly sincere and upset, but his hips were moving
against mine, slowly and deliberately. It was crude and offen-
sive, and I felt an almost painful sensation like a fist clenching
in my belly below the navel.

We found a vacant dressing room with a couch. Simon had
never been with a woman before, as I'd half suspected. Though
I'd had plenty of theoretical training, I'd never had any direct
experience—llerKalten having to be a virgin at her initiation.
We managed all right, considering, though it was probably the
silliest single event in my life, frustrating, painful, and driven.

Afterward, Simon wanted to ease me and I had to show him
how, and while he was doing that he got interested again.
While we were going at it a second time, Simon groaning and
thrusting blindly, I started to get a glimmer of what it was all
about. My first clue was that something was trying to knock the
top of my head off from inside, and I wanted to help it along,
primarily by moaning and hitting Simon. This inspired Simon
to complete insanity, and we nearly fell off the couch. He got
offended when I started to laugh, but it didn't stop him.

Afterward we lay in blank silence for a while, then helped
each other dress. Simon's eyes were heavy-lidded, and he
touched my skin all over as he dressed me. We drifted back out
to the tail end of the party, and Jens waved Simon over as we
entered the room. I went to get some more food. My hair had
fallen down. I felt like I hadn't been introduced to myself. I
was a stranger. I had looked in my first mirror, seen the blind
mad god in the rational priestlike eyes of Kaihan, and lost my
virginity in the same day. I wanted to go to sleep for a week. I
sat down at a table and ate as much as I could hold.

Kaihan sat down next to me, straddling the tiny chair backward with his arms folded on the back of it. I looked at him
warily, but the detached, amused expression was back. I felt as
if I wore Simon like an amulet, to protect me against this man.
He said nothing. I looked back across the room at Jens talking

animatedly to my guide, and my earlier question came back to me.

"Master Kaihan," I said, "how is it that Jens can be King if he is a mage? And how can he be married to Annesil? I thought mages had to renounce all offices and attachments."

He raised his eyebrows, and his dark eyes sparkled like a child's with obscure delight. "On some rare occasions, we must take away the only son of a king. If the king continues to have no heirs, and the child survives school and his Quest and is willing to reign, then the son is returned to him, to serve as heir and King, and sire heirs in his turn, until his successor is of age."

He was perfectly poised on his delicate chair, his face glinting with unspoken pleasure, his mouth curving secretively. I asked, "Why are you so pleased I asked that particular question?"

I will swear he looked startled for an instant. I had only met him three times now, but I was willing to wager very few people ever surprised him. I wondered what I was doing right, or what I was doing wrong. Twice in one day I'd taken this man unawares.

He sat unmoving for a moment, and then said, "Did you know that I am the great-grandfather of your guide's great-grandfather? I am a trifle older than I look." It was my turn to be surprised. Somehow, I had assumed he must be in his fifties. The non sequitur distracted me from my previous question, which might have been its intention, while I tried to figure out how old his claimed relationship made him.

"Your guide, on the other hand," he said, "is younger than he looks and far too serious for his age. Would you watch over him for me? He will have some hard decisions, and you will be traveling together for a while yet." He appeared to be completely serious.

"I could no more look after Simon than I could look after . . . after you," I said severely. "I can barely look after myself." He was still watching me, his chin resting on his arms and his eyebrows raised.

"You are not an utter fool, my dear," he said in his velvet voice. "You won't get to be a total idiot until you are at least my age. So don't try to weasel out of this. I put him in your care." I turned away from him in exasperation, in time to see a haphazard group approaching.

Simon, the Queen, and the King, with Detter following closely behind, processed across the floor to us through the thinning crowd, zigzagging slightly as Simon attempted to loose himself from Jens' left arm and Annesil, similarly restrained, bumped her ample hip exaggeratedly against Jens' right side. The Emsadorn royalty, as manipulative, capricious, and arbitrary as they were, reminded me a little of home.

The King released his captives, and the Queen reached me before Simon could, cutting him out neatly and leaving him to Kaihan's mercies. Jens slipped his arm through Detter's again, turned, and led him away. Detter's golden head gleamed in the streaks of sunlight from the high windows. He was dwarfed next to the King's huge bulk.

Annesil and I went upstairs to change our clothes for dinner and submit to the exasperated but hilarious ministrations of her ladies. Annesil raised her ginger eyebrows at the condition of my borrowed gown, and apparently I blushed, for they all began to tease me without mercy.

Now I was wearing a rose-colored gown with about a hundred buttons down the front, which, though high-collared, was somehow even more suggestive than the green dress. I checked the mirror again, guiltily. I still had green eyes, and they stared back at me shadowed and tired. I came down to a more intimate dinner, only fifty or so at a long table. Annesil was wearing an incredible bouquet of a dress in cream and burgundy. Jens kissed her hand, then started kissing his way up her freckled arm. Simon was staring at me with smoky eyes, his forelock flopping down, and I stared back at him across the table.

If he was younger than he looked, he must only be in his

twenties. I looked at his intense gray eyes and the wide, confident mouth, and thought, I bet he's no more than twenty-five. A great physical rush of tenderness and amusement poured over me. His solemnity, and his inexperience, and what we'd been doing that afternoon made me feel much more kindly toward him.

Toward the end of dinner, Kaihan leaned over and spoke in Simon's ear. Simon reacted as if he'd been slapped. "Sir!" he said, outraged. "That's not fair to me or to my students! We're most of the way there already. If we turn back on the western road, it will take twice as long." Kaihan looked unmoved.

Simon tried again, "My lord, I'd have to pass through Betzindahl. You know what happens to any mage who's fool enough to venture there. You know I am forbidden its borders."

Kaihan looked back at Simon like a weasel at a rabbit hole, calm, cheerful, and utterly focused. "It's not open to discussion," he said. "Detter needs the time, Lisane needs the time, and you need the time. Do it." He turned his implacable gaze away. Simon, dismissed, looked wounded and frightened, but he collected himself with an effort. I didn't know where we were headed in the first place, though I figured it had something to do with Sassevin, wherever that was, and the Beast, whatever it was. So I didn't know enough to care whether we went the long way or the short. I could have done with a little less of Detter's company on the way, though Detter at the moment was looking stupefied, harmless, and oblivious while the King stroked his downy neck with a free hand.

After dinner, the King escorted Detter off, and Simon, watching them leave, said to me, "Do you know what my reputation is here, why the guards knew my name?" I shook my head, and he said, "Jens was my guide, when he was on his Sorcerer's Search and I was questing for my ring. I wouldn't sleep with him at all. It drove him crazy. He's still talking about it and still pretending to try to seduce me."

I said, "Why did you turn him down?"

Simon said, "I was very young, and I was in love with another Student. I was going to be faithful." He looked morose and romantic, but spoiled it by saying, "Besides, Jens isn't to my taste. I like them smaller." I laughed. I pulled him upstairs, and made him unbutton my one hundred buttons, one by one. When I asked him, he told me reluctantly that he was indeed twenty-five. This time we didn't come close to falling off the bed, but I got my head banged against the wall and Simon was very contrite about it later.

Simon fell asleep, and I sat and wondered for a while how I did feel about him. Then I wondered if I knew how he felt about me. I poked him with my foot to wake him up and ask him, but he just grunted and turned over. I managed to button myself up again, and went exploring, though I was utterly groggy with tiredness and unexpected experience.

The palace was smaller than I'd thought, but a wonderful little place, all back stairs, extra rooms, attics, and closets. Most of the people who'd been at the reception must have lived somewhere else, and had now all gone home. I found the entrance hall again. The color guard was down to three men, who flirted amiably with me.

I poked around some more, found the steps down to the kitchens, and encountered Jens there, without Detter, taking ungracious lessons from a chef on how to make vanity cakes. I found a high stool and enjoyed the entertainment. He had an incredibly colorful vocabulary, which he used freely on the chef, the cakes, the cookstove, and all the utensils. I didn't think he noticed me in the shadows, but when the last batch of hollow cakes was pulled sizzling from the oil, the King wiped his greasy hands on his thighs, turned, and offered his arm gravely. I slipped off the stool and accompanied him silently back up the stairs and outside to a lamplit terrace.

It was quiet and hot, a slow humid breeze barely stirring the air. I could see that we were at the top of the city; lantern light flickered dimly all below us. The King settled his enormous bulk on a wooden bench, and I sat down in what space remained. I was feeling blank, drained, and only half conscious. My Voices were whispering sibilantly.

"The boy's in a bad way," he said, as if continuing a conversation.

"Which one?" I said dimly.

"Ah. I meant young Deteras. Simon is bad enough, but he's more cautious than anything else. Deteras is practically baying at the moon. My usual methods don't seem to have much of an effect."

I wondered what his "usual methods" were and what purpose they served. "The students all seem to learn only to hate one another, to fear their masters, and to despise themselves. How did you manage to survive the school? You still seem to like people and enjoy yourself."

He sighed gustily. "I was bigger than anybody, I'm a powerful mage, and I wasn't taken to the school until I was nearly ten. Nobody noticed my Power until then. Simon was brought when he was seven and Deteras was only five. The younger they start, the crazier they are. Kaihan tells me you spent only a year there, so that makes you a paragon of sanity. Advise me, paragon. What should I do with your young friend?"

What was I, everybody's all-purpose aunt? I didn't want to even think about Detter. I was silent. The King waited. My thoughts drifted, and the Voices muttered half-audibly in the back of my head. To my surprise, I heard myself eventually saying, in the flat voice of guided speech, "There is nothing that needs be done with him. He is as he is, and as he should be. He can master his pain, and it comforts him. He loves and he follows his truth. Let him be." It was probably the looniest thing I'd ever heard come out of my mouth, and I've issued some peculiar pronouncements at the prodding of my Voices. The massive shadow beside me didn't move. Maybe he wasn't listening. Maybe he was asleep. No, maybe I was asleep, and dreaming.

I was asleep. The King half woke me picking me up to take

me inside, but by the time he got me to the guest chamber that had been prepared for me I must have gone under again. I awoke in the morning to muffled voices in a courtyard below my window, and looked out to find Master Kaihan, well-groomed, on a glossy black horse, taking his leave of Jens. I didn't make any noise, but they both turned and stared up at me for a long minute, with enigmatic expressions. Then Kaihan cantered out and the King turned and went back inside. I felt as if I'd been struck in the face; I wasn't sure why.

I looked down and found I was still in my rumpled dress. I seemed to be making a habit of ruining other people's clothes. With a tinkle and a crash two maidservants bustled into my room with breakfast, and I put off any thinking until after I ate.

Annesil, red hair flying loose, came in wearing a dressing gown as I was finishing. She laughed herself into hiccups at the condition of my costume, and summoned one of her ladies to undo me. I had red welts from sleeping on seams and buttons. I missed my traveling clothes. She wouldn't let me have them again, but dug up a comfortable dress for me, not too fancy this time. She made me look in the mirror again. I was fascinated that the exotic stranger in the glass remained the same, with black hair and green eyes, eyebrows tilted wryly as if what she saw amused her and saddened her at the same time. I guessed the image wasn't going to change.

We sat and talked for a long time, and then went outside and walked around the grounds. She told me that her marriage had been arranged; that when Jens returned to the court two years ago, just before his father's death, his father had held a dance for eligible girls and her mother had made her go. "I didn't want to," she said, "but my mother said she would never make me go to court again if I went this once." She stayed by the re-freshments all night, stuffing herself and flirting with the stew-ard. Jens spent the evening dancing with, stepping on, pawing, and offending every young woman in the hall except Annesil. He never even talked to her that night.

Two weeks later the old King began negotiating with

Annesil's older brother for Annesil's hand, "which drove my mother nearly insane," said Annesil. "She was so used to being disappointed in me she didn't know how to handle it. She hasn't talked to me for two years."

She didn't really meet her husband until the wedding. "He'd never been with a woman before that," she said, and shook with remembered amusement, "because mages aren't supposed to sire children or indeed to lie with the Powerless at all. He wasn't incompetent, but it was an extremely odd experience." I could see why Jens had married her. She was candid, unaffected but not innocent, and she seemed to have little desire for power. I wondered why the old King had negotiated with Annesil's older brother for her hand, if she had a living mother. It didn't seem proper to let men get involved with the business of marriage, but nobody did things right on this world.

"How do they expect to get more mages if they forbid them to breed?" I asked.

"Oh, mages just pop up here and there like toadstools," she said vaguely. "You don't need to encourage them. There are too many of them as it is."

I knew, though I wasn't supposed to know, that on Mennenkaltenei the inheritance of Power depended on a complex pattern born to the body, a pattern that had little chance of appearing by accident. If they didn't breed for Power, either the potential was dormant somehow in most of the people of this fierce little world, men and women alike, or things worked differently here.

There were so many things I wasn't supposed to know, like the sciences and other things people only discussed in hushed voices when I was near. Mennenkalts keep their deities far from the dirty business of technology.

No, Jens would have fat Powerful babies with Annesil. Suddenly, I remembered something Kaihan had said. "Annesil," I said, "if a mage tells you he's somebody's great-grandfather, what does that mean?"

"It means he's a liar, a cheat, or a king," she said promptly. I tucked the information away in my head. Kaihan might be any one of the three, but I'd put my money on the third.

We lazed about in the sunshine until lunchtime. She was the first woman I had talked to in four years, so I was grateful that she seemed to be as attached to me as I was to her. Other people joined us now and then, all seeming jovial and cheerful as their King, dressed grandly and gaudily. Though all the other women I met were underweight, and were trussed up and bound in yards of fabric like ovenbirds, they could laugh loudly enough, and they were friendly to me. The men, broad in the cheekbones and with twinkling eyes, tended to be fat and avuncular. I didn't trust them completely. All too often, the people who seem most hearty and kindly are those who don't admit even to themselves that they have impure motives.

Simon, looking handsome, peeved, and possessive, found us in early afternoon but I ignored him. I doubted that ignoring him would help me figure out how I felt about him, but it made him so uncomfortable I couldn't resist. Besides, I had begun to suspect it was not only the unlikely sight of the Lisane in a dress that had spurred him to action. He finally got angry and left.

Annesil said, "Are you afraid of him or was that just an exercise in meanness?"

I considered and said, "Both," and she grinned at me. Later in the afternoon I tried to apologize to Simon but he was being mature and obtuse. After dinner he followed me out to the garden as if by accident. We sat on a stone bench and kissed and quarreled and hugged and fought. He tried to tell me what I should do, and I told him he could either be my guide or my bed-cozy but not both in the same breath. He tried to be stuffy and self-sacrificing. I started unbuttoning his flies. We ended up on a patch of grass behind an ornamental bush. I ruined yet another dress that belonged to somebody else.

Afterward, lying beneath him, I grabbed his ears and said, "And just who told you yesterday it was all right to fool around with a woman if the woman's a mage too?"

His face closed up and he tried to pull away, but I dug my fingernails in and said again, "Who told you? It wasn't your idea and it wasn't just the overwhelming effect of my new dress." He reached up and pried my fingers loose, but I wrapped my legs around him. He propped himself up on stiff arms above me, looking dim and far away in the dusk.

I said, "It doesn't matter. I don't care," and let him go.

He hung there and said quietly, "Master Kaihan told me it was permissible after the reception line was over, and immediately I went to find you. I had desired you for a long time, but above all I am obedient to my order's rules. Are you angry with me?"

I laughed, though I felt bewildered. "Every time I run into Kaihan he sticks a spoon into my life and stirs." I pushed against the insides of his arms and he fell on top of me with a startled grunt. I wasn't going to think about Kaihan or the myriad plans he seemed to be pursuing.

That night I dreamed a true dream. I was flying the ancient and peculiar Master Kaihan like a kite. He was floating black-clad and still in a blue sky with no wind, looking down at me. I let go of the string and he swooped and eddied away into the depths of the sky, but I could still see him, and he felt close by. I woke up feeling oddly reassured, though I could find no reason why the presence of Kaihan could do anything but disturb me.

It was time to leave. I persuaded Annesil to give me my clothes back, and found that they had been repaired and embroidered with flowers that coiled around the sleeves of the shirt and the legs of the trousers. It made me feel terribly festive to wear them. I went down to the entry hall, where our small stack of equipment and supplies sat in a pathetic heap in the middle of the floor. Simon was dressed and ready to go, but Detter wasn't there yet. I occupied myself with repacking my supplies, while Simon paced back and forth.

He was impatient to get going, though he looked very gloomy about the route he'd been ordered to take. "We'll have to go north along the coast, then west across the mountains and through the hills of Betzindahl to the far coast, and take ship there. We'll be hitting the mountains at the worst time of the year, and even if we survive the mountains, Betzindahl is un-friendly to mages."

"Do you do everything Kaihan tells you to do? What's the point of going this way instead of that way?" I asked.

Simon said patiently, "I do as the Master tells me, because it is my duty and my responsibility. If you would learn to stop questioning everything, you would have far less trouble." So he was going back to being a prig now that we were heading back to the road.

Jens and Detter wandered into the hall, looking sleepy and content. The King had somehow managed to get Detter to look as pleased with himself as when he had managed to thoroughly humiliate two or three younger boys. I doubted that the King would submit to such treatment, and wondered for the first time what magical powers Jens wielded. The King embraced each of us thoroughly and enthusiastically, saving his last and best for a struggling Simon, and ushered us out into the morning sunlight. He stood in the flowered archway watching us go, genial and relaxed, and just before we reached the perimeter I looked back and saw Annesil slip up beside him and lean against him. An odd arrangement, but they seemed comfortable.

We left the city by a different route, exiting through a high gate in a mighty wall as the morning traffic of coaches and commercial wagons streamed in. The smell in the air was of spices and horses, dust and perfume, the aromas of power and success. We headed north on a road that paralleled the coast. People hailed us in friendly fashion, and I felt optimistic and happy. It was good to be traveling again, good to be free. I thought I could handle everything. It's good to feel that way once in a while, even if it's not true.

CHAPTER SIX

In Which I Don't
Prevent an Accident

Simon sank back into abstraction as we headed away from the city. He walked through the crowds of people and animals as if he were alone on a wilderness path, his long legs swinging out rhythmically and his gray eyes looking toward the horizon. Detter was similarly distracted, though his thoughts were turned inward. He smiled faintly to himself as he walked, and his blue eyes flickered back and forth as if he were listening to a conversation inside his head. The traffic parted amiably enough around us, some of the passersby saluting Simon's neckring with perfunctory bows and eyeing us, particularly me, with curiosity.

I stared frankly back. Though the day was hot, all the women wore full skirts and shawls, and their heads were covered. The men wore baggy pants and long loose overshirts. The colors of their voluminous garments were achingly bright, and the mixed stripes and patterns produced a vibrating, eye-straining effect in the brilliant sunlight. Simon, Detter, and I, in our drab walking clothes, looked like field animals in comparison.

We stopped at midday to rest beside the road and eat a bit of the provisions we'd been given at the castle. The road was less crowded now that we were farther away from Deistel Dom, but there were several small groups like ours taking shelter from the noon sun under the trees. From one such group a man came over to us and patiently stood before Simon until Simon noticed his presence with a start, as if called from sleep. Simon said, "Yes? How can I help you?"

The man, dressed in a road-grimed but spectacular purple and green overshirt, grinned uneasily, showing two missing teeth. He said deferentially, "Lord, you are a Magician by your ring." Simon nodded. "My wife is at her time and having trouble. Could you help her?"

Simon said, puzzled, "Is there no herb-wife handy?" The man shook his head, and Simon grumpily stood up, dusting off his pants and muttering, "This is not my proper work." He prepared to leave but turned to us first. "I may be a while. Both of you morons stay where you are until I come back. And remember the rules."

Detter seemed not to hear him, but I was highly offended. Yesterday he had called me his heart's jewel, today I was a moron. "I'll promise I'll only *think* about turning you into a legless frog," I said snippily as they walked away.

The man with the missing teeth looked back in surprise and said to Simon, "They are both your students? I thought the girl a servant. She is a witch? Has she any knowledge of childbirth?" Simon just kept walking, and the man hastened after him, looking back at me over his shoulder. What a screwball question. Why should I be a servant if I were dressed exactly the same as my companions? Perhaps it was because women were not mages here, though the thought was worrisome. How could men have Power and women not? And what was a witch, and what was an herb-wife?

Detter sat cross-legged on a protruding root, meditatively chewing. A couple of days out of the sun had taken most of the boiled look from his face. He'd gotten a hat somewhere and was wearing it, so his skin would probably recover. He was still lovely and looked utterly innocent and fresh. He swallowed his mouthful and focused abruptly on me. "What did you say to the King about me? He said he talked to you."

So I had indeed spoken aloud to Jens. "I don't really remember, Detter. I wasn't listening to what I said to him." I often didn't listen to my guided speech, especially if it ran counter to common sense.

An expression of impatience crossed his face. "You needn't fear insulting me."

"Honestly, Detter, I really don't remember. I think I told him he should stay away from you." I was beginning to recall what I'd said, but I didn't feel like sharing it with Detter.

"If you won't tell me, it doesn't matter." He started unbuttoning his shirt. "He gave me a message for you, though. He said to show you this and tell you he took the easy way out." He pulled his shirt open with a nasty gleam in his eye. His white chest was covered with fading red welts, as from an enthusiastic whipping. The skin was broken and scabbed in spots. He watched me with detached amusement as I flinched, then he pulled the shirt down his arms to reveal his delectable shoulders mottled with gray-blue bruises. I looked away. I could not believe that grand, jolly, lusty man could have done this to anyone, even Detter.

Detter said, with a peculiar lift to his voice, "He said he left the hard road to you. What's the hard road?" I looked back at him. He was buttoning up his shirt casually but his eyes were dilated. "What's he want you to do, Lise, kill me?"

I didn't know. There was no possible way of answering Detter's question so I sat staring at him blankly, my thoughts revolving. I was an ignorant castaway, dragged by accident into the perverse and long-lived conspiracies of these mages. They were all pursuing their arcane goals, their grand strategies, and I was straggling along blind and witless behind them.

Yet they seemed to think me capable of all kinds of wondrous acts. Kaihan had thought nothing of asking me to take care of Simon, Simon who understood and obeyed all the rules of this world and moved in it with assurance and purpose, if without imagination. And now Jens was asking that I find some way to deal with this impossible blond demon.

Detter was leaning forward, obviously enjoying my discomfiture. I said abstractedly, "Oh, don't worry, Detter. I couldn't possibly do what he wants me to do, whatever it is." But I sat and stared at him, ignoring everything he said, until Simon came back from playing midwife.

He had refused payment, and the new father was following and timidly expostulating with him. Simon whirled on him and said, "I have no need of your money or your food. Accept my services as freely given and leave me alone."

"He'll just come and take the baby back in a few years," said a jeering voice from a group farther down the road. The man backed away from Simon and walked hurriedly back to his family. Simon glared in the direction of the voice. All of the groups of people within earshot began to pack up and return to the road, not looking at us.

Simon said to me, "There's a folk myth that we take children not to educate them as mages, but to kill them in some kind of mystical ritual." He sat down heavily between us. "It's pathetic. Some people even try to conceal their Talented brats from us. It's where most of the renegades come from. Some fool of a village is always raising a boy unguided by the Order, and then they beg us to rescue him when he's grown—if he hasn't already drawn our attention by trying to assassinate us."

Detter said blithely, "Well, don't we kill them? After all, how many boys actually live through school and Quest?" Simon ignored him. Detter said, "The little ones kill themselves off, the older ones murder each other, and most of the rest die from the Quest or the Beast. And then what?"

Simon got up again and shouldered his pack without speaking. I scrambled up to follow, and Detter sat on the tree root smiling cherubically. He continued, "The ones who survive get to travel around homeless looking for more children to condemn, or else they stay forever in Sassevin sucking up to more powerful mages, or they are glorified servants to this petty prince or that, or hated captive sires breeding more princes. We should just kill most of the children off to begin with; it would mean less time, less expense, less trouble . . ." We were out of range of the mocking voice.

Simon said to me bitterly, "Detter thinks he had such a hard time. At least he was leaving no one behind when he went with the mages. My father wept when the mages took me, even though I had killed his trusted friend with my first exercise of Power. He pleaded with them and argued, and when they wouldn't yield he cursed them and said he'd never offer welcome to mages again. He kissed me and told me I was no longer his son, that he had no son. Then he acted as if I wasn't there anymore." He sounded far more sorry for himself than Detter ever did.

I glanced back. Detter was strolling along well behind us, his hat pushed back on his ethereal head. What Jens had said intrigued and repelled me, for I had begun to realize what the "hard road" was with Detter. The easiest thing to do was to strike him when provoked, the hardest to hold back. No, the hardest would be to care for him as for a friend. I wondered if I could ever bring myself to feel anything but irritation and loathing for Deteras Anhand. It would be an interesting exercise of my childhood training, and it would certainly drive Detter crazy.

We walked comfortably for the rest of the afternoon, Detter strolling far behind. Simon and I chatted desultorily, on matters of general interest, and I wondered what would happen between us tonight. He would probably be embarrassed to share my blankets in front of Detter. Or maybe he wouldn't. Maybe I would be.

"Simon," I said, a thought forcing itself forward, "how can you aid a woman in childbirth? I'd swear you didn't know how a woman was put together until a couple of days ago."

He looked offended. "I don't have to stare at someone's private parts to cast a birthing spell."

"Why not? There could have been any number of different things wrong. Didn't you teach me the spell must be specific to the situation? What did you do, then, just rip the baby out whole with one spell and heal them both with another?" He nodded. "That's really sloppy," I said.

He was silent. After a moment he said stiffly, "You're right.

It's how I was taught to do it, but you're right. I suppose the herb-wives do it differently."

Well, well, I thought, give yourself a medal, Lisane. You're right for once. I didn't push the topic any more. Detter caught up with us around dusk.

We'd passed through two small villages during the day, and gone past several small homes in between, but Simon decided to stop in the middle of a long desolate stretch of road with no signs of human occupation. We walked off the road to a level spot among some trees, well sheltered and dry, and unrolled our blankets. Simon put his bedroll apart from mine and from Detter's. I cocked an eyebrow at him and he pretended not to notice. He sent Detter off to gather some wood, and cleared a patch of ground for a fire, since with darkness the air had suddenly chilled. We all sat around the small crackling blaze and stared into it, our faces hot and our backs chilled, until we couldn't stay awake any longer. I wrapped myself up in my blanket all alone, and fell asleep almost immediately to the flickering glow of the banked fire.

Some time later somebody was nudging my shoulder. I opened my eyes to complete blackness. The fire must have gone out. A voice hissed gently next to my ear, "Lisane," and I realized it must be Simon. I extricated an arm from my blanket and gave him a firm shove. With a startled exhalation he rolled back. I snarled at him, "I won't pretend I only know you in the dark." A light chuckle sounded from the direction of Detter's blanket, and Simon went away. I heard no more of him that night. I wouldn't skulk around Detter as if he were a children's chaperon.

Simon looked gray and grouchy in the morning. Detter hummed to himself irritatingly. I set my jaw and decided to detest them both after all. We set off again on the road north. It took three days, during which I ignored Simon, Simon ignored me, and Detter strutted along behind us cheerfully, before Simon would condescend to lay his blanket next to mine at night. And two more days before I forgave him enough to enjoy myself.

Soon after that we crossed the border between Emsadorn and the next small country to the north. I thought at first it must be Betzindahl, because the people there obviously cared less for mages, but Simon said it was a minor kingdom called Telique. We were left strictly alone on the road and off it. People stared at us from the corners of their eyes, muttering to themselves and occasionally spitting not quite at us. They were dressed less colorfully than the Emsadorn peasants, and the whole countryside seemed less prosperous and confident. In our plain clothing, we might have stood out much less in this country were it not for Simon's plain brown neckring, but that was apparently enough difference for the locals.

When we camped for the night, Simon said, "If it's this bad in Telique, it will be impossible for us to travel openly in Betzindahl."

Detter laughed and said, "Why not just set a few of them on fire or turn them into animals? That would make the rest of these filthy peasants respect us."

Simon looked at him with a bitter light in his eye. "Why do you think they detest mages on sight? Some fool probably has done something like that to them already. Once you start trying to frighten people, you must keep on your guard forever."

Detter answered unrepentantly, "It's just because there aren't enough mages to keep the normals in line."

"How many mages are there altogether?" I asked, idly flipping a glowing coal over with a stick and watching bits of bark shrivel up in smoke. When I didn't get an answer, I looked up to see Detter smiling at Simon and Simon's face closed and still. I had asked an unfair question again, obviously.

Detter drawled, "There are a lot less than there used to be, aren't there, Simon?"

Simon didn't reply.

Detter said, "Didn't you say there were mages on your world, Lise? How many did you have?"

"They weren't mages, Detter. They were just people. Some had more Power than others, but I guess about half the population had Talent of some kind. None of them used it the way you people do, though. It would be considered rude."

Simon's lip curled. "Half a world of mages? Come on, Lisane, don't fantasize."

Detter said, "You should hear what she says about her family. Her father was a professional suicide, her mother was a prostitute mage, and Lisane herself is a cannibal."

Simon said wearily, "That's enough, Detter."

"It's true enough," I said. "Though you could describe all of us, my father, my mother, and me, as professional-suicide-prostitute-cannibal-mages." It sounded terribly funny in this language, not dignified or glorious at all. I snorted involuntarily, triggering myself into a fit of giggles.

Simon waited, his eyebrows raised, until I stopped being amused by myself. "Would you care to explain that, or is it too humorous for words?"

Since it was the words that made it so funny, I spluttered again, but said, "All right. I'll try." I collected myself, folded my arms, and said formally, "Kindly hear me now," as if they were a group of children being schooled.

Detter started to say something, but Simon waved him down. I waited until they were both still, then began, as far as I could in this language, to formally explain Mennenkalt government.

"We are a practical people," I said. "Like you, we understand that life, strength, and power are bought only with death, weakness, and submission. Unlike you, we prefer to pay afterward instead of in advance."

Simon started to object but I glared him down firmly.

"Our world is called Mennenkaltenei, meaning roughly 'male joined with female,' or 'union of gods,' though the most direct translation is 'this and that.' It is ruled by llerMennet, the Year-King or Father, and llerKalten, the Queen or Mother.

"The Mennet is chosen by his predecessor from the young

men called Postulants, and rules for only a year. He has ultimate power of decision over the world, wields immense strength by reason of complete possession and mastery of magic, and lives life to the full, eating, drinking, dancing, loving, and siring countless children during his reign. He is gloriously alive and majestic, utterly wise and dangerous, fearfully transfigured and childlike. At the end of his year, he chooses a successor, and is then by him ritually slaughtered, going to his death insane, debased, and helpless, in payment for his reign. His body is cooked and consumed by his subjects as a celebration of life and an acknowledgment of death. My father was one such Mennet, and I have heard his reign was glorious."

Simon looked mildly revolted; Detter's eyes sparkled.

"The future Kalten is chosen as a young child by the reigning Kalten from among all Talented girl children of a certain generation. The child is raised to understand her duties, to learn the necessary skills, and to observe certain strictures. She is rigorously trained in what you call magic, learns the art of administration, and is taught the various erotic techniques. She remains virgin until her installation, has no real name, carries the voices of her predecessors in her head, and is never permitted to look in a mirror lest she forget her divinity. She is installed as Kalten at about the age of nineteen, when she first couples with the new Mennet and conceives his child. Where the Mennet has rights, she has responsibilities. She has ultimate power of administration, wields the strength of complete understanding of and coexistence with magic, and lives life to the full, loving, desiring, nurturing, producing. During her reign she is arbitrary, prophetic, whimsical and practical, comforting, punishing, erotic, and motherly. She continues to bear a child by each Mennet until she has borne twenty children. At the end of her twenty years, she abdicates her rule in favor of her successor, and becomes barren, wordless, and withered. Because she no longer has any interest in living, she usually starves to death in a short time. Her body is abandoned where it lies, ignored. My birth mother was Kalten, wise and good, wild and glorious.

"This is how my world is governed. The Mennet makes the laws, the Kalten carries them out, and they pay for their power with, as Detter has said, ritual murder and suicide, prostitution and cannibalism. The people they rule are peaceful, happy, and productive. There is always enough for all.

"Well, that's the way it was, anyway," I finished lamely. "The Enforcers walked in and blew everything to bits with no trouble at all, so it was obviously not as strong a system as I thought." I relaxed and sat back from the formal story-teacher's pose.

"So your father and mother were king and queen of your world," said Simon, frowning.

"Yes," I said. "For what it's worth, which isn't much anymore."

Detter said, "If it didn't sound so brutish, I'd swear you'd made it all up. It's wonderfully pat—if your mother and father were king and queen, what does that make you, Your Majesty?"

"High office wasn't hereditary." Detter assumed this was either a reluctant admission or an attempt to make my story more plausible.

He said to Simon, "And you thought I was the only savage on this trip. What do you think of someone who could say all that primitive stuff and still sound serious?"

Simon's lock of hair had fallen across his eyes. He looked very young in the firelight. He was thinking about something, and he didn't talk anymore until we were wrapped together in our blankets. I had one thigh over his hip and we were rubbing lazily against each other, hands and lips exploring luxuriously, when he stopped, raised his head, and said quietly to me, "Lisane."

"Hmmm?" I murmured, not interrupting what I was doing.

"You *were* chosen to succeed your mother, weren't you?

Whether or not it was supposed to be hereditary? I could tell by your expression. And you've run away somehow."

I stilled my hands, and nodded silently in the dark.

"Do you ever feel that you should have stayed and done your job, even if it meant your death?"

This was unusually perceptive of Simon, but it felt like a blow. When I struck that soulless man down and stole the ship, I'd known I was leaving my duties behind, those pathetic people who tried so hard to be happy for my sake.

He said, "Never mind. I'm sorry. I'm feeling morbid," and lowered his lips to my neck again. For a moment, I toyed with the image of myself as a tragic, hollow exile, lost to honor by choosing to live. Then Simon said, "Ahh" in an almost inaudible tone, and began moving more purposefully. I put aside my cosmic considerations in favor of more immediate and urgent concerns, such as how to fuse my whole skin to his without losing the blanket. When it was all over, the blanket was crumpled somewhere beneath us and my skin was still identifiably my own, but I had a glowing sense of accomplishment nonetheless, not in the least bit lessened by Detter's strategic exercise in throat clearing at a crucial moment. Simon was a remarkably fast learner.

After a few days of being subtly and not-so-subtly scorned in Telique, Simon began to wear a scarf wrapped around his neck to hide the ring. He dug a coin out of the bottom of his pack when we passed through a village on market day, and bought me a skirt and a headcloth. Simon explained apologetically that he didn't want to arouse any more attention than necessary. Detter seemed to take some satisfaction in my new costume. "What dishonor is there in dressing as other women do?" I asked Simon. "Why do you apologize?"

Simon was uneasily startled. "No dishonor, no dishonor, none at all," he said, waving his hands.

Detter said, "And when shall we see you dressed as a woman, master?"

Simon shot him a look, and Detter batted his eyelashes at him.

I thought about this odd event as I walked, kicking my skirts forward comfortably. It confirmed something I'd been noticing since Emsadorn. Women and men seemed very concerned with distinguishing themselves from each other. The costumes were the most obvious difference, but they also behaved very differently, women tending toward an odd delicacy and sub-servience, and men toward arrogance and physical display. Why would anybody want to make women and men seem any more different than they already were? I put it on my list of things to ponder when I didn't have anything better to do.

Whatever its implications, our slight disguise served to de-flect any further unwelcome interest, and we made our way north through Telique without further incident. The days were getting shorter, though it was still heavily hot while the sun shone. We bypassed a city, though Simon said a fellow mage dwelt there, because we could not afford to lose any time get-ting to the mountains. It was early fall now, but Simon said winter would come on with no warning in the hills. We finally left the broad market road near its end at the northernmost tip of Telique, and struck inland on an unpaved track toward the ragged blue shadows we could see at the horizon. We had not seen the ocean yet, though we had been no more than fifty miles from it the whole length of the road. Were there seabirds and sand on this world? Was the sea salt? Did its waves have froth? I was reluctant to turn my footsteps toward the moun-tains again, and my Voices were suspicious and complaining, though they had no feet to collect blisters.

We passed by a few small villages and then some scattered single dwellings, but by the time we reached the foothills we hadn't seen any other humans for several days. I changed back into trousers, for while a skirt is handy for relieving yourself and making love, it does nothing but get in the way on rough terrain.

The nights were becoming crisp, and Simon drove us

unmercifully toward the two peaks that grew to dominate the western sky. The range was much taller here than where we'd crossed before, and was crowned with snow even down to the join between mountains. The so-called pass we were aiming for looked as if it was as far above sea level as the tops of the mounts in the southern end of the range. This explained some of Simon's dismay when Kaihan told him to take this route.

We were all three in much better shape than when we first left the school. Detter in particular had acquired a long-legged effortless stride that made me look like a donkey scurrying behind a thoroughbred. But none of us was in any condition to take real hardship. I hoped we would have ller on our side— even if I had promised not to speak to ller—when we crossed that pass. My Voices were speaking to me sternly.

As we approached our goal, we kept walking doggedly, but the ground leaned further and further into us. The plants grew scrubby and gray, and there were places where their roots had failed to hold up the earth against gravity and half a pasture had fallen downhill. Soon we had to pick our way carefully to avoid falling ourselves, and when we reached a level spot we claimed it for the night, though it was early still. I listened to the foreboding conversation in my head, watched the sky-spirit swirl and cavort, and listened to the occasional rock or clump of dirt roll down the hillside near us. I suspected the people of Telique didn't visit Betzindahl very often, if this was the easiest path between the countries.

In the morning I unpacked my rope, and argued with Simon for another hour of climbing until he ungraciously agreed that we should tie ourselves loosely together. He made it a condition that he should go up first and I should go last, and that was what we did, though his reasoning was poor mountain-climbing practice. Detter was completely contemptuous of the rope, and it obviously chafed his pride to be attached to either of us in any way. I didn't care how either of them felt, just concentrated on keeping my feet steady and my handholds secure, just in case.

The footing was loose, and got looser. Bare outcroppings of mountain thrust up here and there through rivers of jumbled fallen rock. I tried to have at least one hand on solid rock, my heart pounding, while Detter and Simon scrambled along carelessly. It had been years since my one brief experience, an obligatory pilgrimage to the Solitary Temple.

Improbably, we reached the frozen height of the pass by afternoon, the two great peaks rearing awesomely away from us on either side, glowing rosily in the late cold sun. Simon started to plunge downward immediately, his breath huffing in impatient clouds, but I yelled, "Wait," and made him let me go down first. He and Detter kept trying to hurry me up, because they wanted to get to level ground before dark, but the footing was just as loose here and the incline a bit sharper.

Finally, Detter said, "Stop a minute." He was trying to untie the rope with his half-frozen hands. Holding on to a crevice in a sheer outcropping next to me, I yelled, "No, don't," as Simon half slid down near him.

Detter said to him, "She's holding us up. This is ridiculous. Help me get this undone."

Simon crab-walked across to him. I yelled desperately, "Don't untie him," and Simon put his foot down on a loose flat rock that wobbled, pitching him first backward, then forward, and he fell, arms splayed and headfirst, down the hill. I shoved my numb fingers into the crevice, and braced my feet against projections in the outcropping as Simon tumbled past me, jerking Detter off balance with the rope still tied to his waist. Detter's foot was wedged between two rocks as he fell in turn, and he screamed in pain. Then his bootless foot pulled free, and he slid downhill after Simon. The rope jerked taut around my waist, and I felt an agonizing wrench and snap in two of my fingers as the sudden weight knocked the breath out of me, but I held on and held on and held on.

Eventually the loose rocks stopped tumbling down the hill behind me, but the weight on the rope was still steadily dragging me away from my hold. Detter groaned, and I called thinly, with what breath I could gather, "Can you find anything to hold on to?" but he just groaned again.

I couldn't breathe; my fingers were slipping and screaming. I freed one foot and tentatively planted it into the rubble behind me. It didn't slip much, so I gradually brought some more weight to bear on it and then brought the other foot back until I was standing angled against the slope. Then I slowly let go with my fingers and sank to my knees, hoping my footing was firm enough to resist the rope pull.

Detter groaned once more as I got down on all fours and began shuffling down backward. He slipped further down as I crawled, but finally the rope slackened as he came to rest. I came up against a protruding shelf of rock that was solid, and turned around to look.

Detter was sprawled on his back, head downhill, between two large boulders. His leg was covered with blood and his left ankle was snapped sideways, displaying blood, bone, and shredded skin. His eyes were rolled up in his head but he was breathing.

Simon was farther down the incline, flung loosely like a rag doll, at the end of a trail of blood-blazed stones, blood that must have come from the dark stain on his head. He was breathing, but too heavily, his rib cage heaving.

I sat down on my shelf and thought for a moment, absent-mindedly pressing a loose fingernail back into place with a wince. My Voices grunted and gibbered. I looked at my grimy, half-crushed hands, then down at Simon and Detter unconscious, and laughed, an odd sound in the whistling cold wilderness.

"Lle bevantegihn gehertelkallen," I said quietly. A wisp of ller trailed out of the wind and coiled around my hands in a fig-ure eight, an opalescent silver glowing. "Ekestverten ller an-danfellter, kavelnes ke," I suggested, and lle called more of ller into the loop, until I had a racing double loop the size of a skein of yarn flowing around the poles of my arms. I raised my hands with their speeding halo into the air, and shook ller gently toward the recumbent figures below me on the slope. My hands were partially healed now, the snapped bones straight and whole, the fingernails reattached, but the flesh was bruised and scraped. The silver glow rolled and roiled over and through Detter, then tumbled excitedly down to Simon. Detter groaned again, but now his ankle was merely purple and swollen, no longer shattered, just badly sprained. His eyes flickered open as the mass of ller flowed like a fountain over Simon. I tensed, then remembered Detter couldn't see magic. He probably wouldn't guess what I'd done. Simon's back arched as lle left him, and lle spun back into strands of wind as his eyes opened in turn. Even from where I crouched, I could see something was still very wrong with Simon. His pupils were dilated and he didn't seem really conscious. My spell had been designed only to mostly heal. If Simon was mostly healed now, he must have been nearly dead before. I didn't dare go to him yet until Detter was secured, though.

Detter said, "I think my ankle's broken," to the air. His voice was shaky.

"Hold on, I'm coming down," and I picked my way carefully to him. He pulled himself up to a sitting position and stared blankly at his swelling ankle.

"I could have sworn I felt it snap," he said calmly, his voice firm again. I looked at it, felt it, and said, "No, I think it's just twisted. Don't move it."

I scooted cautiously down to Simon, and confirmed my fears. He was badly hurt, though his skull didn't seem crushed. Detter didn't look so hot himself when I glanced back and caught him unaware. Could I get away with another spell? Detter seemed too alert. Things were very complicated already, and another spell might screw things up even more. It would have to wait.

I said, "Detter, can you slide real slowly down to us on your bottom? Without jiggling your foot?" He contemptuously did so without response, though his foot was obviously causing him incredible pain. His stoicism, if nothing else, was admirable. I inched us forward as a group in the gathering dusk, until we reached a broader rib of rock. I undid the rope and Simon's pack and began to wrap him in his blankets, then sighed exasperatedly, unwrapped him, and made Detter, now shaking and blank-eyed, lie down beside him. I covered them both with the rest of the blankets and the rain capes.

My teeth were chattering in reaction and cold, but I was going to sit and watch over them for a while and maybe sneak in another healing spell. Detter said shakily, "Come lie down, you stupid sow, I'm still cold," and I surrendered, sliding in next to Simon's warm, limp, breathing body. The next thing I knew, it was morning.

Simon was still unconscious, and Detter seemed still asleep. Detter's face was puffy and pale, and he looked sad and ill. I slid from beneath the blankets and hastily called another half-healing spell on both of them, working as swiftly and quietly as I dared. Detter's eyes did not open, but Simon's eyelids flickered and he arched his back gently, stretching his legs. His hair was still matted with blood, but I was pretty sure he would be all right, and I had given Detter's health an overall boost without fixing his ankle. I figured he wouldn't be grateful that I'd saved his worthless life. If he had the slightest suspicion I'd cheated and used magic, he'd use it on me somehow.

I stood up carefully on the ridge of rock and peered down the incline in the cold morning mist. How far was it to the beginning of vegetation and more secure footing? Assuming I could get my companions that far, I could rig some kind of shelter and get some food into them.

Detter cleared his throat elaborately and I jumped. He was sitting up watching me. "Done admiring the view?" he said gaily, his blue eyes shining. "Shall we all take a stroll before breakfast or do you need to meditate further on your sins?" A chill of revulsion ran down my back. I probably should have left him sick, I thought. Less trouble that way. Oh, well.

Simon was lying awake now, squinting and holding his hands to his head. He made a retching sound, but luckily there was nothing in his stomach. I wrapped him securely in blankets and cloaks, and began to drag him slowly downhill. That didn't work, because each bump and slide made him cringe in pain, so I left him and came back up. Some of the rope served to tie Detter's leg to a rolled blanket as a makeshift brace, and I got him started hitching himself downhill. He chattered cheerfully and inanely the whole time, and I didn't answer him. Then I collected the packs and hiked everything down, past Simon and Detter, to the first level patch of grass I found. When I labored back up, Detter had covered a good bit of ground, and Simon was sitting up. I slowly got him to his feet and helped him walk down. By the time I had him settled, Detter reached us, and we all sat on the cold patch of grass in the weak sunshine, drank the rest of our water, and ate the last of the food. Simon looked gray and frail, Detter looked hungover, and I felt like a bucket of mud, but we were alive.

CHAPTER SEVEN

In Which I Don't Get My Man

We were three grown adults shoehorned into a leaf-plastered lean-to night after night, and we smelled bad. At least Detter and Simon smelled bad, Detter like some small carnivorous cat and Simon like a dog with swamp-fever. I assume I had an odor of my own, but luckily I couldn't smell it myself.

The hut, a shaky bundle of branches and brush, was built into a crevice in the foothills of the mountain, well below the snow line, with trees all around us and a spring very near. A real little paradise, considering Simon couldn't walk any farther than that. Detter, though he defied pain, couldn't walk very well on his ankle. The winter rains had arrived, and travel was slimy, cold, and treacherous. I'd built a shelter for myself the year I was alone in the wilderness surrounding the school, which taught me that the smaller, the better. There was less air to heat that way. However, I hadn't had to live with anybody during that time. I'd been better off then than I thought.

Simon wasn't so bad. He slept frequently but restlessly since the accident, and I sometimes got angry at him just because he was sick and weak and recovering so slowly. Detter, though, had me completely on edge. He watched me all the time. Sometimes even in the dark I'd wake up and realize he was leaning on his elbow, breathing regularly, looking at me, though the darkness was total. In the daytime he would hobble around gathering wood or patiently waiting by a snare for some unwary animal, but when he wasn't working he was standing, staring at me blankly. It got so there was a weight on my back even when he wasn't near.

Oddly, he was helpful, restrained, and polite. He spoke only when spoken to, and his insults and sarcasm were mild and rare. That was almost as unsettling. He must be planning something, and I would only know what it was when he had sprung his trap.

I tended patiently to Simon, lost to me as a lover. He was pale, fretful, and childish. He no longer looked like a healthy woodsman but like some lost hopeless natural wandering around the edges of civilization. During the third week, though, a ghost of a smile began to quirk around his mouth when the pain in his head wasn't too bad, and I began to remember what was pleasing about him. It was a pity the rain was so heavy and the shelter so small. I was damned if I would invite Detter in on any activities, and given the size of the shelter there was no way to exclude him.

After we had been there about a month, Detter and I began to build another, larger shelter out of tree branches, sod, and compost, the first one having begun to deteriorate and leak badly. Detter's ankle was almost healed, though he might limp for a long time. I had no opportunity to cast any more healing spells, since Simon slept so lightly and Detter could as easily be awake as asleep. Detter was helping me lift and lash a cross-branch onto the framework, when he said to me, "Lise, what do you think of yourself?"

That had no meaning. It appeared to be a perfectly sincere question, though sincerity was a meaningless concept when applied to Detter. I just made a face at him and kept winding vine around a joint.

"I mean it. Do you ever think about yourself, who you are, where you belong, what you're supposed to be doing? Or do you just react?" His face was dripping with rain, and his hair was plastered to his neck.

That night with Simon on the other side of the mountain, I had wondered for a moment if I shouldn't be dead back on

Mennenkaltenei or crammed in a dim hole on the ship. Other than that, I tried not to think about my purpose in life. My only purpose in life until I was fourteen was eventually to be llerKalten, nameless, fecund, and wise. After the Enforcers came I had no purpose except to survive and keep from upsetting my people, and I had not done very well at that. I ignored Detter, secured the end of the vine under the windings, and moved to the other end of the branch. He stood braced in the middle, his cold hands white and red gripping the crosspiece. He was still looking at me. He was always looking at me. My peripheral vision was filled with round wide blue eyes, as if everywhere I looked there would be Detter staring. I went back to get another branch from the pile we'd cut, and Detter followed me quietly, taking half the load as I lifted.

"Lise, how do you decide what to do? When you're handed a decision to make, how do you make it? What do you think about?"

"Don't talk, work," I said, my voice stupidly strained. He obediently lifted the new brace into position and waited. I knew this was a "don't answer." My tutor Jenneservet, teaching me the art of government, had told me there were two kinds of questions the llerKalten would have to deal with. The first kind should be answered immediately and with certainty, whether I was right or not, and the second kind should be ignored or passed on to the llerMennet.

Jenneservet asked me questions all the time, and slapped me if I answered too slowly, or if I tried to answer the wrong questions. "Make a choice," Jenneservet would say. "Answer or don't answer, wrong or right, black or white, but choose now and hold to your choice." For a long while I hated her, but as a capable and resilient five-year-old I began to figure the game out fairly fast. By the time I was seven, I rarely got slapped anymore. I missed Jenneservet. I wondered if she was still aboard the Enforcer transport, playing her double game.

So I chose not to answer Detter's question. I couldn't have answered him anyway. I tried to make as few rational decisions as possible. The last real decision I'd made had been to throw away my father's finger bone. I still missed it sometimes.

Detter was a wretched sight, no longer the rarefied angel I'd first met. His nose ran constantly, his hair was long and color-less with grease and dirt, and he had the strained gray look of long-term exposure to cold and rain. His eyes were as blue as ever, though, and his voice as dry and cool. He still moved beautifully, despite the limp.

We didn't finish the new shelter that day, and when Simon emerged exhausted from the woods with two limp, dead lizards and a handful of roots for dinner, it was too wet to even dream of kindling a fire. I hate raw meat, no matter how hun-gry I am. That night, still damp to the skin, I struggled out of my clinging old clothes in the wet darkness of the old lean-to and into a blanket that was dry only by comparison.

In the fetid, stinking dark while Detter adjusted the so-called door, I said almost inaudibly to Simon, "I suppose you've sworn some kind of oath not to use magic to help yourself or us, or you would have done something by now."

He laughed huskily next to my ear, and a cold hand found its way to my arm. He murmured almost silently, "Head injuries are hard on Talent, Lisane. Give me a little while yet. Don't say anything. Detter would find a way to make capital of it." His breath smelled like mushrooms, but the cold hand and the thready buzz of his voice in my ear unexpectedly stirred me. Detter crawled along and lay down on the other side of him. I felt my way along Simon's arm through the blankets to his moist chest, but his breathing had already settled into quiet regularity. He was asleep.

I lay awake and listened to the steady spit of the rain and the drip of the leaks in the roof. I'd dug channels and hung hollow stalks under the worst of the leaks to drain the water out, and pegged my rain cape under the center of the ceiling, so the wa-ter didn't hit us directly, but I was swimming anyway.

Simon breathed shallowly, and beyond him Detter began to gasp quietly and irregularly. Sometimes he did that at night, an ambiguous sound. It could have been pleasure or pain, sorrow or laughter. The sounds and the smells and the dampness kept on, and kept on, and I was awake still, queasily alert to the awkward and ugly mundane events of another ordinary, drowned, abandoned, crippled night in the company of my two involuntary fellow sufferers. My eyes began to burn and fill and my throat to close in the weary self-pity I had not allowed myself to feel since I was a small child worn out from too much teaching.

I struggled to hold my breath calm, but could feel my face drawing up in a rictus of grief. I was ashamed. It was not the end of my life, the time when I had always known I would be allowed to mourn. I had no license to weep, no permission to despair, for my reign had not ended. It would never begin. Yet I was lost and useless and hopeless and foolish. Detter's questions had set off all the bleak things I preferred not to think about. I had trained all my childhood to perform an office that no longer existed, and I did not know how to be a human being.

I drew a deep and shaky breath and oddly heard its echo from Detter on the other side of Simon's silent form. It was bleakly absurd. If I couldn't believe that I was weeping, I could even less believe it of the ice prince. The two of us, whimpering silently on either side of the unconscious body of our damaged leader, eventually must have fallen asleep, though I don't know when.

The next day was dry, though gray, and we got the larger shelter finished in time for the next bout of winter rain. Detter started dragging flat stones from farther up the mountain. We slowly built a clumsy fireplace, piecing the rocks together painstakingly against the wall of the shelter. Once we got the fireplace finished, we knocked part of the wall away in front of it so the fire could warm the hut. It seemed insane luxury to have warm, dry nights, though in the dim light of the banked coals I could now confirm that Detter did watch me when he thought I was asleep.

Simon mended faster once he dried out some. He began to seem more capable, and one night he called Detter over and firmly grasped his ankle. Over Detter's involuntary gasp of pain, he spoke two of the Healing Verses and a pallid glow flashed briefly between his fingers. When he opened his hands, Detter's ankle was firm and true, no longer puffy and flaccid, and gay wisps of ller flitted out through the crevices of the roof. Detter's face was stony while all this went on, but later I saw from the corner of my eye that he had his chin in his palm and his grave gaze resting on me.

I faced him, feeling defiant, but his expression did not change. "Lise, how do you decide what you should do?" he asked again quietly.

"I don't know, all right, Detter? I just decide. If I stop to think, I'm dead. How do you decide what you should do? Do you think about it, do you flip a coin, what do you do?"

"I work from a plan. I have goals, and I think about everything in terms of those goals. I'm very systematic. You have to have some kind of system if you want to survive and get ahead." He had dark smudges under his eyes and his lips were chapped. The last light had faded outside. Simon sat with his long arms wrapped around his legs, staring vaguely at the fire.

"What if your goals change? Does that make all your decisions wrong? How can you know you'll always want the same thing?" With each question, Detter's eyebrows lowered farther.

He burst out, "You never tell me anything I can understand. You just tell your fairy tales or ask your eternal questions. You question everything and you give me nothing in exchange. Is there anything inside you or are you just a question?" He was literally hissing at me, and I was bewildered and annoyed. I had managed to anger Detter, and I didn't even know how I'd managed it. Simon's face was buried in his knees, and his shoulders were quivering gently.

"What do you want from me?" I demanded angrily, and

Detter just as angrily pounded his fist on the ground next to him.

"I don't understand you," he said. "I can't figure out why you haven't destroyed me or Simon or both of us, or put us both under your control. You have the Power and the Talent to make us do anything you want, you've shown you're not afraid of wizards or of kings, you don't care anything for conventions, and yet you do nothing. You didn't even choose to heal us all the way, and you could have done that at least. Why don't you use your Power? What good is it if you never wield it?"

Simon was suddenly attentive, the humor leaving his lifted face as he heard what Detter had said about healing. He looked at me speculatively. I didn't care what Simon suspected. But I felt a falling sensation as I realized Detter had known exactly what I'd done on the mountainside, and he hadn't chosen until now to say anything about it. I didn't know what he wanted from me, and I understood him not at all.

He took my puzzled silence for obstinacy and visibly began to collect his defenses again, the lighthearted mask sliding back over his face. No more sniping. I preferred Detter angry to Detter polite and nasty.

I asked, "Detter, what is it you think I should do? Why would I want to control you? Why would I try to destroy you? What would it profit me?" Simon snorted.

Detter said with a hint of his normal glitter, "If you ask me one more question, I'll break all of your fingers one by one."

I breathed in and said madly, "Why would you want to do that?" He lunged at me, Simon grabbed him, and they struggled for a minute. Unexpectedly, it turned into an amiable wrestling match that Simon eventually won. Some of the ceiling fell down, but luckily it wasn't raining.

Simon banged Detter's head on the ground, making his limp hair even dirtier, and said, "It's bedtime. Go to sleep and stop yammering. We start traveling again tomorrow." My face must have gone through some odd changes, for Detter caught my eye and gave me a wry smile. I'm not sure what my expression was in return, but Detter chuckled threadily as Simon let him up. We banked the fire, and the tiny hut darkened as we settled in for the night.

Unexpectedly, as if he had not been a fragile passionless wraith for nearly two months, Simon firmly overlapped our threadbare, greasy blankets and rolled me up in a tight cocoon with him. Though I protested for a minute, the feel of his suddenly insistent hands and thighs, the renewed urgency of his rhythms, made me suddenly frantic with postponed lust. He finally pinned me with my back to the ground, holding me down with his hands and his belly, because he wanted to take his time and I couldn't let him. In the dim red darkness of the hut, I could see past Simon's arm the faint liquid gleam of Detter's eyes as he lay calmly watching us. I turned my head to the other side. Why it should bother me I didn't know. I had once been prepared to mate with a god before a hundred thousand strangers, but sharing more mundane pleasures before one well-known enemy made me squeamish.

Later, still sweatily interwoven with Simon's limbs, I finally fell asleep, but I dreamed, a true dream. I was facing Detter and someone was standing behind me. Detter was naked, as smooth and pink as if he had never set out on this journey. His skin looked as if it had frozen translucently over his bones like a mountain stream in winter, eddying here, rippling there, glassy as the surface of a whirlpool. His eyes were shut, his hands loose at his sides, his chin slightly lifted. The person behind me reached hands forward in front of my face, grasped my lips, and began curling them up and back until my teeth and gums were bared. Then the hands inserted fingers at the back of my jaw as if I were a horse and parted my teeth, wider and wider, aiming me at Detter's face as if my mouth were a pair of scissors. I was forced forward, my head slowly twisted sideways, and I resisted and struggled as hard as I could, retching against the intrusive fingers. My neck was too weak, but I fought anyway, inches away from Detter's nose. I was nearly strangling, and I was afraid my neck would break. The hands couldn't force me any closer. Suddenly the fingers were gone from my mouth, the presence was gone from behind me, and Detter's eyes opened, enormous so close to me.

"Why not?" he asked, puzzled, his milk-white teeth perfect.

"You can't force me to," I answered, as weak and afraid as if I'd been running for my life.

"Oh, all right, if that's the way you want it," he said, disappointed. He started to turn away from me, but I grabbed his arms, leaned forward, and bit his lower lip as hard as I could, tasting blood. He grunted, startled and aroused, and as I dug my fingernails viciously into the skin of his arms, he melted against and into me. It stopped being a true dream after that, but it was a lot of fun in a nasty perverted way, as some dreams can be.

The next morning, after I woke up, and while we got ready to leave, I wondered. I'd never fought a true dream before, never deliberately changed what happened. Maybe my dreams weren't true anymore on a different planet, or maybe my discipline was falling apart. On Mennenkaltenei I would have had to do something about this dream right away, but here I didn't know what to do. There was no one to turn to, no one to tell, no dream teachers, no diviners. I shouldered my pack and set off down the hill behind the men. Simon had already started off, as if he hadn't been my nurseling for so long and I were merely a hitchhiker.

Over the next few days, I realized that Betzindahl was a very different country from Telique or Emsadorn. The country seemed older, tamer, though it was hillier. The rolling, glowing, buff hills were topped by dark trees shooting up like fountains, but the sides of the hills were grassy and rounded. Also, the first building we saw, though Simon steered us wide of it, looked from a distance much bigger and more elaborately constructed than the rustic houses the other side of the continent. It had two stories, a carved roofline, was half-timbered, shingled with slate, and had glass in its many arched windows. It wouldn't have looked out of place in the middle of Deistel

Dom. Betzindahl was a more developed country, or at least had been settled longer.

"Why are we passing by?" demanded Detter, dawdling behind and staring back at the house now half-hidden by trees. "Couldn't we just see if they'd put us up for the night? A bed would feel wonderful right now."

Simon half smiled at him. Getting banged on the head seemed to have loosened him up a little; before, Detter's remark would have earned him a peevish reproof. "Nearly twenty years ago the King of Betzindahl swore an oath to deport or kill any mage who set foot in his country. He has kept his promise so far, though a few Talented children have been removed by stealth. I don't want anybody getting a close look at my neck, or my face for that matter, so we are staying away from people as much as possible."

Detter was scornful. "What are you afraid of? If you don't want people seeing you're a mage, why don't you just cloak yourself in illusion?"

"The neckring can't be hidden with magic, Detter. Illusion doesn't work on it; I'd have to be completely invisible to hide it. What good would the ring be if it could be hidden so easily?"

I said, "I understand why you don't want them to see your neck. But why don't you want them to see your face?"

Simon laughed ruefully. "That is just foolishness. I was born in this country, but I was taken so young I am sure no one would recognize me now."

So he was a native of Betzindahl. Who did he think might know him? He buttoned up his shirt but did not ask me to put the skirt back on.

We came across more houses scattered in the hills, most of them looking solid and well-built but empty. The track we were following became gradually a well-tamped cart road, unpaved, and apparently not much traveled in the winter. The rains kept on, but game was plentiful and we ate well. Both my companions had imperceptibly become much more endurable since we'd left the school, but my loneliness and sadness grew the longer we walked. I didn't know who or what I was. In spite of Simon's affections, the combination of Detter's questions and my strange true dream were making me realize more and more that I didn't know how anything worked anymore, or even how I thought.

We came to a place where the road joined another road, this one paved with gravel, and after a bit we passed through the first village. It looked as if it had once been prosperous, with four small shops and a blacksmith, but two of the shops were empty. The buildings, though solid, all needed minor repairs, and the inn at the edge of town was missing half its sign. The gray rain hissed down on the roofs, and only one or two faces peered out cautiously to mark our passing. When we were half an hour past the village, Simon called a halt and we rested uncomfortably under the trunk of a half-fallen tree.

He said, "Something's wrong here. The houses in the hills shouldn't all have been empty, and that town shouldn't have looked like that. There may have been a plague. We'll have to be careful." We shared some of last night's dinner and walked on, looking for a place to camp. We found a shallow cave in the bank above a stream, and Detter killed a fat bird with a stone for supper. Simon and I rolled ourselves up together, and Detter sat at the mouth of the cave a while longer staring out at the night, until he too lay down with a sigh.

The next morning, I awoke to strange, unfriendly voices. I kept still a moment in fear, feeling Simon stiffen against me as well. I listened until I knew the voices came from outside our cave. Then Detter's voice answered, casual and cheerful, and I realized he was outside with the owners of the voices. I wormed my way out of my blanket and crept to the edge of the cave, Simon following.

Detter was seated facing us with his hands awkwardly behind his head, and a man with his hair tied up, his back to us, was holding a ragged-edged spear to his throat. In typical fashion, Detter looked happy and relaxed, though a thin trickle of blood was running down his neck. Surrounding the two of them were several other men, propping themselves on spears and staves and watching the entertainment.

The man had just demanded something of Detter, and Detter answered him, "Of course I am alone. Who would have me, diseased and vicious as I am?" He laughed, and the man holding the spear to his throat leaned on it a little harder.

One of the men, bigger than the others, said, "Melcom would have you, wouldn't you, Melcom?"

Another of the men, apparently the Melcom referred to, said, "I told you, Rambulf, if you don't slam your hole shut I'll shut it for you." His bravado sounded weak and his companions shifted away from him slightly. Not a favorite with the crowd.

Detter looked at him appraisingly out of the side of his eyes and said, "Well, I think you're adorable. Want to try me out?" The other men laughed, the man holding the spear against him shoved harder still, and Detter's head went back slightly.

Melcom said, "Oh, kill the snot-nosed apple-banger, Slevec, or I'll kill him for you." He moved forward and made as if to grab the spear, and the man holding it pulled back from Detter slightly to give Melcom a shove. Detter puckered his lips suggestively to Melcom, who pushed Slevec aside and swung his fist at Detter's face. Slevec, meanwhile, resented the push and grabbed Melcom's shoulder, while Detter jerked his head back out of the way, smiling and waving his pink tongue at his assailant. The other men were laughing even harder, even when Melcom and Slevec began to wrestle awkwardly with each other, grappling and punching. As they watched the entertainment, Detter backed cautiously out of the way of the two fighters. Beside me I heard Simon quietly chanting. It sounded like an invisibility spell, though since I couldn't use them I hadn't learned them. Lle was flowing lazily along the ground around Detter until lle was coating him evenly in what to my eyes was a glowing shell of royal blue glitter. A similar shell slid between the cave and the men, and if it was also an invisibility spell they wouldn't be able to see any of us if they looked.

Indeed, when there was a brief pause in the fight, they all realized their captive was "gone." Detter lay frozen on the forest floor, watching them carefully through the haze of blue, and luckily none of them stepped on him as they ran looking for their victim. Soon their voices were out of range, but they had left some packs behind and might return, so we gathered our equipment swiftly and left as quickly and quietly as we could, leaving the cloud of ller to disperse on ller own. I saluted ller surreptitiously as we walked away, and lle shuddered gently in reply.

It wasn't until noon that Simon felt it was safe to stop. He said grimly, "There is definitely something wrong here. Betzindahl is the safest and most civilized country in the world, in spite of its politics. Those men were definitely bandits, they didn't fear plague, and they didn't look hungry. They must be doing well for themselves, and nobody is stopping them." He was angry. He seemed to take it personally.

"Who would stop them normally?" I said. "Is there a government here, police or something?"

"The local lord should be policing his domain," said Simon, wiping cold rain off his face for the hundredth time. Detter was standing next to me, leaning weary and pale against a tree. The rain had washed his neck clean of blood over and over, until he finally stopped bleeding. He wasn't talking. I poked his leg, and when he looked down I offered him some cold cooked bird. He shook his head, spraying me with water. I swung my arm around, hit him as hard as I could in the leg, and said, "Eat." He looked startled, but reached down for the morsel I was offering.

Simon approved, or at least he didn't say anything, and Detter seemed to feel better, for a little later he hunkered down and said softly to me, "Dearest one, if you ever hit me again like that, I think we will have to get much closer, and I'm afraid you're not ready for that." He chuckled when I made a disgusted face.

The next village we passed through looked worse, and a small boy threw stones at us as we passed, his pasty mother frantically pulling him inside and slamming the door shut as if to protect him, not us. Simon began to walk faster and look angrier. The gravel road joined a paved road, and there was occasional dispirited traffic, a tinker or two and some solitary horsemen. The paving was crumbling at the edge of the road, and in the dips in the road there were immense potholes full of water. Simon's stride got longer, and he looked as if he were going to war. I finally said breathlessly to him, "Slow down. Wherever we're going, we won't get there today."

He stopped, looked around, and said, "Sorry." We slept secretly in somebody's abandoned stable that night. It was good to be warm and dry, though there were small animals rustling all night in the stale hay.

We entered more populated country, villages coming closer together with less countryside between them. The villages began to enlarge and melt together until they were large market and workshop towns with smaller villages between them. Still, the signs of decay and neglect were there. Doors were barred, some buildings were empty, and we were viewed with suspicion and distrust. It didn't help that we looked like homeless beggars, shabby, lost, and odd, and that Simon would speak to nobody, delegating that job to Detter or me.

Finally, Detter said to him, "You're supposed to be our guide and we're supposed to be students, not servants. Or have you forgotten?"

Simon said, "It is your job to do as I ask, whatever you call yourself. I do not exist here. I am invisible. I will give you no explanation." It didn't sound like pedantic Simon.

He saw me staring at him as if he'd turned into a fish, and I said, "You're going to have to do better than that."

He bit back something, frowned, shrugged his shoulders, and finally answered, "When the mages took me, I was

declared a nonperson, to be shunned. Should any native Betzindahli acknowledge me, he would be punished. He is not
permitted to see me. I would come to no harm, though, since I
don't officially exist. It should be all right for you to speak to
me, since you are not natives, but I don't want to get anybody
else in trouble."

Detter said, "Ever since you got hit on the head, you've been
as peculiar as Lisane," but he went along with the charade of
invisibility after that, as if humoring an elderly relative.

I, however, was beginning to put a puzzle together in my
head, and berating myself for being an idiot. Kaihan had said
to me that he was Simon's ancestor. If he wasn't lying—I knew
of no reason he should lie—and if he had not started Simon's
line illegitimately—I could not see why the Master of Sassevin
Council would want to admit to such a transgression—then Simon was the descendant of a king. I assumed that a king would
trace his seed principally through the line of succession, especially through so many generations. How else would he know
Simon for his descendant?

From what Simon had said, his father had denied him as son
and denied welcome to mages perhaps eighteen years ago.
Likewise, at that time the king of Betzindahl had forbidden the
country to mages. Simon had been born in Betzindahl. Simon
was a nonperson. It was my guess that Simon, like me, had
been torn from his inheritance. Unlike me, his country and his
father still lived, and he was beginning to think he was needed.

I said to Detter later on, "You don't happen to be related to
anybody important, do you?"

"O most gracious majesty, empress of the night skies, I am
the sixth son of a farmer and a weaver, neither of them particularly important, and I know they're dead, because I killed them
both myself," he said. "Other than that, I am the first worthy
person to be born of a long line of nobodies from nowhere, and
I see no reason to claim otherwise."

"That's a relief," I said. He looked enigmatic, and I knew
that meant he didn't know what I was talking about. I thought

I might begin to understand Detter sometime. His lips were a darker rose pink than when I first met him, and he was growing a golden fuzz of mustache. As pretty as a wheat-snake in the sunlight.

Simon, his bones moving smoothly under his ragged brown traveling clothes, his scarf concealing his ring again, had a savage grace I'd never seen in him before, and I didn't think it was my imagination. It was as though he were breathing better air in Betzindahl, as though his pedantry and solemnity had been transmuted to arrogance and confidence. Though he was half-starved and determined to act invisible, his step was lighter and groups of people parted before him automatically. We entered unchallenged through the gates of the harbor city Linz only because Simon led us, his brows knit fiercely and his gray eyes clear and far-seeing. It was almost comic. If I had been in the place of the surly gate guard who waved us through, I would have stopped and arrested all three of us. We looked worse and less trustworthy than any of the bands of brigands we'd hid from on the road. But Simon glowed with purpose like a religious zealot, and besides we probably looked too hungry and poor to be successful highwaymen.

The city was great and grand, bustling and intense, nothing like healthy little Deistel Dom. The buildings were beautifully made, even the frequent inns, some of carved striated stone assembled without mortar, some joined together of smooth-finished woods. The streets wound through the city, down toward the sea and the inner city of tall towers within high walls that was the ruler's castle and the country's center. We could see the towers sparkling in the faint late winter sun, but it was going to be a long walk. I couldn't tell how long Simon planned to keep going. My legs were heavy, my pack dragged, my shoulders hurt, and keeping up with Simon was agony.

There were armed men strolling everywhere in the city, we had no money left, and the closer we got to the castle the less we belonged. The people in their exotic, structured clothing were scurrying nervously toward their homes as the day faded.

Simon found his way assuredly through city squares, along side streets, and down long flights of steps carved into the hill, some kind of back way or shortcut, but it was nearly dark and we hadn't eaten all day.

We were cutting through a nearly empty plaza toward an alleyway when a gaudy figure hailed us. Up close, I could see he was a middle-aged man in a gorgeous burnt orange and brown uniform, a sword in a scabbard at his hip. He bore a scar across his nose, but his expression was not unkind, just indifferent. He spoke to Simon, as our obvious leader, "Son, the pickings are poor for beggars in this part of town. May I direct you to shelter before the night guard misunderstands your presence here?"

Simon stood as if at attention, staring past the man with a face like carved marble. This looked awkward. I said, stepping forward, "Excuse me, were you addressing me, sir?"

The man looked annoyed and said, "No, I was not, you young trollop. I was addressing your shabby friend." Simon was silent.

Detter said brightly from beyond him, "Oh, heavens, I must not have been paying attention. You were speaking to me?" The man's face chilled at Detter's tone, and his hand went to the pommel of his sword. This situation had the potential to become completely ridiculous.

I said with all the dignity I could muster, "It would have to be one of us two, sir, because as you can see there are only two here," and I laid my hand gently on Simon's arm. Simon did not move. I hoped he was right to behave like such a donkey. His black hair was dirty and matted, his broad cheekbones were toughened and gray with exposure, the clothes on his long frame were abjectly worn, but he had never looked nobler or wilder.

The man took a step back in sudden doubt, his eyes on Simon's face. "I am a foreigner here, good sir, new to the city today," I said, "and so is my friend. We are heading for the castle, but we are utterly lost without native guidance." I hoped I was doing the right thing. If my suspicions were correct, and if this man knew what had happened, and if he were sympathetic . . . if, if, if. My Voices were muttering gibberish in the back of my head, and I was on my own.

"If you are so strange to the city, how is it you have found your way to this point? You are nearly at the citizen's door. Who gave you directions?" he said, and I hoped it was working, for he was still staring at Simon.

"No one, sir. No one gave us directions," I murmured. Detter was looking enigmatic again, but Simon tightened the crook of his arm over my hand, and I felt a bit reassured.

There was a silence. Then the man breathed, "Thunder buzzards, I think you're too late, child." I pretended not to hear. Detter shifted from foot to foot, wearily, readjusting his pack and tucking his hair behind his ears. Simon seemed more relaxed, but he continued to stare into space, and the man continued to stare at Simon.

Then, briskly, the man turned to me and said, "The King is meeting with his advisers tonight, but I am sure he would always want to welcome foreigners. Why don't you and your friend follow me?" He spoke as if reciting lines. He turned his back on us deliberately, fiddling with his belt and waiting.

I said to Simon under my breath, "He knows you?" and Simon said in a normal voice, "My mother's brother, Quillas. We couldn't have met up with better. A fair, strong man and faithful to the King."

Quillas straightened his shoulders as if challenged and stepped off toward the alleyway that had been our original destination, not looking back to see if we were following. Everything had to be done according to form, apparently.

Detter said to Simon pettishly, "I'm hungry. Is he going to take us somewhere to change and eat?"

Simon said dryly, "He has his reasons for wanting me in particular to show up ragged and hungry. I may or may not go along with his plans, but it won't harm me to be prepared." We were scurrying to keep up with Quillas, who seemed to be a man of much importance in the city. Guards parted respectfully before him, however doubtful they looked when they saw whom he was escorting, and doors opened to him. We passed through several thick walls on our winding path, past stronger and stronger gates, until at one great iron gate a bearded troll of a man dressed almost as beautifully as Quillas gave him a spirited argument about letting us in. Quillas cited chapter and verse of some dusty law regarding the welcome of strangers, the troll spat in disgust and argued some more, but finally we were admitted. It was night, the sky had cleared, and the stars were out as we crossed a wide courtyard to a great open door ablaze with torchlight.

We entered an arched anteroom widening into a great chamber half full of people where some kind of dispute was taking place. We were half-blinded with the light, but I could see that the crowd looked bored and overdressed, showing scant respect for the frail figure in the high throne who faced them all, arguing with a small knot of people before him. I assumed the man in the throne was the King, but I found it hard to make him out. He was obscured by a malevolent haze of embodied ller, spirit-fire old and maimed and confined by some cruel force.

I said to Simon, shocked and angry, "That man up there is spelled to the gills, and has been for years. It's disgusting." Quillas was looking at me doubtfully.

"I can feel it," Simon said quietly. "Who is responsible? Can you see a source? Find out for me." No one besides the door guards had noticed our entrance so far, and the guards merely inclined their heads to Quillas as he led us in. He moved us to a spot beside the door. I guessed that the layers of gates and guards made these people careless of their safety, though far too many of them were armed for my taste. Quillas stood, arms folded, now looking a little worried. I hoped he didn't regret his decision all of a sudden.

An enraged graybeard was standing before the throne, berating the seated King in an infuriated but tremulous voice, only the graybeard wasn't the mystery mage. There was no sign of spells to accompany his gestures. The King, who through the haze of magic seemed barely conscious, looked bored, weak, and irritated, and responded in monosyllables.

I surveyed the room carefully, and came across a redheaded, black-bearded, lantern-jawed figure watching impassively from the side of the room. He seemed unconcerned with the argument going on, but his hands were rolling and rolling over each other, and between the palms was a spirit-glow, a blob of ller. His collar was open, but I saw no ring around his neck.

I murmured to Simon, "The redhead in the blue waistcoat."

Simon searched the room and found him. "A renegade," he said sadly, meaning the lack of a neckring. Pompous twit, I thought affectionately. I could count on Simon to be annoyed at simple rule-breaking when a major sin was being perpetrated here.

He said quietly, "I am about to betray your trust and my role as your guide. You had both better leave the room, for I have to do something about this, and it will mean I cannot leave ever again. Quillas will help you escape, and you must make your own way to Sassevin. It has been done before."

"Now you've gone completely insane," said Detter, pale with anger.

I interrupted. "Simon, if you really want to stop this, you're going to have to let me do it."

He glared at me imperiously. "You will do nothing. You are a student under oath. I will take care of it." A cadaverous character in purple seated near us turned and shushed us, then peered at us more closely. I was going to have to hurry if I wanted Simon to get off his high horse.

I said in a lower tone, "That's your father, right? The King?" He paused, then nodded, startled by my guess, the sweet idiot. "He's enspelled by a renegade and the kingdom is falling to bits, so you're going to stay and do your duty by him as Kaihan wanted, instead of going for your Sorcerer's ring, right?"

The man in purple was urgently talking to his immediate neighbor, a corpulent man with a nervous tic. Simon nodded again, and suddenly began to smile at me. His face was so much handsomer when he smiled.

I said, "Simon, you don't have the Power to beat this man. The spell is old and ugly, and the renegade is strong. This needs to be done, I can do it, and you can't. Trust me."

Detter said through his teeth, "You motherless offspring of pigs, I'm not going to let you do this to me!" The man in purple was standing up and motioning to a half-dozing guard by the door, and other heads turned toward us.

Simon said to Detter, "You don't have any choice. Since I may not speak until my banishment is lifted, will you be my voice, or must I speak with your mouth through spells? It is most uncomfortable, as I'm sure you know." Detter looked mulish, but as Simon put his hands to his neck, ripping his shirt open to reveal his neckring, Detter nodded reluctantly.

I said quickly to Simon, "Hide me. I need to be invisible." He spoke rapidly in an undertone, and a coating of royal blue entwined itself around me until I knew by his eyes he couldn't see me anymore. It wasn't a moment too soon, for the man in purple was calling out, "Who are you? What are you doing here?" to Simon. The graybeard at the front of the hall was too absorbed in his infuriated oration to hear, but the red-haired man's eyes shifted toward the disturbance. I walked rapidly away from Simon and toward the King.

Detter came in front of Simon. Simon muttered, prompting him, and Detter said loudly and elegantly, "Oh, gracious people of Betzindahl. I am new to the country, but even I can see that your King is under the spell of a renegade mage. Do you prefer your royalty thus enslaved, or do you perhaps not know what has happened? Could somebody enlighten me?"

There was noisy tumult. Half the people in the room went for their swords and the other half dived to the floor or out the door. They were definitely prepared for violence here. I turned to the saffron glowing spell enveloping the slumped figure of the King.

"Lle mehnes pertegressteren ihn beserglemt, san?" I said

chattily to the spell, and the few people still near me recoiled in
horror. Apparently I was invisible but not inaudible. Detter was
shouting something else inflammatory and elegant from the
back of the room. The mustard-colored spell stirred lethargi-
cally, and slowly unwound its long tail from the King's body.
Lle was half-solid, almost material, and must have been con-
gealed like that for years, poor thing.

I repeated, urging ller on, "Lle pertegressteren?" and lle
shook like a jelly and flowed away from the King toward ller
creator. The redheaded man's attention was entirely on the
commotion at the back of the room. He was turning, coming
away from the wall, craning his neck to see what was going on.
I risked a glance backward and saw that Simon and Detter
were half-surrounded by a slow-moving, cautious group made
up of the more courageous gentlemen in the room, the rest having left entirely or cautiously concealed themselves behind
benches. Simon was not without defenses, as I could see by the
flickers of plum-colored ller that kept his attackers at bay. The
redhead reached his hands out into the air and called globules
of ectoplasm to him from the air. He molded them into ominous shapes and prepared to cast the product across the room at
the disturbance. I admired his work. He was extremely good,
the best I'd seen so far.

I turned and said encouragingly, "Yegger ve andersgerteren,"
to the immense spell humping across the room from the King
back to his enemy. The renegade obviously sensed and ma-
nipulated magic by touch, not sight or emotion, so he probably
wouldn't realize what was happening until the spell was on
him. He released his crowd-control spell into the air, but I immediately told the new spell there was no need for ller to hang
around. The renegade swung abruptly around at the sound of
my voice and grabbed for some more magic, but as he grabbed,
the spell he had cast on the King reached him finally and
flowed back over him in rippling waves, shuddering with release. He was drowned in ller like a fly in amber, gasping and
convulsing as lle tensed around him. He must have looked a

sight if you had no spirit-eyes to see what was happening to him. He screamed, choked, screamed again.

With the new disturbance, the crowd was bewildered, fragmented, not sure what was going on. The King, bewildered and half-awake, stirred on his throne and said, "What is happening? Where am I?" No one heard him, and sick as he was, he grasped the arms of his throne, hauled himself to a standing position, and rasped harshly, "What is the meaning of this?"

In the sudden silence that followed, everyone heard the renegade choking and gasping in the corner, including the King. He turned and looked at his enemy, and after a measured moment said, "Whoever started killing off that vile little man, please finish the job."

I told the sulfurous gelatinous mass of ller to enjoy itself, and the redheaded man began to dissolve from the boots up, shrieking in pain and outrage. When he finished dissolving, I told the evil old binding spell its time was come, and lle faded gladly into undifferentiated sludgy streaks until lle had vanished. I turned to look at ller's erstwhile captive.

The King was almost as tall as Simon, and he must have topped him in his youth. The cheekbones were Simon's and the nose, but the face was more barbaric and closed than I thought Simon's could ever be. I made a mental note to ask Simon if all the men in his family lost their hair by late middle age, for the King's scalp shone smooth as Kaihan's in the torchlight. He was flabby and emaciated, wavering, like a man who had been seriously ill for a long time, but he kept himself upright by sheer will.

With a gesture and a word, Simon cleared the blue haze that surrounded me, and people recoiled as I "appeared" from thin air. I walked back to Simon, my head down like an elegant servant's, and he put his hand on my shoulder when I reached him. His other hand was on Detter's shoulder.

The King looked at us, a pathetic and inglorious group now the battle was over, and said to Simon, "Explain yourself. Why are mages here in defiance of law? Surely you must know of

my edict. I am not swayed by the service you have done me."
There were murmurs of agreement. What a bunch of legalistic
loonies, I thought. What were they going to do, march us out
and behead us for saving his life?

Simon did not reply. I started, "Majesty . . ." and Simon
tightened his hand warningly on my shoulder, so I stopped.
The King ignored me, waiting for an answer. Simon was not
going to give it to him. There was a long silence. The King's
arms were trembling with the effort to keep himself upright.

Finally, Quillas, leaning against a column not too far from
us, said casually, "My lord, I should mention that you are once
again without an heir now that Baron Laitallen has so tragically
been taken from us." Somebody laughed sharply, and I
guessed Laitallen had been the redheaded renegade.

"Now is hardly the time to discuss that. You overstep
yourself," said the King angrily to Quillas. "Answer me, or
suffer the consequences," he shouted at Simon. Simon stood
stock-still.

"On the contrary, my lord," said Quillas. "It is time to settle
the succession once and for all, since you have *no natural son*,"
stressing the last words. There was an appalled gasp from several of the people near us, and the man nearest to Quillas actually backed away as if afraid of contamination. The King
peered at Simon more closely and then sat down suddenly.
"Oh. Well then. Bring me syrup," he said hoarsely, but no
one moved. "Quillas. Bring syrup," he commanded. Quillas
sheathed his sword and strode clattering out a side door.

Simon said quietly to me, "It seems I have made a choice
between my responsibility to my students and my duty to my
father and country. I am very sorry."

"Responsibility and duty," said Detter mockingly. "It couldn't
possibly be power and pleasure you desire. It must be responsibility and duty. Being Prince and heir to the most powerful
kingdom of the Lesser Shore is simply your miserable duty."

Simon said gently, "There will be precious little pleasure
and less power for me from now on. You will be far better off

than I, Detter." He must have felt very dramatic and tragic, and all the apprehensive people around us appreciated the little show. Nobody knew better than I how important it was to truly be the character you play when you rule.

Quillas returned, bearing a pottery bowl full of a tea-colored viscous liquid. He said to me politely and pointedly, "Have you eaten today?"

I understood vaguely that the question was not meant for me, and said, "No, sir. We have been traveling empty since last night." I no longer felt very hungry, and wondered why.

"I will endeavor to see that you are fed later," he said, and bore the bowl gravely up to the King, laying it in his lap.

The King surveyed the room solemnly, as if it were not a frozen picture of chaos and battle, with people gradually coming out of their hiding places or falling back from fighting postures. He seemed not at all discomfited by being released from a spell, being presented with a long-lost son, or watching a man die from the feet up before his eyes. He began to speak solemnly in words that sounded ceremonial and dignified. I remembered how nice it was to have something suitable to say for every occasion, one time long ago when I was the straw goat of another world.

"My beloved queen bore one and only one child, a son, but he is dead to me," he said. "It is my right and my duty to declare an heir to follow me as ruler of the kingdom. I did indeed once choose an heir, but against my will and under duress, and the false heir has died in payment for his crime. Let all those present witness that I now choose my final heir, for good and of my own will. Are there any challenges to my choice?" He had blue shadows under his eyes and he was trembling, but I wouldn't have crossed this frightening old man for any reason, and apparently, though his audience shifted and muttered, neither now would anyone else in the room. "Will the candidate come forward?" said the King after the long pause.

Simon kissed my cheek, and unexpectedly Detter's too, though Detter pulled away from him. "This is how I was acknowledged legitimate as an infant," he murmured to us, and left us to walk to the front of the room. He stood before his father, upright and poised. Two sets of gray eyes stared at each other for an instant, and then the King dipped his index finger into the bowl of syrup. He extended the finger, and Simon leaned forward and took it into his mouth, sucking the syrup off as if he were a nursing baby. The sight disturbed me, an annexation of motherhood's nurture to the father, doubtless why the fostered child had to go hungry before the ceremony.

"This is now my son. I declare his name Saimin Leonais tzin Terhal mian Ankheleral, and from today until the end of time he will take the place of the son who was lost to me," said the King, and he was holding Simon's dark and dirty head in his lap. Simon's arms were around his knees. I'd lost a lover to ritual, though not in the way I'd always expected. I couldn't believe I was wishing Simon had been killed instead.

Detter said loudly, "How adorable they look. Just made for each other, don't you think?" and I nodded absently, tears running down my face. I really never would be llerKalten, I realized, and thought I could feel the presence of the goddess leave me absolutely.

Detter stared at me and said, "Am I really the only sane person in the world?" and I nodded again. He probably was.

CHAPTER EIGHT

In Which I Don't Take the Job

The suite where Detter and I were housed was comfortable enough, but lonely. No one but a pair of silent, disdainful servitors had visited us since Quillas led us out of the audience hall. He had said quietly, "We'd better get you out of here before somebody remembers you," and hustled us down a long corridor lit by oil lamps to the small, warm apartment. He shut us in the sitting room, said, "Somebody will come to see to your needs," and started to leave. He paused in the doorway and said, "Please stay here. I can't guarantee what might happen to you if you leave these rooms."

It was my guess that our main offense was not the practice of magic, but that we didn't fit the rules. I knew now where Simon got his legalistic bent and his lack of humor. This court was a web of unspoken laws, and if you made one wrong step you were spider food.

Three days had passed. I'd finally had as many hot baths as I wanted. The highly spiced food, though good, was hard on my stomach. The rooms were elegant and sophisticated, and smelled of perfumed smoke, but there weren't any books to read. The servitors brought clothes for Detter and me, but I made them take the woman's clothing back and bring me a man's costume.

Detter said, "Why do you need to dress like a man? Don't you think you make a better woman?" He himself was decked out in a pin-tucked costume of gleaming forest green, all shirred seams and elaborate beading, and he lay on his belly on the rug like a basking lizard, eating dried fruit. He was happy in this plush confinement. It was odd how much he loved his luxuries, considering he was equally comfortable with pain and deprivation.

"You'll never know how much better," I said, cheerfully. The real reason I wouldn't wear the gown was that it weighed about forty pounds and was as comfortable to wear as a butter churn. It was beyond me how the Betzindahli could be so comfort loving as to build indoor plumbing, yet design clothing expressly to limit motion and cause pain. Even the Emsadorn gowns had permitted some movement.

The servants, mutely conveying disapproval, brought me what I'd asked. I stripped off my worn traveling clothes and began changing. I'd gotten out of the habit of worrying what Detter might see.

Detter watched me pulling the knickers on and said, as if discussing the food or the weather, "Am I expected to be your consort now that Simon's out of the picture?"

I looked at him with such outrage that even he couldn't hold a straight face. I finished knotting my belt, my lips pursed, while Detter buried his giggles ostentatiously in the rug. I got up and kicked his ribs to get his attention. "The only way I would ever lie down in the same bed with you, Deteras Anhand, is if you were bound, gagged, and drugged. And even then I'd worry."

He rolled on his back, smiling relaxedly up at me, and said, "Don't you still have some of that rope in your pack? I'm sure the drugs and the gag could be arranged."

I considered kicking him again, just for the pleasure of it, but it wasn't worth the argument. Besides, that was probably what he wanted of me. I finished dressing, and roamed discontentedly through the apartment while Detter popped nuts in his mouth and hummed irritatingly.

The time went slowly, and no one visited us, not even Simon. That was all right with me. If I never saw him again, it would be easier for me. I could think of him as dead, then, rather than having the uneasy feeling that it was I who should be dead. I had no windows to look out of, nothing to do but eat, daydream, listen to my peevish Voices, sleep, and try not to talk to Detter. I felt as if we were a pair of embarrassing ghosts, fading gradually from reality.

Finally one evening, late, there came a quiet scratching. Detter, sprawling on the hearth, rolled swiftly to his feet and darted to open the door. Simon stood framed in the doorway, grave, dignified, and perfectly groomed. Even his forelock was trimmed and combed into place. He was still somberly dressed in brown, but the rich drape and perfect cut of the fabric made Detter's gaudy costume look shallow and cheap.

"I was unable to come before," he said quietly.

Detter said sarcastically, "I suppose you were held at sword point?"

"No. I couldn't seek you out without drawing attention to you, and there are people here who would leap at a chance to hold you hostage against me. My very existence threatens the plans of much of the court. I have arranged to get you both out of Linz and onto a ship to the Greater Shore tomorrow. There's a captain who's an experienced winter sailor, and he's agreed to take you. He doesn't know you're mages, though, so you must be cautious." It all sounded very dramatic, but his presence was annoying and I wished he would leave.

Detter answered sulkily, "I realize we are an embarrassment to you, but you needn't be in such a hurry to get rid of us."

Simon just made an exasperated sound, and continued, "When you reach Sassevin, you will go straight to the Beast, of course, but when you leave, find Kaihan. Tell him what happened, and tell him I said he is responsible for you."

Detter said, "Whereupon he will have us both locked in ward-chains, and he'll send the Finders to bring you to judgment. I find the prospect of your trial vastly entertaining."

Simon looked back and forth at the two of us, and his forelock escaped from its unguent and flopped forward. Then he sighed, came in, shut the door behind him, and sat down.

"Detter, Kaihan has been trying to make me return to Betzin-dahl since I survived my Quest. I have done as he wished. He will take care of you, and I will not be punished. I thought Lisane had some idea of this. Hasn't she said anything?" He looked at me, puzzled, but when I didn't answer he turned back to Detter.

I was sitting in the armchair, my arms resting in my lap, feeling even more of a ghost than before. Simon sat there talking to Detter like some merchant saying he was out of fruit but the weather was fine. The Voices in the back of my head, my predecessors and prophecy guides, were chanting childhood rhymes in ragged unison. I could get on a ship tomorrow and leave this remote man without regrets, but I was leaving pieces of myself behind wherever I went, and nothing was coming in to replace them. I didn't know how to become anything but llerKalten, and none of what was going on fit in with my training. I was beginning to understand why the llerKalten always died at the end of her reign. She didn't know how to do anything else. I had lost my planet, my position, my pride, my prophetic powers shred by shred like a fish-nibbled corpse in the ocean.

Detter and Simon kept sparring, but I no longer listened to them. I wished Simon would go away. Now they were silent; Simon came closer to me, and I could feel the living warmth of him standing over me. Detter stood behind him, his arms folded, and I realized he didn't want to leave Simon either, though for different reasons. I stared through Simon's midriff, willing him to leave me alone, until he knelt before me and I was forced to look into his narrowed gray eyes. He already looked more like his father, purposeful and arrogant.

"So how is the King?" I asked coldly.

Simon winced, paused, and then answered. "He's already feeling much better, unfortunately. He's an opinionated, dictatorial bully at best. Even though he was enchanted by that rogue conjuror for nearly five years, he's recovered swiftly. I suppose it's good, because he needs all his wits to resist the political maneuvering that's going on, but he's a terror to deal with. He's unbelievably demanding, I'd forgotten how much."

"Didn't anybody here know what was going on?" I was willing to talk about anything but Simon and me.

"Not everybody has your Talent," he said quietly. "No one at court knew there was any magic involved. He just became more and more arbitrary and outrageous, and declaring an outsider his heir seemed only one more infuriating act. There was much dissension in the court, and the country itself nearly came to war. That's why the bandits could run around unchecked, because the lords were all conserving their soldiery for battle. Kaihan knew, somehow. He's been trying to convince me for a long time not to essay the test for Sorcerer, even though my father never requested my return."

He became aware he was rattling on, and stopped, embarrassed. At least he hadn't become completely pompous, though the potential was there. I didn't say anything more, but I put Kaihan on a list for painful revenge. It gave me something to live for, the prospect of flaying him alive. He'd planned all this with exquisite care, granted permission to Simon to seduce me so I'd support him, gave me just enough of a clue so I'd guess what was going on at the right time, and ordered Simon to pass through the country of his birth. He'd known I would be abandoned to make my own way with treacherous Detter as my only companion, and he'd cold-bloodedly condemned honest, well-meaning Simon to a political balancing act for the rest of his life. I closed my eyes. Simon put his hands on my knees, and in a sudden inexplicable burst of rage I swept them aside.

As I did so, the door flung open with a crash, and the King strode in. "I told you to come to me after dinner," he said coldly to Simon. "Instead I find you creeping back to your slut and your catamite. Are they merely your secret advisers, or are you their puppet? If you can't keep away from the kind of slime who stole you from me, I might as well throw you back to them." Simon, eyes slitted, sat back on his heels and waited out the tirade. Still furious, I had no such patience, and struck out at him with my harshest command voice, dredged from my oldest training.

"What rat-faced sludge of turtle spawn has beslimed this chamber uninvited?" I snarled. I was lifting, translated, from one of Jenneservet's better speeches. The King paused, his cape still swirling around him, and regarded me with alert attention.

I continued, "Were you not hairless, brainless, ancient, and badly addled, I would stir myself to be annoyed with you. Since your mother was obviously a kitchen drain and your father a festering rag, I must assume you do not know you have been rude. You may beg my pardon or remove your presence and its unbearable odor from the room." It was pleasant to feel anything, even rage, though both the King and Simon were watching me like snakes. Detter had edged halfway out of the room and was observing with prurient fascination.

Simon said, low and amused, "Father, she technically outranks you. You'd better do as she says."

I wasn't sure how he meant that, or if it were true, but the old man, astonishingly, took my instructions literally, a calculating glint in his eye. He inclined his head to me, said, "I do beg your pardon, madam," and I said, "Granted. I see I may have been deceived as to your character." I indicated the couch and he crossed over and took a seat, adjusting the skirts of his robe.

He said to Simon, who still sat on his heels before me, "You didn't tell me this adolescent would-be witch was actually a hundred-year-old queen with years of rule behind her. How did she make her voice do that, or is her appearance deceiving?"

Simon said cautiously, "You'd better ask her." The King waved his hand negligently, with no apologies. Simon rose, bowed to me, bowed to him, and left the room shooing Detter ahead of him. The King followed his progress with cat eyes but did not move. I'd never used command voice in a real situation before, and I was not sure whether it had worked or not, though it had certainly gotten his attention. For an exiled, dethroned ghost, I still had my resources.

The King turned to me with a rustle of fabric and said, "I thought you merely a witless, perverted, female apprentice conjuror. I must apologize. May I know your name and your station?" The old buzzard wasn't under any illusions, just looking for a different way to do what he wanted. My only recourse was truth, which might be counted on to disconcert if nothing else.

So I said frankly, "As for my station, I am indeed a student mage, which I assume is what you meant. However, I am in a manner of speaking the exiled, uncrowned queen and deposed deity of an invaded, defeated land. I have no name to give you, but you may call me Lisane. Your name, gracious sir?"

He said, "I am Terhal Leonais tzin Segevan mian Ephemener, and I am the previously bewitched and incapable King of a long-standing but heated permanent argument." We sat in silence for a moment. The fire popped and sent out a shower of sparks. I reached for the fire-tongs, and Terhal said, "I assume you are fairly close to my son?"

I looked up and in the flickering firelight realized I saw a man who was in some ways very like me. He'd been raised all his life to be a ruler, a human collection of strategies and policies who occasionally allowed a stunted emotion to rise to the surface. Though the question he'd just asked had all kinds of motives, he'd not been able to keep from showing a protective, fearful affection for his lost child. So I told him what I knew of Simon. Some of it he didn't like, but he was relieved to know for sure that Simon had been my lover.

"At least he's capable, then. I feared he was as twisted as most of the mages. He must be married soon, and I thought I'd have to find him some girl to marry who wouldn't mind spreading her legs to a man whose interest lay elsewhere."

He sounded like a cattle breeder with a reluctant bull, and I laughed, thinking of Jens and Annesil, and how complicated the practical romances of royalty must be here. It would have been so much easier for me. My consorts would have lasted only a year.

"He's a romantic, and naively honorable, so you'll have to

choose well. He'll need a woman with spirit and brains, I'm afraid, or his eye will wander, whether to women or men I couldn't tell you." Terhal cocked an eye at me and I realized how cynical I sounded. I gazed at him levelly. His eyes dropped first, but I suspected from the creases around his eyes I'd lost the skirmish somehow.

We talked for another hour, and finally the old man lifted himself out of the sofa and kissed my hand. "You had better get out of the country fast," he said, "or I will find myself fighting my own son over the right to court you." The crafty old demon managed to make me blush, though I knew how much calculation went into the statement. He looked at me for a moment as if he were sorry for me, then left.

I went to bed. I added to Kaihan's list of offenses. I'd thought I had no illusions about the Master's reasons for mating Simon with me, but now I saw I had mainly served as evidence of the heir's potency. In the small hours of the morning my door swung silently open, and Simon climbed into my box of a bed, cold and shivering in his nightclothes. When he left at dawn I felt less solid than ever.

Quillas came after breakfast and escorted us down to a carriage, which took us the short distance to the harbor. He transferred us to a two-masted ship, manned by a silent, efficient crew, and loaded two chests of clothing and food for us as well.

Detter vanished in search of our quarters, and I said to Quillas, "Take care of your swell-headed nephew."

He leaned on the rail comfortably. "Saimin will be fine. He's already fitting in. He was a well-behaved child, and the courtier he killed all those years ago was a scheming pervert who deserved to die, so those of us who remember him support him." Seabirds were mewing shrilly, and wind-blown ropes slapped against the masts and dock in a pattering clamor. It was bitter cold, and I would have to go below soon.

Quillas reached into a pouch at his waist, and handed me two small boxes. "One is from Saimin and one is from the

King," he said, and then dug out another box for Detter from Simon. Sentimental tokens of esteem, I thought sardonically, and considered tossing them in the water but refrained from politeness. Quillas grasped my shoulders and kissed me firmly on the forehead, then loped down the gangplank as the crew began to cast off. It was so cold I couldn't smell the sea, and I'd lost feeling in my fingers, so I sought out Detter and our cabin.

Detter's gift was a pair of earrings, small gold hoops. I watched fascinated as he matter-of-factly pierced his ears with them, leaving beads of blood on the wires. He left in search of a mirror, and I opened my presents. Simon's box contained a signet ring, sized for a man, with an elaborate dragon incised in intaglio. I was uncomfortably certain it was some kind of state seal. Also in the box was a tiny rosette of interwoven human hair, two kinds, both black but one coarser than the other. I wondered when he'd stolen my hair and found the time and the skill to fashion a love knot. I stared at it angrily for a while. He was an idiot and a romantic, and he did not deserve to be anybody's sovereign.

In Terhal's box was a locket, filigreed on the outside. Inside was an exquisite miniature, a mosaic in almost invisible chips of semiprecious stone, a portrait of a very young boy. He was solemn and innocent, perhaps five years old. The luminous eyes were silver gray and the forelock curling on his forehead was onyx black. I looked at that for a longer time, my eyes dry. Detter came in and went to his bunk, humming to himself.

We were the only passengers, no one else being so imbecile as to travel by ship in the pit of winter. Detter and I shared a mushroom box of a cabin with two shallow slots for bunks. As we inched out of harbor, the raised sails shuddered in the wind, and we began endless days and nights of pitching and rolling. Detter's stomach failed him for nearly two days, and my balance was unsure for a while, so it was some time before we ventured out.

The crew was a quiet lot, endlessly occupied with ship's

chores or their handiwork, and they seemed to view us both with suspicion. There were no women among them, which startled me. I was used to women sailors, mostly. This whole planet seemed to have peculiar notions about gender.

The captain, a youngish man with a cruel mouth and remote eyes, avoided us altogether. After I had essayed polite conversation and been ignored, a young sailor told me gruffly, "The captain doesn't mix with passengers. Best leave him alone." I thanked him for his advice and he turned from me with a grunt.

So I didn't try to approach the captain anymore, just watched him covertly when I had the chance. There was a constant coalescence and dissipation of ller going on in his vicinity, never very intense. Every once in a while he would make a vague gesture and the spirit-fire would dissolve away into smears and blobs. He ate with his arm wrapped about his plate, as if someone might steal his food. He had no neckring, but he was obviously a product of the mage school, unless there was a similar prison for mages elsewhere on the planet.

The ship groaned and creaked, shuddered and plunged, day in and day out. The water was salt. Sometimes the wind sprayed ocean water on the deck like rain, tasting of salt, death, and life. Sometimes the rain poured down on us from the sky instead—bland, cold, and sweet. Either way it was deathly cold. We stayed in our cabin much of the time, driven out for meals and air. Detter was itchy, bored, and vicious, but I couldn't stir myself to fight with him.

In the daytime, the Voices in my head spoke in counterpoint to the wails of the wind. They had been making less and less sense, and now they spoke in fragments, irrelevancies, malapropisms. Sometimes I sat and listened to them for hours, as if waiting by a deathbed, pressing Simon's ring into the skin of my arms to make raised welts in the shape of a dragon. At night I dreamed in my confined bunk, but they were dreams that began in solemn ceremony and ended in intimacy with people I hated, or dreams of giant walking corpses bigger than the world itself.

One day in our cabin, Detter stood up suddenly and shouted, "What are you trying to do to me, drive me insane? Well, it won't work," and left the room. I was puzzled. I hadn't said a word to him for days. People kept acting as if I were a human being with motives and desires instead of a waking shell full of tools and training, voices and dreams. I still had obligations to Detter, I supposed, and a promise to keep to Simon, so I wouldn't lie down just yet. I wasn't sure I could even manage to die properly, if I had never reigned and never passed on my reign to another. I kept apologizing to Jenneservet in my head.

It was almost spring of the year I would have succeeded my mother. I kept forgetting to eat.

Detter took to sitting with the off-watch crew, though they ignored him completely. His mustache was growing out nicely, a delicate gleam on his upper lip, refined, slick, and absurd as a baby with a cigar. One day I saw the captain speak to him briefly and move away, Detter's eyes following him like a dog's. It happened again a few days later, and in spite of the bewildered deadness in my head, I vaguely thought I should do something, I didn't know what. The third time it happened, when the captain spoke and turned away, Detter stood and followed him to his cabin. The sailors playing cards did not change their expressions, though I could feel astonishment in the air. Detter did not come back to bed until late at night. I lay in my bunk listening to my Voices when he crept into the dark swaying room and clambered into his berth.

The captain ignored Detter again for some time. I could guess why, for the captain had fresh scratch marks on his neck and he walked as if something hurt. The flickers of luminous spirit were stronger about him and stayed coherent longer. Detter looked cold and self-satisfied. He thought he had gotten away with something.

I couldn't seem to rouse myself from lethargy, but one day when I had left my cabin with the half-formed and soon forgotten idea of getting something to eat, I saw the captain speaking to Detter again. I made my way across the deck to them, my Voices chorusing contradictory instructions to me, and was in front of them before Detter could finish standing up. The captain eyed me with a cold gleam, his harsh mouth compressed:

I said, ostensibly to Detter, "How often does a guide lose a student on the Quest? How often does a student lose his guide? What happens to mages who slip through the cracks?"

Detter, his eyebrows raised, thought I was threatening him, but the captain reacted as I thought he might. Small explosions of ller like fireworks were appearing around him. He was backing away from me imperceptibly, as well he might. I had no patience anymore with people who ran from their duty. No patience at all anymore.

I hissed, "What does happen to lost mages? Where do they go? Are they afraid of being caught? How can they possibly hide and whom do they have to hurt?"

Detter said, "Lisane?" bewildered.

The captain was backed up against the bulkhead. A crew member looked up from his knitting and began to rise. I don't know what he saw when I looked at him, but he sat down again, slowly.

I wondered what I was doing there. I said to Detter, "Just keep it in mind," and went back to my cabin. I shut the door and sat cross-legged in my cold bunk, with the beams creaking and the wind moaning overhead. My Voices inside had silenced for a moment. I felt weak, odd, and temporarily sane. What had I been trying to do? Keep Detter from running away? Where could he go? Was I trying to tell the captain I knew what he was? What purpose would that serve? I didn't think I was going to survive this voyage, and just as well.

Detter didn't come in and I didn't go out. In a while, my Voices came back in a clamorous rush. I moved legless and armless through true dreams, arguing with an old woman, chasing an animal through the dark, but I was wide awake for days and days, I think.

Finally, someone was apparently feeding me soup, and doing a clumsy job of it. I was very hungry, biting at the spoon, but he wouldn't hurry up. I tried to grab the spoon, but my arms were bound up in a rough blanket. The food went away. Someone wiped my face roughly.

I opened my eyes and Detter's absurd face hovered over me, looking irritated. "Are you awake, bitch?" he asked. I blinked and nodded at him yes. He said, "Good. Because I'm going to feed you until you get well, you'll stay alive till Sassevin, and when we leave the Beast I'm going to kill you."

I smiled up at him, absurdly happy to see his face. He screwed up his mouth and brought the spoon back, shoving more soup in my mouth. "What were you trying to do, kill yourself?" I nodded, my mouth full, and he continued, "I didn't think you cared that much for Simon." I swallowed, and shook my head no. Affection for Simon hadn't had much to do with it. My Voices weren't talking. Maybe I'd managed to kill them off. Detter shoved another spoonful in my mouth, and I didn't quite throw up.

Detter tended me carefully, though he disappeared for long stretches at night. He looked happy, and I kept seeing new bruises and broken skin here and there. I guessed he and his new friend were still hitting it off, as it were. I asked him, "What happened to the captain?"

Detter said, "You scared the stuffing out of him. Did you know your eyes were glowing and you were spitting sparks out of your mouth when you spoke to him?"

No, I hadn't realized that. No wonder that sailor had looked frightened. "That's not what I meant. He was obviously a student some time. How did he end up a merchant captain?"

"He and his guide took the route south to Perchel, but then his guide slit his own throat at the seaport. It happens. When he was on his own, he realized he didn't want to face the Beast, and he didn't really want to be a mage anyway. So he signed up as a sailor on the first ship out. A lot of students disappear that way on Quest, and there are so few Finders left, nobody came after him."

"Do *you* want to be a mage?" I said seriously.

He looked at me as if I'd lost my mind again. "Of course, darling. It's the only thing I'm good at, and I'll make a marvelous practitioner." I should have known. He was the perfect product of the school. "I'll apprentice myself to a Wizard in Sassevin for a few years, then become Sorcerer myself. I'll have students and apprentices of my own when you're still barking in the wilderness." He chucked me under the chin, and left the room. The ideal nurse, someone who liked making people do things they didn't want to do.

I made my way out of my cabin eventually, and found that spring had arrived. I must have been out for a while. The captain saw me pass by, but he didn't react. I felt helpless and inarticulate, but my Voices were still silent. Detter helped me up the ladder, and I surfaced on deck to a scudding wind and a deep blue sky. There was a darker blue streak on the horizon, land. We were almost there.

Without comment, the captain brought the ship close to land, and then, instead of mooring in the harbor, steered the ship up the wide river that fed the sea. We were heading into the heart of the Greater Shore, going straight to Sassevin. It took several more days.

We disembarked at Sassevin. I was almost a human being again, though my edges felt raw. Neither Detter nor I knew where to go, but we set off at random, leaving our boxes with the harbormaster. Could we just go up to someone on the street and say, "Could you please direct me to the Beast?" No one in sight seemed to be a mage. We wandered around like tourists as the sun rose pale and warm in the brisk spring air. It was a bewildering city, all dead ends, side streets, buildings on buildings, and crowds. I have never seen so many different types of clothing in one place. We were impolitely ignored by all and sundry.

Suddenly, as we paused near a thriving livery stable, I sighted a steady purposeful stream of spirit-fire condensing from thin air and pouring off down a lane out of sight. I grabbed Detter's arm and we followed the current. It wound from street to street, and was joined by other flows of ller, all different colors. Detter, resigned to trusting my peculiarities of vision, allowed me to lead him.

Eventually, the glowing torrents converged on a shabby stone building with an unfinished wooden door, standing alone on a hill overlooking the river. No one seemed to be going in or coming out. Detter said, "That can't be what we're looking for." He argued with me but finally consented to have a look.

We opened the door, Detter stepping in ahead of me, and entered a large cool chamber. A man, wearing a purple-striped single-strand neckring, sat at a desk. He looked up from his writing briefly and said to Detter, "You go ahead," gesturing to a set of ebony doors, then, holding up a palm to me, "You wait." Were we expected, or was this how all were greeted? As Detter walked forward, the doors swung open. A similar set of tarnished brass doors was revealed just beyond, before the black doors closed behind him. I sat down to wait, feeling like a customer at an expensive fortune-teller.

A moment later, a terrible harsh scream reverberated through the room, and a thunderous boom sounded. I jumped to my feet. The mage continued to write, ignoring the commotion. The screaming and pounding continued for a long time, and then there was a hideous silence, followed by the slamming of doors. I was shaking with shock and fear, but the mage just said, "All right. Go ahead." He didn't look up. So I stood and passed through the black doors. They closed behind me.

The tarnished brass inner doors parted slowly to the darkness like the inside of my eyelids when closed. A deep thrumming sounded, the dying echo of a gong, and a smell of raw meat and salt embraced me in thick folds as I passed through

the opening. Once inside, I found to my surprise that my eyes
were indeed closed, and when I opened them stickily and
sleepily, I was standing naked, pale, and alone in a great warm
crimson chamber the shape of an egg and the size of the entire
Enforcer transport. Its walls were soft and moist, succulent,
covered with a fragile membrane and pale veins as far as I
could see. This room was far bigger than the outside of the
building, and somehow more real. In true dreams but not in
waking life, I'd felt this awful certainty of underlying reality,
but even in true dreams I'd never noticed the small confirming
details, like the dimples my feet made in the soft, wet, red floor,
or the prickly rising of gooseflesh on my exposed skin.

A shudder ran over me, and I chafed my arms with my
hands to make the startled hairs lie down. I stood for a minute,
arms wrapped around myself, waiting for something to happen. It occurred to me to look for the door again, but when I
turned around, the walls stretched just as far in the opposite
direction, smooth and glistening and breathing gently. So this
was the dreaded Room. Where was the famous Beast? I
walked around, aimlessly, then stopped. There wasn't much
point in moving around if the whole place was all the same.
Whatever was going to happen to me, I was sure it would
come looking for me, so I might as well relax. I felt somehow
queasy about slapping my bare bottom down on the fleshy
floor, as though that organic substance might somehow grow
up into my insides. I stifled the nightmare thought, but com-
promised by sitting on my heels, my hands resting lightly on
my thighs. Nothing much happened, very slowly and for a
long time.

There was a sense of presence all around me, remote and
uncaring. Something or someone was thinking big rolling
thoughts, thinking about things much more significant than
me. I didn't like it. This, after all, was supposed to be my moment of truth. What if whatever it was never got around to
noticing me? The room pulsed and glowed steadily around me,

somnolent and inattentive, and eventually my left foot went to sleep. I was beginning to feel decidedly miffed and unwanted.

What if this setup didn't work for women? I was the first female mage these Wizards had acknowledged, after all. Maybe the Beast only came out to chew on lame-brained violent punks like Detter. Was he dead? There was no sign of him here. I hoped he had survived somehow, the nasty worm. He was my only family.

My back was starting to hurt, and the warm moist surface of the floor, though it rolled gently like the deck of a becalmed ship, showed no signs of intent to molest me, so I stretched forward on my front and laid my head on my arms, my breasts flattened beneath me. The floor quivered and gave gently around me.

Where was the big confrontation, the grand battle, the chance to prove my magical strength and wisdom and my natural fitness to rule something somewhere? Barring that, where was the door? Though being a ring-bound mage wasn't even my last choice on the list of desirable jobs, I had at least thought I'd have the choice of attempting to prove myself. I might not be able to die properly, but my training shouldn't go completely to waste. I think I had completely recovered from my funk at sea, for my natural arrogance was returning. In fact, it seemed amplified in this improbable room.

These dunderheaded mages, with their pettiness and caution and their perverted cravings, wasting their command of the spirit on mundane magical contrivances, these self-important misogynistic soul-shriveling snakes, had no idea who it was their Beast was ignoring. My destiny was greatness or death, but the Universe seemed determined to thwart me. Having managed to place the blame for my sidetracked life squarely on someone else besides me, I proceeded to work myself into a state of rage at each and every man with Power in the world, especially Kaihan. I spent a stimulating half hour figuring out a spell to give them all permanently sealed assholes and a case of galloping diarrhea.

The Room continued to swell and shrink imperceptibly like a giant heart, while I, the very important would-be llerKalten and Wizard, grimaced and twitched like a beached fish at the bottom of it, extracting the last teaspoon of satisfaction out of my imaginary revenge. But after that wore thin, I lay still, thinking of nothing at all. I had run out of paranoid fantasies and grandiose dreams. There was nothing I could do to occupy myself except worry, and I couldn't see much purpose in worrying, so I just lay and watched the Room pulsate, feeling useless.

An hour or a day or a week later, with a gasp and a sigh, an enveloping wind poured over me from the other end of the chamber, and I jumped to my feet. I now saw a dark misshapen figure ambling toward me from a distance. As it approached, I could not make sense of it, until with an adjustment of my sight I realized it was an immense centaur, with the squat upper trunk of a giant man and the massive black barrel and legs of a dray horse.

I stood waiting, shy and flushed as if just awakened, and the creature plodded steadily toward me, swollen-muscled arms swinging with each ponderous shift of his legs, until he paused a body's length away from me. His size and overwhelming masculinity overshadowed me, and I had to bend my head back to look into his face.

It was a blind, wild, ecstatic face, with great brown eyes all pupil like a stallion's, a hard strained mouth, and a blunt, flat, flared nose. I knew that face, though I'd only seen it before in diluted form, glaring through the mortal flesh of the Year-Kings who coupled with my mother. I felt a fierce pride in my knowledge, so fierce a pride that I didn't think to wonder why the avatar would show up in a glorified final examination room on the wrong planet.

"King and Lord, are you in this world as well?" I said. "I saw no signs you were awake among these people."

"I am in all human worlds," he said in a harsh voice like the scream of a horse. It was so loud and formless I could barely understand him. "Why should I not be here, whether people know me or not?"

"Where is your Kalten, Mennet? How can you be alone?"

He laughed, a cold booming sound starting from his horse's belly, and reared his forelegs in the air. His splayed hooves came down on the red membranous floor with a wet thwack and he danced sideways, looking down at me with his transfigured face.

"The Wizards called only me to this form, woman. They don't know of the Mother. How could they? They don't know their own mothers, they take no wives, they beget no daughters. They don't know the Mother, though she surrounds them entirely." He sidled back closer to me.

His skin was so white it was almost translucent between the black curls of his body hair, and blue veins rode over the threshing muscles of his belly and chest. At the base of his human half, coarse curly pubic hair blended gradually down into glossy horsehide. He was offensively, blatantly masculine and ugly, and my skin goosefleshed painfully at the sight of him. He switched his long coarse tail so it cascaded back over his haunches. The crimson walls of the curved chamber quivered imperceptibly all about us, with a repetitive thud like a distant heartbeat.

He began to move away from me again. He was going to leave me. I helplessly raised my hands as if to call him back. The centaur grinned fiercely, cantered back to stand before me, then knelt slowly so that his wild and hairy head was bent over me. Up close, his face was even more terrifying, savage, and remote, and his acrid sweaty smell made my eyes narrow and my nostrils flare. He spread his arms around me, and drew me half-willing to his curl-thatched chest. My brains were coagulated with lust and love and with the pride of the destiny I'd thought I'd lost forever, and I wanted to merge with him as with no mortal male, but a small cold voice was speaking dimly in the back of my mind, and it was not one of prophecy. It was a very mundane, stupid voice.

He slapped himself against me, front to front, like some humping animal in heat, and seized and sucked at my lips with his mouth, tasting me and groaning. My legs were straddled over his kneeling forelegs, and my whole body arched and peeled itself insistently against his, with a feeling like hot fluid pouring from my groin, up my spine, to my skull, where the small voice said, clearly and simply, "No." Against my whole desire, and with no clear understanding of my change of heart, I struggled, suddenly completely ashamed and fearful, against his grasping arms and groping lips, until, disgusted, he thrust me away from him at arm's length, dangling me in the air. "Don't you want to do what you were born to do? Why, then, are you here at all?" he demanded.

His unknowing animal eyes were wild and hot, his clutch was excruciatingly painful, and my throat swelled in regret and lust for him, but I knew I could not do it. The red walls beat steadily about us, looming somehow closer.

"I don't think this is my job anymore," I said inanely.

"Job?" he said, and laughed, jeering, in my face, his spittle spraying me. "You think you know what your job is, little bag of blood? If you want to be Mother, your job is to be my vessel, as mine is to pour myself into you." He flung me to the ground without effort and stood looming over me. I shrank back, afraid of his hooves, but he did not follow, just stood with his hairy knuckled fists on his hips and his tail arched high.

"I'm sorry, Lord," I said, knowing that I was blowing my last chance at eternity, "but you're talking about the real Mother, not me." His hard wide mouth opened, showing his teeth, and he was panting like a dog, but I lurched on: "You'd burn me into cinders from the inside out if I tried to join with you. I'm not enough for you, I'll never be enough for you. I'm just an ordinary woman with delusions of grandeur."

There went my childhood dreams of glory, and his great bared teeth shone, grisly and coarse in the crimson light of the encircling chamber. He hunched down and lifted me above him with his stone-muscled arms. His jaws gaped wider and impossibly wider as if he were going to gulp me down whole, and I felt I was about to die, my womb now forever empty, but my mind was saying inanely over and over, "No, I can't do it, no, I can't." I dangled limp and helpless in his grip above him as he rose, lurching and swaying, to all four feet. The egg-shaped chamber had closed completely about us, now so small it barely cleared my head, and it glowed with a hot ruby light, pulsing and flowing.

With a gasp, the membranous wall rushed in completely and wrapped us both in moist warmth and darkness. I was dropping down slowly, his hot arms still cradling me, and his dark wild voice, in unison with another, thicker, softer voice, whispered into my ear, "So you are only human, little one? Did you think we didn't know that? And now you know as well. Be well, beloved. Remember we are bound here when the time comes."

My feet were suddenly on a hard, bare floor, my eyes were closed, in a cold, silent space. I opened my eyes to lamplight appearing between two slowly opening doors. I stepped forward, staggering a little, and as I passed through the doorway I felt a sudden smooth cold weight settle around my neck.

I was in an ordinary hallway, with worn wooden floors. Down the center of the hall ran a thick congealing trail of blood, smeared with naked bloody footprints. A freckled red-haired Magician in a tunic and a single jade neckring, lazily mopping up the blood, gaped at me in silent consternation. His expression made me look down self-consciously, but it seemed I had my clothes on again, after all. I reached my hand up blindly to find out what had happened to my neck, and found a thick triple-ring collar bound seamlessly about it. Apparently, even if I was not a failed goddess, only a human woman and a cowardly one at that, the Beast had given me the badge of a Wizard.

Behind me the doors finally closed with a prosaic thud, and before the red-haired Magician could pull himself together, I strode past him down the hall, passed through the door at the end, and found myself back outside the shabby stone building. I didn't look back, just kept moving as fast as I could without running.

CHAPTER NINE

In Which I Don't Poison Myself

"Rounderbean. Now, that's easy enough to remember. 'Round' for 'comes around,' for a woman's cycle. Takes the bloat away, that comes before your monthly flow. Chew till all the taste is gone, but don't swallow, and never take more than one a month." Charonne slipped the hard round bean back in its bag, then fumbled again with her wrinkled, spotted hands in her wicker medicine box.

I said, "Is that because it could be poisonous?"

She drew her mouth in, annoyed. "Lisane, is your head just on holiday or are you planning to think like a rock the rest of your life? I've told you and told you, everything in this box is poisonous if you take enough of it. You have to assume your customers will take too much of their medicine and take it too often. Though they're just as likely not to take it at all, but that doesn't poison them, just doesn't cure them." She found what she was looking for in the box, a creased packet of paper, and began painfully to unfold the end.

I was learning a trade. Since I'd chosen against being either a goddess queen or a practicing mage, I had to acquire some different skills if I wanted to keep on eating. Charonne was peevish and impatient, but in a way that was familiar to me. She reminded me of Jenneservet. She had agreed to teach me and lend me her vendor's squat on the pavement by the horse-dealer, if I would conduct her business for her so she could retire. She was getting too old to stand the cold, didn't want an enclosed shop, and, she said, was planning to die toward the end of next winter, so she wanted to take some time off before that. She'd spent half a lifetime selling medicine on Tinker's Hand Street in the Frog Belly quarter of Sassevin, and it seemed as good a trade as any to me. Though she was very careful to distinguish between her trade and that of the country herb-wife, she didn't explain the difference. I supposed it mattered to her, but I was content with the job, whatever it was called.

Now she spilled a little pale powder from the packet into her puffy hand, touched a moistened finger to it, and held her fingertip up for me to lick. The taste was bitter and lingered. She was stern-faced, which I was learning meant she was going to lay another trick on me. I worked my mouth and wrinkled my nose. She waited, impassive, for perhaps a minute, then darted her hand out, firmly twisting a pinch of skin on my arm. I laughed, amazed but completely relaxed. Though the pinch was viciously painful, the pain felt as if it belonged to someone else.

"What is that? It works fast," I said.

"Works fast, wears off fast. Called foster-pine. Good for short, hard pains—tooth pulling, bone setting, suchlike. Take a whole spoonful, it'll give you half an hour without pain, but you pay with shivers and spasms." She tipped the palmful of powder back into the packet. "I don't label it, so remember what the packet looks like. People like to steal it—an overdose is a good clean way to kill your enemy, or yourself for that matter."

It was afternoon, a merciless blinding summer day. Even dry old Charonne was sweating, and I kept blinking the salt out of my eyes. My three black neckrings chafed my skin red and raw in the heat, and I would have taken them off if I could. Charonne disapproved of them. Though I'd seen other nonmages in Sassevin wearing costume jewelry styled after the mage's mark, Charonne thought it poor judgment and bad taste for anyone to wear Wizard's sign. I hadn't tried to convince her I had earned it; I suspected she would think no better of me. She did not care for mages, nor did she see much use in magic, saying it was like harnessing sun's fire to power a candle flame. That was part of why I trusted her, in spite of her skin-scorching tongue. The innkeeper, Bielo Massim, had put me on to her after I'd been cleaning his stable for a couple of weeks. He said he was sorry to lose me, but I knew I really didn't do that good a job, and besides I distracted his customers from the working girls, who paid him tithe.

Charonne's pitch on Tinker's Hand Street was smack in the middle of one of the sweeping torrents of ller that met in the Beast's shabby shelter, but there was a little peaceful eddy around Charonne's pavement mat, where magic, it seemed, did not dare trespass. Lle had no such respect for any others, coursing through the crowds as if they were light-shadows, in frantic haste to supply the Beast. I wondered how the spell that bound the Beast had ever been set, and what would happen if it were broken. It didn't seem to me that any mage I'd met so far was capable of such an act.

I was here because when the Beast had finished with me, I decided I was finished with magic. I kept walking until my legs wouldn't work properly, which happened just outside the Cat and Apple, Bielo Massim's inn. I sat down, right there against the stinking wall. I was still wearing men's clothing, my hair was tangled and matted, I was only half-recovered from my confused attempt to die properly, and my neck was stacked three high with black mage-rings, but one of Bielo's drunken patrons still thought I was worth an effort. Bielo himself came out to see what the noise was, and after a series of misunderstandings, he ended up giving me a bowl of soup, a corner of the stable to sleep in, and the cleaning job. It all seemed so amusing to him I never felt the need to thank him.

"Lisane! Stop mooning about. You look like a chicken in the feed bin. Lesson's not done." Charonne was holding up another fingertip-full of smutty black dust. She had a terrifying gleam in her eye, though she was attempting to look sterner than ever. I began to stick my tongue out to lick the powder off, then backed up, uneasy.

I said, "That stuff looks evil. I'm not tasting that until you tell me what it is."

She cackled and waved the finger at me. "Spelldamp flour. Illegal as murder. I don't sell it, I don't have it, you haven't seen it. It wouldn't do a normal person any harm, but you give it to one of those insufferable mages and he's not a mage any-more. Can't do magic, can't cast spells, no matter how many chants he's memorized. Go on, taste it, it won't hurt you." I shook my head at her silently. "Aaah, I should have known. Do you think you were somehow born a mage but got overlooked somehow? Are you waiting for a Wizard to walk by and say, 'There she is—that one'? Even if you did have Power, girl, you'd be better off without it. Taste it."

"How long does it last? What's the dosage?" I said. The smudged finger was too near me, and I tried not to flinch. Though I had decided not to practice magic as a living, I found now that I didn't care to lose my abilities either.

She pulled it back, wiped her finger thoroughly in the dirt, and closed up the small black envelope. "At least you're be-ginning to learn what questions to ask. With this stuff, I don't know. When I was young, I was more than half a witch myself, so I've never dared taste it," and she cackled. I felt better. "The woman who gave it to me said enough to cover a fingernail would cripple a mage long enough for an enemy to knife him. Keep it in mind if any of those boil-faced mudthumpers causes you serious trouble. Not that you're the right sex for that."

Pelleter Tailor walked by, snapping her fingers briskly. Charonne unhurriedly stowed the envelope away and closed her medicine case. The finger-snapping was a signal that meant mages were coming. At all the stands, carts, and shops on Tin-ker's Hand Street, similar calm concealment occurred.

"Isn't it useless to keep secrets from the mages? One of them could walk through here invisible, for all you know, or cast a truth-telling spell on all of us," I remarked.

Charonne said impatiently, "The idea is to avoid rousing any attention in the first place. We're not important to them, and they're blinded by arrogance. They won't waste their energies on us if we don't do anything out of the ordinary. That's why your stupid neckrings are such a bad idea—they draw attention."

I obediently wrapped my headscarf around my throat, though I was instantly sweating twice as hard. Two mages strolled into sight, absorbed in their conversation and paying no heed to the colorful cacophony around them or to the relentless flow of ller that coursed over and through them. It was not usual for mages to stray from their luxurious quarters in Seven Snakes, but they did wander through occasionally. One was a dark-haired young single-ring Magician, and the other was a double-ring Sorcerer with curly white eyebrows and too much finger-jewelry.

As they passed us, the Sorcerer glanced aside and said vaguely, "Ah, Charonne. How goes it?" Charonne bobbed her head and smiled, showing too much brown tooth but not moving the rest of her face. The Sorcerer had already forgotten her, and the Magician had never looked at her. They kept walking and talking, and when they were out of sight Charonne calmly opened her case back up and I unwound the sweat-soaked scarf with relief. "You seem to have drawn the attention of at least one mage yourself," I said.

Charonne scowled at me, embarrassed. "If I haven't always followed my own advice, that doesn't mean it's bad advice. I'd be better off if no mages knew me." She started digging through her disorderly box again.

I lifted my rings up to let some air circulate on the abraded skin. According to the pocket mirror I'd bought with my first spare money, the rings were black as ebony, dull, smooth, and almost alive, the same color and texture as Kaihan's, though I would have preferred emerald green. With my long braided black hair, the rings formed a lustrous frame for the vivid face that still appeared to be mine. I spent a lot of time gluttonously, guiltily staring in the mirror, memorizing that face.

The afternoon wore on, hotter and slower, and finally Charonne latched her box shut, rolling it away with her back bent over. I stood, arching my back and stretching, feeling the flow of the indifferent spirit as I stepped into the stream. It was time for dinner. The air was thick with smoky food smells, sideways shafts of sunlight needling through the haze. I couldn't decide whether I should get sausage from Nicot's aunt or meat pastry from Sibby Gomm.

I set off down the street, winding my way between the buyers and sellers, the strollers and lookers. I knew about one in ten by sight, one in twenty to speak to, which wasn't bad, considering how new I was in the city. Working Charonne's pitch on Tinker's Hand and knowing Bielo Massim counted for a lot in Sassevin. I had been very fortunate in my flight from the Beast.

A little later, licking sausage grease off my fingers, I stopped and looked into the Cat and Apple. It was as busy as ever, but dark stocky Bielo stopped to talk for a moment. He always found everything vastly entertaining, as if all humanity were performing for his benefit.

"Mages are all stirred up. Something up north is eating them, one by one," he said gleefully.

"Eating them? You mean chewing them up and swallowing them? There's nothing big enough to do that." Bielo scurried across the room to serve a customer. "Who's been spreading tall tales?" I demanded of the room at large. I knew most of the customers there.

Dour Argevin looked up from his table. "It's true enough they're disappearing, but whether or not they're being eaten, I couldn't tell you." Argevin was Sorcerer Tilloke's manservant, an ill-natured, drunken gossip, but his information was generally reliable. It was Argevin who'd told me that Wizard Gelmas, a Council member notorious for his fits of cruelty, had a new apprentice, a blond-haired, blue-eyed novice Magician who'd already outlasted the three previous apprentices and earned a nasty reputation of his own. Detter's long-term plans were still working out, it seemed.

I came further into the room and sat on a stool by the wall, but Argevin went back to his greasy gray stew. He knew I was waiting to hear more, and he might tell me more in a bit if he felt like it. I leaned back and closed my eyes. It was as hot in the tavern as it was outside, or hotter, but the darkness inside made the heat feel friendlier somehow.

Argevin swallowed a mouthful, wiped his chin with a piece of bread, and finally said, "Any mages take the Dicedipper Road all the way up through Belmire to Asterman's Wood north of Falconhill, they don't come back. It's been happening for a long time now, but Council just decided to notice. Council's been fussing and gibbering all week." He stuck his spoon back in the bowl and put his hands on the table. "They won't do anything about it, though. Too busy scoring off each other to get any real work done, Kaihan or no Kaihan." He pushed his chair away from the table.

Before he could finish getting up, I said too eagerly, "Kaihan? What's Kaihan doing?"

He stood and shoved the chair back in without replying, then went out the door, a sullen, sour, gray-haired mutt of a man. I didn't know how his master could stand him. I certainly couldn't. I sat on the stool watching Bielo scurry about merrily among his customers playing innkeeper until the inn was too crowded, then left. I didn't drink and I didn't hook, so I had no real business in the Cat once I'd already eaten.

The day was cooling slightly now that the sun was low, and if I walked slow and loose my clothes didn't stick to me. I turned down Tinker's Hand and decided not to go home yet, but to sit in Charonne's spot and watch the pretty men go by. Since Simon I had become even more wary, I was chaste again for the time being, but that didn't mean my thoughts were pure. I sat on the pavement and relaxed. My Voices had come back soon after I started with Charonne, unfortunately, but they seemed to like man-watching too, and I caught them some-times making rude rhymes. They were becoming a giddy bunch now that I was no longer anybody important.

In the smoky dusk I didn't see Charonne and her unlikely companion approaching until they were almost on me. I rolled sideways and scrambled behind Aggi's clothing stand, which annoyed Aggi. I peeked around the corner of her stand, my heart pounding, my mouth dry. Charonne strolled past, com-placently arm in arm with a graceful Wizard all in black, the eternally unexpected Kaihan, who smiled down at her as if she were a lovely young girl. The expression on his face made me short of breath, and I could feel my face reddening. She smiled back, stumping along next to him like an animated bag of pud-ding. Aggi crabbily poked me with her toe, and I desperately ignored her until I was sure they were well past and that they hadn't seen me.

"What is wrong with you, girl?" demanded Aggi as I got back to my feet.

"Was I seeing things or was that Charonne and a mage?" I said weakly. "I heard no warning."

"Oh. I keep forgetting how new you are in town. That's Kai-han. He doesn't count—we don't warn for him." A customer claimed her attention, and she promptly forgot me.

I walked out into the street and stared after them. The Master of Sassevin Council and an elderly, poverty-stricken, mage-hating, acid-tongued street herbalist were ambling like a courting couple through one of the roughest sections of town, and nobody turned a hair. Something was skewed. This was the man for whom the King of Emsadorn held a recep-tion and everybody came, all thrilled to share in his glory, but on Tinker's Hand he didn't count as a mage. I could see no logic to it.

Flat-footed in the middle of the road, I watched Kaihan and Charonne disappear into the crowd and thought how in-triguing it was that men can perform the complicated act of walking without swiveling their hips at all, as if their legs were swinging loose from an axle. Somebody had been thinking well when they put that man together. Or maybe he put himself together. I wouldn't put it past him.

I sat back down at Charonne's spot, feeling stupid and depressed. I'd made the mistake of thinking I understood Sassevin just because I'd found myself a place and made a few friends. I wondered now if my concealment in plain sight had worked as well as I'd thought. Maybe Kaihan had known where I was all the time, and Charonne was his agent. He'd been able to make me do exactly what he wanted before, while all the while I'd thought I was on my own.

I was still sitting there in the half dark when Charonne herself sat down next to me, with a groan as her arthritic knees bent down. "I wish I had your body and my experience," she said querulously. The image of Charonne as anybody's agent dissolved in my mind. Then she saw my face. "Hey, spitfire, who died? What's the matter?"

"I just found I don't know as much as I thought I did," I answered shamefacedly.

She cackled. "Is that all? I've been telling you that all along." She reached out a puffy old hand, the skin swinging loose on her arm, and thumped me on the back reassuringly. "I just found out I don't know that much either, but ignorance is a much lighter sin on an old back like mine. What took you by surprise, then?"

I sat mum for a minute, but she prodded me impatiently with a forefinger. "Come on, out with it."

"I saw you walking with Master Kaihan. I thought you hated mages. It looked like you were old friends."

"We are. I've known Kaihan all my life. He's an old-style mage. He follows the old laws and even some he made up himself, but he never let a bad law get in the way of what's right. I respect him for that, though it's a waste of good meat for that man to play the celibate."

Celibate? The dark Master looked about as chaste as an old tomcat. "You've known him all your life? How can that be?

He's only been here a year." It was almost dark. The vendors were packing up and moving off all around us.

Charonne grumbled, half-visible in the dusk, "Kaihan was Master in Sassevin before he ever played schoolmaster, and not just the once, either. He was Master before even I was born. You know him, don't you? And you're the young woman he's worried about, aren't you, hellion? No wonder you turned so white when I brought out the spelldamp." She reached out a finger and flicked my neckrings. "Those are real."

I nodded, watching her. She gathered herself up to stand. I stood myself and helped her up. "Well, it's time for us semi-respectable types to turn in before the fun starts," she said. "Do I have your illustrious Wizardship's permission to tell Kaihan you're all right? If I promise not to tell him where you are?" I nodded again, feeling weary and probably looking sulky.

"See you in the morning, you bat-brained young twerp," she said, and hobbled off in the direction of her room above the draper's.

I went home myself, out of sorts. Home was a lean-to on the side wall of the horse-dealer's yard. I liked having my own place. It kept the vermin down when you didn't share a bed or a room with anybody else. I had a hard time getting to sleep that night, shifting and turning on my lumpy straw-filled bed. I wished I could sleep on the ground as I had on my travels, but there were rats in the stable yard and I didn't care to be a rodent racetrack.

I did sleep, finally, and dreamed my first true dream in months. A rabbit-cheeked boy was sitting at a table with a mixing bowl before him. He took a jar, unscrewed it, and poured colored sand into the bowl. He put the empty jar and its bulbous lid to one side, and the jar grew arms and tried to screw its lid back on. Meanwhile, the boy was pouring more sand in from a different jar. I moved closer and saw that the jars were men and the lids their heads, with blinking eyes and moving lips. He poured out another jar, and another, until the table was full of feebly grasping jars and the bowl was a swirl of colors.

The boy smiled openly at me, grasped the last jar, unscrewed it, and upended the contents. When he put the jar down, the domed lid gleamed smooth in the dim light. The jar reached out nimble hands and grabbed its lid, leaping aside on agile legs. The head looked up at me with glittering empty eyes, and it was Kaihan. I struck the boy heavily behind his ear, and he fell, stunned.

I grabbed the bowl, but Kaihan's powder was inextricably mingled with the others. I poured it all out on the table, and the empty men leaped on it, scrabbling desperately among the grains.

It was hopeless. I stood holding the huge bowl in my arms, watching the antics on the table. At my feet the boy stirred and groaned. I looked down, knelt, and methodically began folding him legs first into the bowl. I might as well get some food for the Beast out of this mess, I thought. I folded and folded him until only his head stared up from the bowl, smiling at me. As I bore the bowl out of the room, I looked back. The manikin Kaihan stood at the edge of the table, watching me leave.

I woke with a foul taste in my mouth, and pried my body painfully out of bed. I'd hoped I was done with true dreams. I pasted myself together and walked to work, trying to forget the dream and wondering what Charonne was going to do with me now that she knew I was a mage.

She saw me coming and wheezed cheerfully, "Look what got swept off the outhouse floor. How much did you pour down your gullet last night?"

"You know I don't drink," I said defensively.

"So why do you look like the pig's dinner?"

"Bad dreams," I said, and sat down like a gross of potatoes.

Charonne hauled her wicker case next to her thigh, and dug through until she found a vial full of crimson liquid. "Stick out your tongue," she said, and put a single drop on it when I obeyed. The liquid tasted like cinnamon, so aromatic my eyes watered painfully. "For bad dreams," she said, and patted me clumsily. It seemed my open secret was still safe with her. A customer with palsy sat down before us, and the work-day began.

The only other thing she said to me about it was a few days later. "A well-meaning innocent like you shouldn't have ended up with the mages, no matter how Powerful you were," she said. "Where was the herb-wife when you were born?"

"It's complicated," I said, and she let it go after a moment. I wondered what she meant, but I didn't want to raise the topic again.

That summer, I finished learning all the names of Charonne's medicines, and began to understand her system of diagnosis and dosage. Fall came, a blessed relief. The skin of my neck healed under my rings, and the streets smelled less like stale sewage. Charonne was letting me treat all the customers while she watched, and since fall was her busiest season, I had no time to think.

One afternoon after we had packed up early, I walked back along Tinker's Hand Street after dinner. The Hand was in full throat, all the vendors shouting out their wares and the customers discussing the merchandise in passing. I wound between the people, and almost collided with a man pulling a white shirt over his head at Aggi's cart. He had a small but appreciative audience cheering him on, and I was annoyed I couldn't find my way around them. The man's head emerged from the neck of the shirt, and I found myself face-to-face with Kaihan.

He was as startled as I was, his face for once unsure. His neckrings were entirely gone, though there was a ring of pink, smooth scar tissue where they had abraded the skin. He tugged the hem of the shirt down awkwardly over his surprisingly flat belly. "Lisane," he said quietly. The people who'd been watching him try on the shirt, three of them friends of mine, melted back into the moving crowd as if they had all just then remembered an urgent errand.

My stomach turned over, but rather than stand there gooping at him like a lackwit, I said, "What happened to your rings?"

Kaihan turned, flipped a coin to Aggi, and offered me his arm with urbanity. I looked at the arm in astonishment, but he waited motionless until I caught on and clumsily slipped my arm through his. Off we went at a leisurely pace, people making way for us calmly. He wasn't much taller than I, which made me feel not that he was small but that I was a great galumphing galoot of a horse. My Voices were making indecent suggestions.

"I went for a fourth visit to the Beast," he said. Rings or no rings, his voice was still velvet. "I found out what outranks a Wizard."

"What possessed you to do that?" I demanded, and felt immediately even more awkward. We jerked to a stop to let the vegetable hawker trundle by us, then proceeded on, Kaihan deftly guiding me past a puddle.

He said ruefully, "I couldn't get Council to do what I wanted, though the fools should know by now I only put my foot down when the survival of the brotherhood is at stake. They called enough challenges on me that I could have fought twenty duels before breakfast. So I resigned as Master in a dramatic and satisfying way, with a rousing speech, and paid a call on the Beast." His tone was light, but I knew he'd intended suicide, not from self-pity but as a last political maneuver. I could understand that. Jenneservet had told me it was always a last resort, but an effective one if done properly.

"You must have felt very odd that the Beast didn't kill you. What are you going to do instead?" I asked.

He pressed his lips together and tucked his chin under, staring down at me over his nose like an owl, then spoiled the peculiar effect by snorting a stifled laugh out his nostrils. We had to stop while he searched for a handkerchief, and his eyes were watering with the attempt to keep from laughing. Finally he sat down on the curb and put one hand over his eyes, his shoulders shaking.

I was miffed. I hadn't meant to be humorous. Obviously I'd played the ignoramus again. I shifted from foot to foot, bored and irritated, while he recovered from his bout of laughter. Finally he dropped his hand, leaned his elbows on his knees, and said to me, "Yes, I felt very odd indeed, you horribly penetrating young harridan. Stop looking so mulish, I wasn't laughing at you. Sit down." Now I really felt foolish, but I uncomfortably lowered myself down to sit next to him. "As for what I'm going to do, I didn't lose my Power along with my rings," he said, "so I'll do what I wanted Council to do, and go north to stop whatever's taking mages. There are few enough of us as it is; we can't afford to lose any more, or the renegades will be the only abstract practitioners left and there'll be nothing but trouble."

"If you go north, you'll be taken as well, you egotistical rooster, and what will that prove?" I said, still irritated with him.

"Don't be so certain," he said, not in the least stung. If Sassevin Council was anything like the madhouse Council I'd seen at school, he was fed a steady diet of insults far sharper than that. "I have had nine of your lifetimes to perfect my skills. I should have gone north alone to begin with."

"You will be taken as well. You should take somebody with you," I insisted. "What do you want me to do when you don't come back? Should I tell somebody?"

He started to say something, then stopped and looked down. I remembered again who I was talking to, and cursed myself for a dumb donkey. "No," he finally said. "Council doesn't believe you exist, because you never showed yourself to them after you left the Beast. They all think I conjured you up out of some perverse desire to humiliate them. And the herb-wives have no use for mages, or I'd send you to them. No, better off leaving well enough alone. My friend Charonne says you are learning a trade. I wish all mages would do so; they would then at least be useful for something besides conspiracy and mayhem."

He began to get to his feet. He'd assumed I was worried about losing his protection. He must think me very young and selfish indeed. I could take care of myself. "It's you I'm worried about, you pigheaded, arrogant, self-absorbed, power-hungry old tyrant," I shouted up at him from my seat on the pavement. "You think you're free to do as you wish, but that doesn't mean you have to behave like an idiot and get yourself killed for no reason other than lack of common sense." I couldn't see his face against the sun.

"If I were free to do as I wish, I would have become a horse-coper in Linz a long time ago," he said harshly. "We are not all permitted to make Charonne's choice. Power carries responsibility, and I do what I must. Nor are you so free yourself, but you'll find that out without my help." He hesitated, bowed lightly to me, then said, "But thank you for your concern. I have to go," and left, walking very fast as if running away, his new white shirt rippling in the breeze of his motion. I was so furious I could barely see, so furious my throat burned and the bridge of my nose felt hollow. Mother's milk and Father's blood, how I hated that man.

"Lisane, what's the matter? Why are you crying, dear?" said Sibby Gomm's mother, a woman I couldn't stand. I wiped my eyes casually, said, "Nothing, just smoke in my eyes," and went home to lie on my bed, argue with my Voices, and wonder what "Charonne's choice" meant. When I asked her the next day, she pursed her mouth up and said, "None of your impudent business, and Kaihan should keep his mouth shut."

I found out what it was at the end of the winter. Charonne died on a day she'd picked out, at the end of winter as she'd warned me, of heart failure. She'd wrapped up her affairs, given notice to her landlord, told her closer friends, and gone to bed to get it over with. She was mildly surprised I didn't object, but I said it made sense to me. I sat with her before she went to sleep, watching the flickers of spirit-fire that circled cautiously out of her reach, and said to her, "One thing before you go, Charonne."

She flapped a spotted hand at me impatiently. "I'm done. No more. Ask somebody else," and she pulled up her covers over

her face. I put my feet up on the end of her bed, and waited until her curiosity got the better of her, and she peered out at me
grumpily.

"Why does magic avoid you, make a wide circle around
you? Wherever you are, there is a gap, an eddy, a hole."

"Oh. I thought you were going to ask how old I was, or why
I'm going to die in half an hour, or the difference between pow-
dered lungfish brain and puppy shit, or something important
like that." She snickered and coughed, pleased with herself. I
waited. "Magic doesn't avoid me. I avoid magic. I told you before; once I was more than half a witch, but I gave it up for real
life a long time ago." She blinked her almost translucent eyes
sleepily. "Anything else before I finally get some rest? I won't
say I'll miss you, because I'll be dead and won't care."

"Kaihan told me he couldn't make 'Charonne's choice.'
What choice is that?"

"What I just told you, silly girl. I gave up magic. I finished
what I had to do, and chose to live, grow old, and die like a human being. Now let me get on with it." Her wrinkled mouth was
turning downward, so I let her be. "You are such a silly girl,
you'll never make a good herb-wife anyway," she mumbled,
and closed her eyes for good. Half an hour later, rushes of spirit-
fire tumbled through the walls and swept over her like yarn
around a ball. Her body lay there glowing to my spirit eyes in
the evening-darkened room.

"Zhe sselenter, devaghtel ains ye Charonne," I said to ller,
but lle didn't even reply. I got up and left ller alone to mourn,
telling the knacker on my way home that he could collect
Charonne's body whenever he wanted.

A week later nobody mentioned her anymore, and her old
spot on the street was "Lisane's pitch" in casual conversation.
I heard no news of Kaihan. The winter rains poured down on
the tarp over my space, I cured those of my customers who
bothered to take their medicine, and the uninterrupted stream
of ller poured over and through me down Tinker's Hand to the
Beast, now that Charonne's protective shield was gone. My

Voices sang harmonies with the melodies that formed in the river of magic, and sometimes I thought I heard answering voices in the rushing swirl of ller. But though I lived my days in an ocean of magic, I had never felt more real. I thought maybe this was real life, the thing that normal people lived. I hoped I was doing it right.

CHAPTER TEN

In Which I Don't
Mind My Own Business

I lasted until spring. Once the novelty wore off, I tired fast of squatting on my haunches on Tinker's Hand, dispensing muddy-looking powders and murky liquids to people whose ailments could have been prevented by drinking less or taking one bed partner at a time. I tried hard, but one morning between customers I thought, what use am I? I can't do this for the rest of my life, I haven't the patience. Perhaps I had reached the limits of my maturity. I had turned twenty and therefore should have been grown-up, but I couldn't bring myself to settle down. Kaihan was right: I couldn't make Charonne's choice just yet.

I kept thinking about Kaihan striding away from me, his new white shirt flapping loose. He'd been afraid of something other than death, and he'd looked as foolish as I'd ever seen the man. He must have bought the shirt to celebrate losing his rings, for if he'd been a mage as long as Charonne said, he'd worn only black for centuries. He hadn't come back, for Asterman's Wood had swallowed him whole like the others, pretty new shirt and all.

I supposed it was really none of my business, as he had so clearly told me, but I had the uneasy feeling I should do something about it; I didn't know what and I didn't know why. My dreams at night mixed truth and wishes, and Kaihan walked in and out of them enigmatically. Sometimes I struggled to distinguish what they were telling me, and sometimes I simply refused to care.

This cold spring morning, with the wind high and damp, I

felt restless and worried, and the torrent of magic that poured
past me day and night was fragile and itchy llerself. I stared up
at the sky and realized I'd always depended on passing disasters to make up my mind for me. It was time I stopped waiting
for things to happen to me and started making things happen.
As another customer, uncomfortable and stone-faced, stopped
before me, I made an appointment with myself to discuss my
plans that night.

The evening was even colder, with hovering moisture
crawling under my clothes, when I entered the Cat and Apple
and found my stool. Sometimes between rushes of patrons
Bielo came and sat on another stool next to me, silently study-
ing me when he thought I wasn't looking. I realized I might
have to find another place to eat dinner soon, for something I'd
done the week before had made him take an interest in me, and
I didn't think he was looking for another working girl. There
had been an argument about the star patterns in the spring sky,
and I'd let it slip that I thought they were just faraway suns.
Everybody laughed at that, except Bielo for once.

Bielo wasn't the only one who was behaving oddly. All the
patrons of the tavern seemed to be in a scummy mood tonight,
though I marked most of that to the change in the weather.
Twice arguments broke out in the other end of the room, and
from the conversation I could hear, most people were doing
nothing but complaining. After dark, Wizard Tilloke's servant
Argevin came in with another mage-servant, a clean but sullen
young woman I'd seen with him before. She had a bruise on
her face tonight, and Argevin looked more than usually truculent. I hadn't been able to get any gossip out of him for months;
he just stared through me. I was heartily tired of him and half
the people in Frog Belly by now.

Argevin shoved my stool deliberately as he came around to
his table. Taken by surprise, I nearly fell off, and grabbed at his
jacket for support. He wrenched away from me, so I ended up
slipping the rest of the way to the floor. He bent and lifted an
arm to slap me, and I cringed. Bielo said curtly from two tables

over, "Hold, Argevin." Argevin lifted a sour eyebrow at him but straightened and turned away from me.

He addressed Bielo instead. "I'm sick of the scum that hangs around this tavern. Especially this trull. Why do you defend her? She's a fool for mages, Bielo. Look at her, wearing those sham rings. She should be ashamed to show herself, wearing those things in this town of all towns, but I've never seen her without them." His companion frowned in agreement, looking at me sideways.

Bielo said, "She does no harm, man."

"She's always pestering me for stories about the mages, like they were bedtime tales. If I have to work all day for miserable backstabbing spell-weavers who give me half my pay in bruises, I don't want to think about them at night. My nerves are so shot I'm thinking of going to the Gutter Pony from now on, Bielo." Funny, he sounded really anguished. I hadn't realized I'd annoyed him as much as that.

Bielo said nothing, just looked at me in amused and embarrassed apology. Apparently, the accusations were fair. I said, "I'm sorry, Argevin. I didn't realize I was bothering you. I'll stop," but Argevin glared at Bielo, grabbed his companion by the arm, and left when he realized Bielo wasn't going to throw me out. "I'm sorry, Bielo," I said. So much for my quiet evening spent considering my future.

"Lisane, I know you don't care for conjurors any more than Argevin. Why do you have to wear those stupid rings?" said Bielo reasonably. "They'll only get you into more trouble. Come on, I'll get a cutter and do it for you if you like." Bielo's eyes glinted with his usual humor and more than his usual sharpness. I looked toward the door and realized that there were too many people between me and it. I wouldn't be able to escape if I ran, and I didn't like to think what would happen if someone tried to remove my chokers without the blessings of the Beast.

"You can try to take them off if you like," I said reasonably to Bielo. "I'd be happy to lose them." That was truthful enough, and might buy me some time.

As he turned to get his tools from behind the bar, I turned to run, but Onion Susa the water-broker, someone I'd thought a friend, grabbed my arms. I tried to pull her hands off me, my cheeks burning, but the tavern crowd had closed around us to watch the argument. Some there were friendly, but mostly they were just well-oiled idiots looking for amusement. It looked like I didn't have any alternatives. The rings weren't going to come off and I didn't want to be in the middle of this spring-struck mob with a sharp object near my throat when they discovered their mistake and my true nature.

So, as Bielo pushed his way back through the grinning audience with a rasp and a small latch-bladed jeweler's bow-saw, I said in a whisper, "Keff est perenteren, keff ge lesieg." They all roared, and Susa gasped with laughter, "She thinks she can even cast spells." Bielo by his expression was not so amused, and meanwhile a slender rope of faint green ller shot in through the roof, looping and twining like the lash of a whip around the body and arms of each person in the room, even the spectators still sitting, though none of them knew it yet. Then Bielo tried to come at me with his tools, and found he couldn't move, and the rest of the room erupted into shouting and fruitless struggle. I mouthed "sorry" at Bielo through the noise and snaked my way between the wriggling bodies to the door, nearly losing my dress and some of my skin in the process for they were standing too close together. I looked back. Bielo's face was completely alien, stiff and strained, and he was shouting nonsense at me. I left at a run to get my things before they could come after me. I had not asked the spell to last very long.

I didn't have much to take. I upended Charonne's box into my battered pack, put Simon's ring, my mirror, and the miniature into my waist-pouch, and threw my cape over me. When I emerged onto Tinker's Hand Street, I said farewell to the fountain of ller, and was shocked to hear ller sing me glad farewell and good journey in turn, very clearly as if in words. Lle had never spoken directly to me before in ller natural state.

I looked to the right, to the left, and found that my Voices already knew where I was going. Seven Snakes, the mage quarter, was all the way on the other side of the city to the northeast. It wasn't walled or guarded by anything but its foul reputation. All right, I'd go there first and look around, though I doubted I'd find much help there. I hadn't found yet what use the mages were in this world anyway. Magic to them was only subject for research or useful as weapon in war against each other. But I thought I might stir up some trouble and see what happened—in other words, look up Detter.

If I lived through that, I'd head up the Dicedipper Road. Why not? It was spring, another passing disaster had ripped me from my temporary respectability, and no matter what Kaihan had said, I was free to do what I wanted. And what I wanted to do was find him and curse him out for treating me the way he had. Even if I had to rescue him first to do it.

I walked briskly north in the dark through Frog Belly, more slowly through the workshops of Sunken Trunk, and cut east across the merchant's quarter. I didn't fit in here at all, either, and more than one window slammed shut as I passed by wishing I was anywhere else. It was too cold, my stomach hurt, and my knees were developing some kind of weary ache. Who did I think I was anyway? Maybe I could just hide in the country, and this wasn't such a good idea after all.

Before I knew it and before I could convince myself to give up, I was on the street that led into Seven Snakes from the south. I didn't feel any different crossing the invisible line. I just continued to be quite sure I wanted to be somewhere else doing something else. There was nobody on the street, nobody at all. The houses got bigger and bigger as I penetrated into the quarter. I was floating in cold blue shadow, all alone in the still, tidy, mage-lit streets. There were pale yellow lights in occasional windows, but though I was near the heart of the quarter, still I had encountered no one. It was late, but not that late. Did they all lie down and die when night came? Where were the mages?

Some of the buildings toward the center of the quarter reminded me of the school, all gussied up with useless ornaments, but occasionally I came across a treasure glowing dimly by the mage-light. One such was tiled from top to bottom, each tile a masterpiece, and each tile fitting perfectly into the whole. Another building seemed to soar eagerly like light into the dark sky, all arches and flying buttresses in cream-colored limestone. Each of these edifices followed a different taste, and I supposed belonged to the elder Wizards, members of Council.

I finally came into a gem of a square, a jeweled blooming garden full of lush trees and flowers, lit by a single flaming torch. Four buildings surrounded the square, four small castles. My Voices shared a joke about the spiritual significance of four, but I ignored them. One building was white, one was black, one was red, and one was every color I knew and some new ones. The multicolored edifice rose from a bulbous base to a point that glittered and sparkled in the fading sunlight, an impudent spire of no apparent function, too narrow to contain stairs. The base of that building was fenced in with curlicues and vines of wrought iron. The whole thing was in appalling taste, and exuded grotesque exuberance and good humor. Facing it across the square was the red structure, a massive lowering hulk like a giant's chiseled brick. That building was preposterously threatening and grim, a court or a prison.

I was standing next to the black palace, which reminded me of the Master's chair in Council. Made of a dull and porous stone, it grew from its base like a black flower, all its lines like those of living things. In the shuddering light of the torch, I could see that projecting windows swelled above my head like nodes on a stem, delicate and succulent, but there were no lights inside. The high-arched front doors hung open, abandoned. I put my hand on the wall, and it was warm and smooth and curved. I could almost feel its life. Nothing so obviously strong should feel so fragile. I leaned against it for a moment, then took a look across the square at the white building.

I didn't like it. It was restrained and clean, form following function, very explicit, very reasonable. It had doors and windows, and I felt that every door was where it was supposed to be and every window placed to let in precisely the right amount of light. It exuded clarity, purity, spiritual peace, and enlightenment. It was the smuggest building I'd ever seen. I crossed the tiny square and stood facing the peaceful white palace. The front door, set beneath a front arch, was white as well, a sedate marble panel with a white porcelain handle, and light gleamed invitingly through its windows. I turned the handle out of curiosity, the door opened, and so I walked in, though I hadn't planned to.

There wasn't anybody here, either, it seemed. It was annoying, though I had no right to quibble. My nerves, my heart, and my mind were geared up for confrontation, but apparently it was an off day for my visit. The entry hall was high-ceilinged and dignified, almost dowdy. Two stairs went up either side, bent back, and joined in the middle with self-important precision. I started toward the stairs, and heard a far-off clatter of metal. There was a kitchen somewhere here, and somebody in it working. How mundane. I took off my shoes, and padded up the stairs. I reached the top, and was looking down a long hall that led from the top when behind me the front door crashed open. My chest collapsed suddenly in panic. I dropped down on the waxed wooden floor and peered down from the landing.

A long-nosed, scholarly-looking, white-ringed gentleman Wizard with a cold glint in his eye was striding in, his white robes whirling around his body, and behind him Detter loped imperturbably, his face as sweet as ever. Detter's new neckring was a divine speckled blue like a bird's egg. He was carrying a satchel full of books over his shoulder that looked like it outweighed him, and he managed adroitly to avoid being hit by the backswing of the door. The two of them headed at the same furious pace for the stairs, and I scrambled in a panic down the hall in my stocking feet, devoutly invoking the Mother's intercession. I turned a corner, almost slipped and fell, and jerked open the first door I found. Behind me I could hear footsteps. I slid into the dim room, shut the door behind me, and looked around for a hiding place. It was a storage room or library of some sort with freestanding shelves full of books, objects, and stacks of paper. A pallid light came from the solitary window, half-blocked by a shelf. I stood with my back to the door, listening in complete paralysis to the approaching footsteps. They turned the same corner I had, came closer, but then continued past my door.

I took a breath and realized it was my first in at least a minute. My breathing sounded harsh in my ears, and the door behind me creaked as I shifted my weight. I froze again, but a door slammed indifferently farther down the hall. I cautiously took a step into the room. Mage-lights flared into life in sconces on the far wall, and I dove behind a shelf, barking my shin painfully. I felt like a fool when I realized the lights were lit by a captive spell reacting to my movement.

I got my breathing back under control and settled my back against the wall. I could hear muffled voices through it, one acrimonious and acid, one deferential and sweet. A door slammed open again, and the irritated voice shouted, "Then go get the right one!" I heard footsteps again.

The door to the library opened, and Detter came in, cradling a crystal globe. Behind him, the older man swept up and stood impatiently in the doorway. Detter was as sure of foot as ever, and visually musical in his movements. He passed down a range of shelves silently, carefully placed the lucid ball on a velvet stand, and more casually plucked a smaller one from the shelf below. Out of my field of sight, it slipped somehow through his fingers and smashed into the unforgiving floor, spraying glittering curved fragments out like a fountain. One must have passed his face, for a bleeding line appeared on his cheek.

"Clumsy, useless troll," came a tense and despairing voice from the doorway. The long-nosed one was half bent over, holding on to the jamb. If this was Gelmas, I was sorry for him. Detter had obviously been having his way with him. "How can such an oaf be so conceited and so inept at one and the same time?" Detter smiled at him beatifically, standing in the midst of the strewn shards. The Wizard straightened in fury and took an involuntary step toward him, then halted, his head back as if resisting a physical drag.

Detter said gently and impersonally, "I'm sorry I broke it, master. I'll try to be more careful next time." The older man surrendered to his fury and lunged at him, his hand raised to strike, and in the same instant Detter's face, indeed his whole body, seemed to rise triumphantly toward the falling hand. The Wizard checked himself with an effort and a disgusted noise; Detter's face fell and his eyes opened. Then the man hit him after all, as hard as he could, across his scored cheek.

"Clean it up, you calculating third-rate lump of gutter filth," the man said with contemptuous intensity. Except for the blotch where he was struck and the smear of blood, Detter's face was white, but he gracefully bent down and began to gather the shards together with his bare hands, ignoring the frost-thin curbed edges that made beads of blood appear on his palms. Light tinkling sounds were the only noise in the room aside from my back creaking in the effort not to move. His master stood over him, now looking cold, bored, and disdainful. I wondered whether Detter would get the reaction he wanted, or whether his master could stand to watch him systematically mangle his hands forever.

Detter straightened, holding a scintillating mound of broken glass firmly in his cupped hands. A thin line of blood promptly ran down his wrist into his sleeve. He looked the Wizard straight in the face, his blue eyes reflecting yellow in the lamplight, and held out his hands as if presenting a precious gift. For a moment they stayed like that, both of them pale, the young mage solemn, the older mage's lips drawn helplessly back, and then the Wizard swung around and swept out as if summoned. The front door crashed again below us. Detter let his hands open slowly, and most of the glass fell out to the floor; two pieces lightly embedded in the skin of one hand still jutted out, trembling with the intensity of his pulse. He let his head fall back luxuriously, smiling.

"I see you've finally found your proper home," I said dryly from behind the shelf. Detter whirled toward me, banging his elbow on the first crystal globe, knocking it off its stand and catching it in midair in one motion. As I suspected, he hadn't let the other one drop by accident. I stood up and stepped out into the light.

"Lisane, what are you doing here?" he said in a low voice. He was flushed now, perhaps embarrassed, but he looked me up and down with an attempt at elegant distaste. "I thought you were dead. I thought the Beast killed you off. What do you want?" He put the globe back and dusted the glass from his hands.

I shook out my rusty black skirt and sat on a towering pile of papers. "Was that charade all part of your long-term plan, Detter? For the apprentice to drive the master mad? You've got him well tenderized, I see. You should have him frothing, gibbering, and cutting your throat any day now."

His face was red. "This is my home, and you are not welcome here," he said. "You're dirty besides, and you've chosen to plant your stinking rump on some very important papers. Tell me what you want or get out of here, before I lose my temper." I laughed at him, for he was as disconcerted as I'd ever seen him. For Detter to resort to simple insult and open threat!

"I stopped by to say hello, Detter. I'm going off north on an expedition to rescue Kaihan from the mage-eater, with no plan, no backing, no equipment, and no companions. I thought I'd admire your face once more before I left, since I'm so fond of you. The Beast didn't kill me off, but I sure saw a lot of blood left behind from your visit. Was it yours or his?"

"I'm going to call Gelmas," he said, and turned to the door.

"Oh, good," I said. "I'm dying to meet him." He stopped.

"I never thought you would actually do that," he said. "All right. I'll do as you wish. What in the name of the septic weasel that spat you out do you want?" He sat down on a stack of books. Now I was off balance.

"You never thought I would do what?" I said blankly.

"Oh, don't play coy. You know, and I know, that you could take Gelmas, me, and any twelve other mages in spell-battle and plait your hair at the same time. Get on with it." He looked complacent and satisfied now.

"What are you talking about, Detter? I stopped by to say hello, and to tell you I was going north to find Kaihan. I'm not threatening you."

We sat and stared at each other. Detter said, "You're not threatening me." I shook my head. "You're going north to find Kaihan, and you stopped by to say hello." I nodded. "You don't want *anything* from me. What is *wrong* with you?"

"Well, actually, I did want one thing," I said cautiously.

"You may name your firstborn spawn after me, but I refuse to be the father, lizard lady," he said, flapping his hand at me contemptuously.

"I wanted to find out if you knew anything about what's been taking the mages in Asterman's Forest. I'm not up on Council affairs, since my source dried up."

Detter absently sucked on his mustache. I was afraid he was getting an idea, for his face changed, lighting from within with joy. "Take me with you," he said suddenly. "I'll tell you whatever you want, but you have to take me with you. I'll lend you a horse if you want. I don't believe it, what a wonderful idea, I'll run away with a street woman. It will infuriate Gelmas, absolutely demolish him. He thinks I adore him and want to be just like him, could you tell? He thinks he's corrupting me, the old toad."

"Detter, what happened to your master plan? I thought you were going to be the perfect apprentice."

"As far as Gelmas is concerned, I *am* the perfect apprentice," he said gently, as if I were short an upper story. "And he's the perfect master for me, a man who plays the hardest, highest game, and the next Master of Council if Kaihan's really gone. This will just teach him not to take me for granted."

"He's not dead," I said, and realized I knew that much. The Master was still alive somewhere, or I would have dreamed him dead. "You can come with me if you really want to, Detter, but I won't play your games."

"I don't think you can, sweetness. You're not equipped for it," he said lazily, rubbing his hands up and down his thighs suggestively like the golden boy I'd first seen in the school. Detter was all cheered up now. I couldn't imagine why I'd thought seeing him was such a good idea.

In the small hours of the morning, as our horses plodded jingling through the empty streets of Seven Snakes, I said to Detter, "Doesn't anybody ever go outside here?" There was no one to see us leave, as there had been no one to watch me arrive, and Detter had conducted our departure as if we were leaving on a Council-sanctioned errand in the middle of the day. He must have been very confident Gelmas wouldn't be back that night.

Detter looked at me through his lashes. It wouldn't be long before he stopped bothering to answer me at all, no matter what he had promised. "Hardly anybody actually lives in Seven Snakes, frogling, and the servants go home at night. You really haven't been in touch, have you? There's only Council members here, their apprentices, and a few working Magicians. Everyone else is teaching, traveling, holding down outstations, and finding wild Talents." I stared around me at the strange buildings. Most of them vacant, then, like the mostly empty school. Once this world must have seethed with mages. We left the mage quarter unchallenged.

Detter rode easily, long legs embracing the horse's flanks, his hands relaxed on the reins. He had adapted quickly to Sassevin luxury. I, on the other hand, rode like a getterhopp clutching a half-hatched shuss-lizard egg, slipping, sliding, hanging on for grim life, my skirt straining over the saddle neck and my calves sticking out. Back home when I traveled by palanquin, it had looked so much easier than it was to ride a horse. A horse is entirely too far off the ground. I would rather be closer to the point of impact if I fell.

The weather had changed. It was a good time for riding, the stars out sharp, hard, and high in the heart-stopping spring night at the northern edge of the city. No wind blew now, and sounds echoed close and still in the streets, in a foretelling of the intimacy of the summer.

Something caught my eye. "When your master knows you are gone, what will he do?" I asked.

The faintly lit figure beside me answered, "He won't do much for days, because he won't believe my message. Then he'll explode. I hope the pompous old gas-bag has a heart attack."

He apparently believed it. But a dimly not-glowing ward-spell gathering over his oblivious head had not been there a moment ago. His master knew he had left already, and was not stopping him, just keeping track of him. The sight made me sad for that baffling, furious disgusted man in the library. Unlike slim velvet Kaihan, Gelmas looked like my idea of a proper Wizard. He wore white robes, collected magical manuscripts, used crystal balls. His deep-set hood-lidded eyes and contemptuous mouth belonged with the sonorous chants they used for magic here. If he were senior Council, he must be controlled and canny. Along had come baby-blond Deteras Anhand in his precious speckled blue ring, and the powerful mage took his measure. He knew, but Detter didn't, that their war was being fought between equals.

We rode out of the city in the dark and kept on going until the horses were weary and we ourselves beyond weariness, riding into the light and the cold dew. As I expected, we didn't talk much, and Detter knew less than I'd hoped about the mage-eater, little more than I already knew myself, just the names of those who were lost and how long they had been gone. He wouldn't tell me what had happened between him and the Beast, just showed his teeth and smacked his lips unpleasantly. There was news of Simon, from three months ago; he was handfasted to a highborn woman, tall and homely, independently wealthy, notorious for her strong-mindedness, and three years older than he. Detter told me this gleefully, assuming that I would immediately go into a jealous decline, but I was pleased to hear it. Simon seemed very far away and long ago.

The horses were gentle saints, brown-eyed and soft-mouthed. They needed little guidance or urging, and by the third day I began to think I might like riding, though I still found them unpredictable. My mount's name was Amlik, and when I was grooming him at the end of the third day he unexpectedly knocked the length of his immense head flat against my side, landing me splat on my hip in the grass. Detter, done with his horse and sprawled on a moss bank, laughed at me, but after a couple of days' travel, Detter no longer looked so refined or elegant himself—or so driven, for that matter. The ward-spell still hovered over him, though, a reminder that Gelmas had not surrendered him.

At the end of two weeks' leisurely travel, we inquired and found we were within a day's ride of the forest, and that the local people went in and out of the wood with impunity. Whatever lurked in there, it took only mages. I still had no idea of any strategy, and Detter didn't care, for he said he was turning back as soon as we sighted the forest.

His masquerade ended even before that, for as we tethered the horses that evening, I heard hoofbeats on the road. Over a rise came a blue-eyed, sweating white horse, and on it was Gelmas, looking like a close relative of the plague. He reined up when he saw us. The horse's sides heaved in and out, and its eyes showed too much white.

Detter, absolutely glowing with suppressed satisfaction, looked up at him calmly. Gelmas addressed him, ignoring me completely. "I look for you to fulfill your bond, and find instead you have pranced off without permission in the company of what is either Kaihan's infamous nightmare or a diseased trollop with horrible taste in jewelry. Is this mere rebellious- ness, major delusion, or just another instance of your ineffable ineptitude?" Detter looked innocently aside at me through his lashes as if to savor the description, but stayed silent, turning back to his horse.

Gelmas waited for Detter to answer his rhetorical challenge. He was quite a sight in the sunset, proud and cruel with long strong bones and paper-thin skin, all dressed in white on the half-dead white beast. I said, "You'd better see to your horse, it's nearly foundered," and pulled off Amlik's sweaty blanket.

Gelmas continued to pretend I wasn't there, watching Detter move off, then slid off his heaving horse, his back contemptu- ously to me, and began unsaddling it. It was like having two Detters to deal with at once, the group of us grooming our mounts as if each was alone in the wilderness.

I got my comb and my mirror out of my pack and rebraided my hair while the two of them ignored each other. I really was an awful sight, my black dress gray with dust. I had slit the skirt up the middle so I could ride better, and the edges were unrav- eling. I took off my battered shoes, wiggled my toes, and set about building a fire as dusk settled. Gelmas sat himself down regally, still not looking at me, still silent. I began to understand that I should be afraid, for Gelmas was jockeying his forces for battle.

We ate in silence, equidistant around the flames. I noticed that Gelmas' long fingers flickered in the shape of a summon- ing as they lay in his lap; I spoke languidly to the glimmer of spirit-fire that started to form, it dissolved, and I realized Gel- mas thought I had Detter under spell. He didn't understand Detter any better than Detter understood him, then. Gelmas looked at me under his brows, moved his lips in the beginning of a chant; I requested the approaching hesitant tendrils of plasm to leave. He straightened his back and glared, beginning to speak; I hastily interrupted, convincing a shell of ller to form a space all around us free from other spells. Gelmas closed his mouth as he realized how strong the spell was. Neither of us had yet spoken above a mutter, but Detter was beginning to look sulky. I finished off my melted cheese and licked my fingers.

Gelmas sat staring into the flames. Detter unrolled his blankets and prepared for sleep. Soon his breathing was regular, his sweet lips relaxed, one broad hand pillowed beneath his face. I didn't believe him. I began cleaning my toenails with my knife, with great concentration, hoping to irritate Gelmas into some action. Gelmas did not move, but stared silently at the campfire. It was as relaxed in appearance as a catfight in the making. Any moment the squalling, spitting, and scratching might start, or then again it might not.

I put the knife away and hugged my knees. I didn't have anything left to pretend to do, but I knew if I were the first one to speak, he would have me on the defensive. The fire hissed, and glowing honeycomb coals shone hotly beneath the burning branches, while all around us, like a soap bubble about to pop, evanescent spirals chased each other in the spell I'd set, humming inaudibly as they swirled. Magic is so happy, I thought, gentle, willing to oblige if asked, pleased to be of service, even to harsh, irascible old mages like Gelmas and grubby, half-baked bawds like myself.

Gelmas got to his feet finally, but I didn't. The fire was dying. I resisted the urge to feed it just for something to do. He stood there, waiting or thinking or preparing a spell, I didn't know what, but then he spoke aloud to me. His voice made me leap inside, so bemused had I become with the fire and the silence. "Why steal this particular apprentice, witch? If it was only to call me out in battle, you could have done it much more easily. I admit I am puzzled. I could name you ten other young Magicians you might find more suitable."

I said to the fire, grinning inside, "You have made an incorrect assumption. I did not steal your apprentice." He'd made the first move. Apparently he was reasonable enough to want to negotiate, in spite of his bad temper. There was a long silence. The fire really was getting too low now, so I got up and put some more wood on it. The blaze leapt up again soon. Gelmas folded himself down on the ground again, staring at me over the flames. That was better. I relented enough to look him in the face, and regretted it immediately, for it gave him license to look me over in a way that made my skin crawl, but now I could not look away. Round two to him.

He tired of his game when I did not waver, and with a flicker of his deep eyelids dismissed me, looking away. Detter was truly asleep now, his face slack, his closed eyes fluttering. We were both watching him dream, and Gelmas said, "You must be a powerful mage indeed, to make this wretched mongrel obey you." His voice was amused and almost tender, but I did not let it deceive me. He thought to flatter and distract me.

"I haven't spelled him," I said. "And he wouldn't bother to obey me unspelled if I had a knife to his groin and a rope round his neck. He came away with me only because it amused him to. I didn't try to prevent him." Gelmas did not look convinced. I was getting a cramp in my calf, and massaged it wearily. My face was drying up in the heat of the fire. "We have traveled like this before, when we made our Quest, in company together but not as friends. You of all people must know how impossible he is."

Gelmas looked sharply over his nose at me. "You claim to have earned your rings honestly from the Beast, then."

"I make no claims, and would prefer I didn't have to wear the rattling things," I said impatiently. "I have no desire to play Wizard."

But he did not believe my disavowal. He couldn't, now that I confessed to Power, the Talent to use it, and the blessing of the Beast. He couldn't imagine someone having those gifts and not finding them valuable. "Kaihan has made the claims for you. Are you true life, or did he conjure you for some purpose of his own? If so, now that he has gone, there can be no value in your existence. Why do you linger on, plaguing the world like an unsatisfied ghost?"

"Kaihan didn't make me. And he's not gone. He may be a twisted schemer, but he's the only mage out of all of you who doesn't see me as a threat." I was horrified, for my throat was swelling in a wave of sentimental self-pity at the thought of Kaihan dead. I must be more tired than I thought. I found I was either going to have to wipe my eyes or sit there with tear tracks on my grimy face.

Luckily, Gelmas looked not in the least swayed by my histrionics, or I would have broken down completely. He said grimly, "Then this is yet another of these hasty, ill-thought rescue trips? A woman and a lackwit against strength that has vanquished ten of our most powerful mages. I begin to believe that you are human, woman, for you are a fool. You should have simply killed Detter and yourself in Sassevin and saved yourselves and me this useless trip."

I wiped my nose on my ragged sleeve and smiled blearily at him, saying, "Detter wasn't planning to help. He was just coming along for the ride. It's too bad you're not human enough yourself to stay and help me, because I'm going to get Kaihan out one way or another." I knew how insane it sounded, but it was the truth.

His head went back as if I suddenly smelled bad. "I am here only to reclaim my assistant; he may be deranged and deficient but at least he's trained. If you have any brains, you will let us leave."

"Leave, then, old man. You can have Detter if he wants to come with you, but I have nothing to say about that. He probably will go back with you. You're made for each other. Suspicious, vicious, and warped. Go ahead and leave." I stood up and shook out my blankets. "Now, if you want. I'm tired, I'm going to sleep. If you want to argue with me, can we do it in the morning?" He didn't move. I turned away for a minute, and when I looked back he was futilely trying to form another spell.

"Keff ge lesieg!" I said sharply, and the shell of ller collapsed around him like a net. Encircled with veins of crawling not-light, he sat glaring at me, immobilized. I sat down again facing him, and rubbed my puffy eyes with the heels of both hands. "Please," I said. "I'm tired. I want to go to sleep. Can we fight in the morning?" By his expression, he refused to surrender, so I asked ller to make him sleep, and soon was drifting to sleep myself. Detter slumbered, mouth open, between us, the picture of peace and contentment. It must have been relaxing to have no conscience.

CHAPTER ELEVEN

In Which I Don't
Perform Any Magic

I couldn't move, and I couldn't open my eyes. Not my favorite way to wake up, no matter how fine the morning. "Thank you for the restful night," came Gelmas' voice bitingly from above me. Detter must have awakened early and released his master from his enchanted sleep, the petty, perverted little wretch. What for? It ran against his grain to curry favor. He probably just awoke, saw an opportunity to cause trouble, and couldn't resist.

Gelmas' foot nudged my side ungently. "I know you're awake, you needn't sham. If you tell me the truth now, I'll cause you no pain. Why did you steal my apprentice? What did you need him for?" I heard an annoyed intake of breath from farther away.

"She didn't steal me, you old fool, I left of my own will. You think too well of yourself. Didn't it occur to you I might not want to stay with you?"

"Be silent when you've nothing to say, boy. You'd never have gone off with this simpleton witch on your own. She's not devious enough to please you; you'd be weeping of boredom if you were in your right mind. She's just got raw Power. I have to find out what's going on. Go tend to the horses." Detter wheeled and strode off, far too agreeably, I thought.

I worked my mouth and found Gelmas had not sealed it, but as I opened my lips, he said, "If you start to conjure, I will break your teeth. What were you going to use Detter for, bait?" I started to laugh, and a hand came out of nowhere and belted

184

me in the face. "I warn you, child, I'm going to enjoy this," he said austerely, and then I heard a sudden jingle of tack and the sound of hoofbeats going away.

The Wizard inhaled sharply, started to rise, then roughly lifted my head and gagged me with some kind of sweaty cloth, knotting it tightly behind my head. He ran from me and I heard another horse, but soon all the sounds faded into the distance. I was left behind snug in my blankets with my eyes closed, the picture of lazy serenity, and feeling like an utter idiot. I didn't know if something had scared them away, but as nothing came to eat me I realized Detter must have decided to demonstrate his independence by running away.

As the sun rose further, I began to feel even more uncomfortable. I was too hot, my bladder was full, and I had lost sensation where I lay on one arm. I was too distracted and upset to think clearly, but I could hear a background hum, peaceful and soporific, like bees in summer. Finally, when I stopped berating myself long enough to listen, I realized it was lle singing gently as lle held me immobile. Fascinated, I listened harder and began to make out a tune, and lyrics that weren't exactly in words. I forgot my discomfort.

It was a song about comfort, and pleasure and obedience; it celebrated closeness, and was thankful for direction. It pleaded for intercession, forlornly questioned fate, asked for forgiveness. I was enthralled. It sounded like lle was singing a hymn.

Lle noticed I was paying attention, and lle was grateful. I couldn't move my mouth to speak to ller, but while I framed a tentative wish in my mind, lle loosed ller bonds and whirled away. I sat up awkwardly, opening my eyes, and watched ller dance about me and slowly dissipate. I gazed up at the fading vestiges of the spirit-fire that had held me, and wondered at the way lle seemed to know and speak to me, more and more as lle had on Mennenkaltenei. Was all of ller connected, from world to world, as some said? My arm began to wake up, all flaming prickles, so I put theology out of mind, eased the gag out of my mouth, and tended to my mistreated body.

Amlik grazed nearby, still tethered from the night before, and possessions lay strewn about the cinders of the campfire. Detter had acted like an ass, but it was all the better for me. Gelmas really did seem to value him, though I couldn't see why. I was better off with both of them out of my hair.

Ten minutes later, I was up on Amlik and back on my way to the forest. The sun was warm, the road was smooth, and the sprouting baby leaves were throwing a green haze over the countryside. It was earlier in the day than I'd thought, not yet noon. I must not have lain bound as long as I'd thought.

The road came to a ford, and almost by chance I noticed a mess of splattered drying muddy hoofprints on the far side of the stream as Amlik lumbered out of the water. With a queasy sense of foreboding I realized Detter's escape had led toward the mage-eating forest. I kicked Amlik to a trot, but soon admitted neither he nor I would last long at that rate. I let him slow to a walk. There was no sane way I could overtake Detter or his master before they got to the forest. Maybe they would stop, maybe Gelmas would catch Detter, maybe they would veer off. I don't know why I didn't think they could take care of themselves, or why I should care, but I was even more worried than I'd been before Simon and Detter fell down the mountain, and this time I didn't have any rope.

Abruptly I reined the horse in. I was going at it all wrong, I thought. This was a problem in magic, and I was trying to outrun it mechanically. Why not take advantage of my Power for my own purposes, for once? I settled my thoughts, opened my mind and my mouth, and a cataract of elemental power poured eagerly over me before I could speak. Lle came with a rush and a glad roar, understanding what I wanted before I could get the words out. I found myself and my frantic horse surging into the air like froth on a breaking wave. As we soared giddily forward, high above the ground like a misshapen, improbable bird, I lunged forward to get my hands over Amlik's eyes; it helped, but not enough. The horse was shuddering, whinnying, and flailing his legs. I felt like doing the same.

It was awe-inspiring, what we were doing. We were a good thirty feet off the ground and racing along like a tidal wave or a grass fire. The only thing suspending us in the air was the massive curling crest of a wave of elemental fire, invisibly flaming in crimson and orange. The ground raced past so fast we must have covered a good twenty miles in the time it took me to remember to breathe. Then, slowly, we drifted down, skimming the surface of the turf and gradually slowing, until Amlik's dangling hoofs touched delicately down. We came to a halt, and Amlik, head down, sweated and breathed as if he'd run the whole way. Lle circled with me as ller center, rising and roaring like a tornado, and dissipated back into the sky with a whoosh. I was exhilarated and terrified, feeling the same way I had as a child being blanket-tossed.

I looked around, and found myself perhaps a hundred feet from the first trees of a dark, thick forest starting above me on the hill. Detter and Gelmas, still mounted, were almost beneath the branches of one immense dark tree, arguing. Improbable as it seemed, they hadn't noticed my apocalyptic arrival; I supposed it hadn't been visible or audible to them. I approached cautiously, for I could see that a miasma of ller filled the forest like water in a bowl of pebbles, reaching out all along the border between grassland and tree to the very tips of the tender leaves. Lle seethed and simmered, dark, sad, confined, and malevolent, and Detter was within arm's reach of it. As I came into hearing range, Detter was shaking his head sadly, his face set and cold, while Gelmas said, "You are defeated. Admit it. If you come back with me now, you will at least have understood your limitations. That's part of growing up. Only children think in terms of pure victory, and you are no longer a child."

Detter said, "You're so blind, old man. You're so sure the woman took me against my will, you can't see the truth. *I will not* go with you." His lips were parted, and he was enjoying himself, but his restless horse sidled sideways one step, backward one step, even closer to the forest.

Gelmas said irritably, reaching out one hand for Detter's

reins, "You should know by now that inner certainty is just as easily inspired by bewitchment. Come on, grub, I'll take you back and straighten you out. There is no use in running from me."

Detter wrenched his horse's head vindictively away, and it pranced back another step. He was almost within the circumference of the straining spell, totally unaware of its nearness. "Stop trying to control me," he said, and then he saw me.

"Oh, dead gods, Lise, go away and leave me alone!" he shouted, and his restless horse backed him full into the arms of the enchantment. He stopped in midsentence, chirruped to his horse, and rode gaily, utterly enspelled, into the woods. Before Gelmas could follow, I kicked Amlik forward and around him, forcing him back as he struggled to control his offended horse.

Before he could collect himself enough to get nasty, I hissed, "Lle got Detter, whatever lle is, and lle's one step away from taking you too." He stared at me wildly, not comprehending, and I said, "The spell, idiot, the spell. The mage-eater. Get away from the forest—can't you see, fool?" But he couldn't, of course.

"If Kaihan isn't already dead, I'll kill him myself for bringing you into the world, you miserable abortion," he said, and tried to wrest his horse away from me.

I lurched forward, grabbed a handful of his robe, and said with utter sincerity, "There is one evil grandfather of a spell extending all along the edge of this forest. I don't care what you do, turn blue, just as long as you don't throw yourself in there too. I've got enough to do as it is."

He was red in the face. "You've done what you wanted with him, haven't you? Let me go, rot you," and he tried to beat me off. I fell unexpectedly off my horse, dragging him with me, and he hit the ground heavily beneath me. I found myself intimately entangled with an enraged but breathless bag of bones.

Before he could get his breath back, I gabbled a hasty incantation to hold him for a minute. I extricated myself from his legs, and turned back to look at the forest. Detter, oblivious, had gone out of sight by now. The forest trap obviously took any mage lle could get. Lle was bigger and meaner than any spell I'd seen since the Beast's. I spoke to ller, and lle didn't even quiver. Lle was massive, indifferent, answering to something far stronger than me. It was far beyond any one mage's Power to dispel. I'd been afraid of this. It was going to take something other than magic to break this spell.

I didn't have time to play any games with the Wizard, and I didn't want to think about what I was going to do, so I turned away from him and rummaged in my pack. I found the small black envelope. What had Charonne said—enough to cover a fingernail would take away a mage's abilities long enough to knife him? How long did it take to knife a mage? If the mage-eater's source were at the center of the forest, I'd have a good long way to go. I'd better take a larger dose, just in case. I tipped the spelldamp, black and feathery as mold, into my palm. There was a healthy spoonful.

Gelmas, his eyes wide and wild on me, writhed away from me on the ground. He obviously knew what I had there.

"It's not for you," I said disgustedly. "It's for me. This disgusting forest captures mages," and licked the foul stuff off my hand. It was hard to swallow, clinging to the inside of my mouth, and it tasted bitter, oily, and decayed. In fact, it tasted like long-dead animals smelled. I looked up, waited for the medicine to take effect. Gelmas was gray in the face. I said, irritably, "Don't gape," and realized I had to release him from my spell or leave him bound until I recovered. I let him go.

"What are you doing," he gasped, "killing yourself?"

"What I'm doing should be obvious to one of your discernment and intelligence," I said sarcastically. "The forest only eats mages. I have to get Detter out now, as well as Kaihan. If I'm not a mage, I can go in. So I'm taking spelldamp."

And then the dose hit. I said, "Uh," and "Uh," again, as if I'd been hit in the belly. It was like being struck blind, deaf, dumb, and sterile all at once.

I dropped the black envelope and groaned. I felt like I'd

been spun in a circle and left staggering. All around me, things were just things, just lumps with no life. Colors were flat and were only colors, sounds were crisp but tuneless, the sky was empty blue space. There was no spell in the forest, and Gelmas was a skinny old man with the stupidest look of chagrin on his face.

"Oh, Mother and Father, I just killed the world," I said in dismay. It was too awful. I wanted to dig a hole and bury myself, but the stupid old man was suddenly holding me by the arm and slapping me. I tried to stop him, and instead he started shaking me until I was forced to look at him.

"Pull yourself together. It's done now. Don't waste it," he said. Everything looked like it was made out of wax, including his pop-eyed, intense face. I almost laughed at him. He shook me again. "I was wrong. You're even more naive than I thought. You actually didn't plan to use Detter, did you?" I remembered why I'd done this incredibly foolish thing. It was worse than I'd imagined anything could be. "Oh, girl, you're worse than even Kaihan," he said. I nodded vaguely at him, and he thrust me from him roughly. "Get that fool Detter back first," he said. How nice, I thought. I'll go get Detter for him to beat up and at least somebody will be happy.

I clambered back up on Amlik, and Gelmas in his rumpled robe watched me with something like fear in his face. I turned and rode back under the trees. Nothing changed. The trees were just trees, dark damp boles and high branches, leaf mold and rotten logs. My head was empty. It was impossible to believe that a few minutes before I had been riding in the sky on a wave of joy.

I caught up with Detter in a few minutes, for he was riding slowly, blank-eyed and content. I grabbed the reins and turned his horse, but he slipped off its back and strolled in his original direction, ignoring me. So I dismounted myself, found a smooth rock, and hit him behind the ear with it. He fell to his knees, holding his head, and I hit him again. I hauled him up, staggering under his weight, and managed to lay him across his horse without rupturing myself, though it was a near thing. When I emerged from the woods, Gelmas rushed to him and got him down, cradling his head in his lap and doing something that made the blood on his scalp disappear. Astonishing, I thought. Magic really looks like magic when you can't see ller. No wonder mages take themselves so seriously.

"I guess I'll go look for Kaihan now," I said, "before this stuff wears off."

The Wizard, startled, remembered my existence. He took a deep breath, paused, and took another. "I don't know if it wears off or not. I've seen it used, twice. It's Council's ultimate punishment, and both mages killed themselves after taking it, so . . . I don't know."

"Oh. Well, then I've got all the time in the world, don't I?" It didn't seem to matter to me. I felt drained. Everything was meaningless. How did normal people navigate in the world, with all the intention taken out? I aimed my horse back at the boring trees anyway.

Behind me, Gelmas said stiffly, "Before you go." I twisted around and saw him staring up at me with his arms around his unconscious apprentice. "What are you, girl? Are you human after all?"

"Last time I looked," I said. He was silent. It took far too much work to win an argument with that man. I wished Detter joy of him.

I rode off into the idiot forest on my mindless horse on an empty day in spring. I rode alone in dark silence, though it was a sunny day filled with birdcalls, the hiss of breezes, and the steady crunch of Amlik's footfalls. I'd never known how much my perceptions were colored by the spirit that sang and flew in and through all there was, all that lived and died around me. Now I was moving in a cardboard world, shallow and sketchy, the scenery for a play. It was as if I were a character in a story-singer's tale, a shadowy puppet of the mind aping the action behind the words.

So I was a puppet in a story-song, going through the

motions. Who's singing the story, I thought tiredly. Let's get to the last verse so we can all go back to real life. At least in the songs people knew where they were going and why. Maybe this was supposed to be a funny song, and I was the goat.

Not feeling particularly amusing, I meandered generally toward the north until I came to a well-cleared trail, then followed that. After a bit, it joined a road, and by early afternoon, Amlik and I were standing looking up at a translucent castle, delicate and airy in the sun, impossibly perched like a bird in the arms of the trees, with the road passing beneath it and the sun shining through it to the ground below.

I wondered whether for the first time I was seeing an illusion as others might see it. I rode closer, unsaddled Amlik and tethered him, then walked up to take a look. It still looked real enough. I found a tree with low branches and climbed up to rap the base of the building with my knuckles. No, it was solid stone, and rough enough to scrape my skin. I couldn't see any way to get in. There were doors enough and windows, but they opened out far above the ground.

I walked underneath it, between the trunks of the supporting trees, staring up through interlaced branches at the watery image of the sun and faint body shadows moving far above me. The castle was inhabited, apparently. I came to the center of the base, and nearly walked past a crystal spiral staircase wafting delicately up to a square opening in the foundation like a trapdoor. The stair was the only part of the building that actually touched the ground. The rest was all impossibly borne on the inadequate shoulders of the trees. I put a tentative foot on the bottom step, and the entire structure rang out, singing, like a bell. I backed up in haste and hid behind a tree, but no one came to investigate. After half an hour I made up my mind to try again, and this time put my foot on the second step. This time, there was no sound. I tiptoed up the treads cautiously, holding on to the insubstantial railing, and poked my head up into the building to investigate.

Once I was inside the castle, its walls were perfectly opaque. I guessed the light of the sun was somehow routed through the castle to emerge unaffected beneath. It seemed a lot of trouble for an aesthetic effect. The entrance hall was shadowed but solid, lit by glow-lights of an eerie steady blue. I came the rest of the way up, and cautiously opened the far door. In the next room, there were more glow-lights, but they were green. Somebody had an odd taste in decoration; the color made everything look putrescent. I had seen no lights from beneath the building, either. I wondered what those moving shadows had been—birds, perhaps.

Growing bolder, I crept through the hallways, checking side doors and looking for stairs. All the rooms were furnished fancifully, like pictures from a child's book, and each was different. When I opened one door, it gave me a horrid turn to be looking into a torture room, complete with tools and equipment. The next chamber I looked into was a sprightly sitting room, its absurdly affected furniture upholstered in maroon silk, with fussy pictures of landscapes on the polka-dot papered walls. It went on like that, an endless variation of unexpected contrasts.

Finally, one narrow door I tried opened into a cramped back stair. I trudged up, peered out at the next landing, and decided to go as far up as I could. Three more floors and the stairs ended, opening out into a light and airy gallery full of plants and sculpture. Feathery arching branches nearly swept the high ceiling, vines trailed from hollows in the walls, and stone creatures peered out here and there from between the greenery. I walked along, trailing my fingers through the leaves and caressing the smooth stone sides of the carved and polished animals. Hot sunbeams slanted through the moist and dusty air, and dead leaves curled in the corners. The soporific atmosphere made me feel languid and careless, and I made more noise than I should have. I nearly walked past a lattice archway opening off the gallery, then I glanced aside and realized I saw human forms moving there in a darker room.

There was no way to hide; I was standing in the middle of the doorway, backlit by the sun. I stood frozen in indecision for an instant that felt like an hour, but as I stood, I realized that no one was paying attention to me. Were they also illusion? I couldn't make out faces, my eyes were dazzled still, but the shadowy figures were moving casually, sitting, standing, shifting about, gesturing. Something was very wrong with the picture, something besides the fact that they were ignoring me.

I stepped farther into the room and stood beside the door, waiting for my eyes to adjust. It was cooler than the gallery, a square room with a fountain in the center, stone platforms ranged around the fountain, and a darker arch-framed passageway running around the outside wall like the roofed porch in a courtyard. Low tables were scattered around with food on them, and the people occasionally selected something to eat.

Still no one acknowledged me. I realized that they didn't acknowledge each other either. Though no one collided, they walked as if they were blind or seeing something other than what lay before them. As my own eyes finally began to work, I saw that their eyes were all closed.

I had found the captives, still alive, still healthy, and still thoroughly enspelled. There were more of them than I'd expected, perhaps twenty. Half bore no rings and three of the ringless ones were women; the spell saw no distinction between recognized mages and those who had never sought the Beast. Their restless movement dizzied me, and it took me a while to pick out the man I was looking for. Kaihan was seated, relaxed and still, on a stone platform, his chin on his hand and his eyes closed. He was still wearing the white shirt I'd seen him in last, though now it was worn and stained. I wove through the pacing figures toward him.

I passed a hand casually in front of his face, if only to confirm what I already knew. He didn't move, he didn't see. I shook his shoulders gently, and his head rolled forward and back. When I was done, he was still entranced. I sat down next to him and poked him in the side. It was like poking dough. I tried to wrestle him up, and managed to get him standing, but as soon as I let go, he sat down again. Maybe I could hit him with a rock as I had hit Detter, but then I'd have to get him through the halls and down the stairs, hoping he would stay unconscious. Even if I managed to get him down to the ground, I'd still have to get him out of the forest, and still all these other mages would be captive.

This was no good at all. Everything was wrong. I hadn't thought through the consequences of giving up my Power. Here I was at the center of the enchantment, exactly where I planned to be, and I was useless as the eyes on a mole. I sat next to Kaihan, kicking my heels. At least I could rest a little while before I decided what to do. I snagged some bread and cheese from a nearby table and had a meal. Kaihan continued to meditate, oblivious of me. It was a small comfort, but comfort nevertheless, that he was still alive.

A shadow came across the blazing archway I'd entered by; someone stood there as I had. I tried to duck behind Kaihan's body, but Kaihan, like everybody else in the room, was standing and turning to face the newcomer. I slid behind the platform, sure I'd be discovered, but the man strode into the room as if everything were normal. He stood by the fountain in the center of the room and waved to the spellbound mages to be seated. They obeyed. This man must be the maker of the spell, then, though he was not marked as a mage.

He gestured, and the fountain vanished; in its place stood a jewel-encrusted throne, and sunlight haloed it from above. Fresh flower petals appeared beneath his feet, still glistening with moisture. He took his seat, and surveyed his thralls, still not seeing me. The room began to change shape weirdly, as if sleeping life was waking beneath the surface of the walls and floors. I realized that if I were still a mage myself, I would not be able to see past the magic that must be surging and boiling in this room. Somehow he was using and channeling the power of his twenty slaves.

The man's face was eager and glad as windows appeared in

the walls and the mages slid from their seats to kneel before him. He didn't look evil. In fact, he looked more like a boy than a man, someone who hadn't reached his full growth. He looked familiar to me, and I remembered my dream of the jars with heads. This man's smooth childish cheeks and innocent eyes were those of the boy in the dream. He looked passionate, visionary, and prophetic, as the ceiling rose higher above us. He was doing something he believed in, whatever it was. I began looking for something I could use as a club.

There was a heavy pottery jug on one of the tables. It was awkward, but maybe it would do. I hefted it in my hand, and walked boldly up to the man on the throne. He still didn't know I was there. I felt free to circle around him looking for the right angle, and finally poised myself behind his left ear, jug upraised, like a vengeful brewer's god. I swung as hard as I could, praying that it would work.

He fell on his face, landing full on his nose and scrabbling in panic on the floor. I stooped and hit him again, not caring if I broke his skull. The blow took effect; he collapsed limply. All around us in a vague supplicant circle the mages knelt, in hushed unison.

I grabbed hold of Kaihan's slack arms, trying to wrestle him out of the room. He came with me to begin with, but the closer we got to the door the slower he moved, until I could force him no farther. I tugged and tugged until I had to stop and catch my breath. Then, serene and sightless, he swiveled and paced back to catch his place in the circle surrounding the felled spell-master, who was starting to move again. It was worse than chasing a room full of half-swatted bugs. I grabbed up the jug and swung it again at the head of the boy. The jug shattered. Finally he lay still, and stayed there, but everything else began to come apart.

The captive mages groaned in unison, a sorrowful chorus. Two fell to their sides, backs arched, twitching. Several others simply clutched their heads, and a small hardy group, Kaihan among them, stood up and began purposefully walking away.

As they walked and as I watched, they looked as if they were striding into swampland, sinking lower somehow. I looked closer and realized they were up to their shins on the floor, which was gelatinously softening and yielding to their feet. My own legs were half sunk through the surface, like standing in the surf at the beach while the sand wears away beneath. The walls were sagging, the ceiling drooping down to us in the center, everything was turning gray, and I was afraid I was going to drown or be smothered in the disintegrating building.

Now I was up to my hips, and I felt a falling sensation. I held on to the nearest body, which turned out to be that of the renegade conjuror I'd hit. He and I both continued to sink, and the stupefied men around us were half-covered with the cloudy translucent slime everything had turned into. The ceiling drooled over the top of my head and trickled into my hair just before my nose disappeared under the surface of the floor. In the dark miasma, still clutching the unconscious mage, I sank holding my breath forlornly, faster and faster, until my feet hit something solid with a wrenching thud and I fell to my knees. I thought for a moment I'd broken both my legs, not that broken legs would matter if I suffocated to death. I lost my grip on the boy as he fell farther to the bottom, and just as I was about to surrender and gasp gray sludge into my aching lungs, my head broke the surface and I could breathe.

All around me, the building continued to dissolve and disappear, a shallow gray pool broken by the trunks of the trees and rapidly settling into the ground like water in a desert. A scattering of large lumps revealed themselves as human beings, crouching and lying on the ground, moving feebly. In a short while the dregs of the castle were gone, and there in an unsullied, sunny clearing in the forest were twenty mindless mages, an unconscious puppet-master, and myself, battered, breathless, shabby, and sweating. My horse, still tethered, placidly tore with his teeth at the undergrowth not fifty feet away.

I wavered on my feet. My head swam, my ears roared, and I

nearly fainted. I sat down and closed my eyes, wondering why I wasn't dead and not sure I wouldn't prefer to be. I put my head between my bruised knees, waiting for the feeling to go away.

Finally, I felt I could raise my head again without passing out, and to my horror saw only myself and the renegade still in the clearing. There were three men still staggering out through the trees, all three in different directions, as fast as they could force their half-useless legs. I jumped to my feet and again nearly passed out. I stood swaying in the sun, ready to throw up. I wanted to do something but I didn't know what; I didn't know which direction Kaihan had gone, and I knew I would lose him if I went the wrong way.

At my feet, there was a scratchy wheeze. The renegade turned over with an effort, then lay flaccid again, squinting his eyes painfully up at me. "What happened?" he asked weakly. "The kingdom is gone. Am I dead? Is this the afterlife?" Then he threw up on himself. He really was no more than a boy, a young man barely showing a beard. I turned him on his side with my foot so he wouldn't throw up on himself again. He began to cry like a bullied child, hopelessly and quietly. I walked over to the horse so I wouldn't have to listen to him, but as I untethered Amlik I could still hear the occasional painful gulp.

I wanted to kill him to shut him up. I sat on my horse staring into the forest, wondering where Kaihan had gone and knowing I had lost him again. At least he was alive, but if he'd been himself he would have known me and stayed, not run off into the forest like the rest of them. And I was a mage no longer. I couldn't send a search spell after him or call him back to me. It would start to get dark soon, too.

I turned back to the renegade, walking the horse back to loom over him. His chest was still shaking, and he stared out in complete despair. He didn't seem to be afraid of me, just completely hopeless and incapable. I must have given him a bad injury with that last blow; like Simon on the mountain, he had no magic for the moment. I considered trying to kill him now before he recovered, but I didn't have the stomach for it. Besides, in my true dream I hadn't killed him, though there was no sense in the dream for me.

I got down, and kicked and shoved him until he hauled himself up onto the horse. I got up before him, kicked Amlik's sides, and set off back down the road. I'd let Detter and Gelmas figure out what to do with him. Maybe they would kill him for me. Maybe they could find Kaihan for me, too. I couldn't do much for myself or anyone else at this point, and my dress was an absolute mess as well. The monster-boy-mage clung to Amlik's mane, shaking, looking as if he'd never ridden a horse before.

It was a long ride back to the edge of the forest. I took the path, turning right when I emerged from the woods, to skirt the trees and find Detter and Gelmas again. It occurred to me to wonder if they had waited for me. The light was low, the grass and trees glowed in the dusk, and I could see a few stars shining through the mother-of-pearl sky when I finally came on a low campfire, two men relaxed beside it, two horses placidly grazing. It was so hard to see through the dusk. I realized that if I no longer could see ller, nights would be even darker. No wonder normal people preferred to travel in the day.

"Well, if it isn't what the dog wouldn't eat," said Detter, healthier than ever. "What's this grimy piece of fluff?" he said as the boy slid off the horse and fell weakly to his knees.

"This is what set the mage-eater spell," I said. The boy stared up at me glassily. He hadn't said anything since the clearing, though his shoulders shook occasionally in stifled sobs. I didn't know if it was the head injury or if his mind just wasn't too well assembled in the first place, but he was not my idea of a malevolent necromancer.

Gelmas still sat by the fire. I lifted the boy to his feet, walked him over to where he could get some warmth, and sat him down. Gelmas looked him over without interest, while I wrapped him in a blanket. The boy sat huddled, shivering. "I don't understand you," said Gelmas. "Why haven't you killed him? Where are the lost mages? Are they all dead?"

"You're never happy, are you?" I said to the long-nosed old bastard, and flopped myself down on the grass. Detter came over and sat beside his master, not quite touching shoulders.

"Oh no, Master Gelmas is always very happy, aren't you, Master?" said Detter with his eyes very wide and innocent. An even sourer expression settled over Gelmas' face, but he didn't move away. Detter sat tucked up into himself, self-contained, smug. Although I'd explained it all to them in my head on the way back, I realized now that they probably weren't going to believe my reasons, my dreams, or my Voices.

"The spell is dissolved. The lost mages are alive but mindless, walking in every possible direction at great speed in the forest, and I don't know whether they're going to recover. The only one who stayed behind when I broke the enchantment was this one. I hit him pretty hard in the head. He's harmless for the moment." I paused. Gelmas was barely visible in the firelight, but what I could see of him was unreceptive. "What do the Finders usually do with renegades?" I asked.

"Take them to the Beast and throw them in unprepared," said Gelmas. "Sometimes they live."

"Oh." I was very tired, my head hurt, and I had little hope, but I went on anyway. "Can I ask two favors of you?" He didn't respond, but I went ahead anyway. "Could you take this creature back to the Beast for me, that's one. The other is, would you cast me a search spell so I can find Kaihan? I'm worried he'll hurt himself."

Gelmas said coldly, "Ask me no favors." Beside him, Detter lifted his eyes to me luxuriously. "It is not my place to give ear to your petitions, woman. You should not be asking favors of anybody. That is a serious error of judgment." Detter turned to him, puzzled. "I have been listening to my apprentice attempt to slander you for hours, and from that I have gleaned a few things. In everything you have faced, whether disabled or no, you have managed to tear success out of a situation where any mage of sense and ability would lie down and die, and you try to cut your own head off between times. You disgust me. You have obviously been very badly trained, and I am glad I had nothing to do with your upbringing, or you would have been killed a long time ago." Now I was puzzled too. He took a breath, and continued, "If you *command* me, I will take this pathetic slug back to the Beast, I will provide you with a search spell, and I am afraid I must also insist on providing you with some different clothing. You are about to fall out of that disintegrating rag, and while I am immune to your dubious charms, I am sure you wouldn't want to frighten any unwitting passersby with the appalling sight of your flesh."

Detter said disgustedly, "You're raving, man," and Gelmas said, "Shut up, hotheaded thug."

I wiped my nose on the sleeve of the maligned dress. The halfwit renegade mage was weeping again, silently, inattentive. I said, "I am really very hungry. Is there anything to eat?" Gelmas chanted a change spell, and my clothes shimmered and changed on my body. I was now wearing something suitable for my purposes: trousers, high boots, and a warm tunic. Detter got up and walked away. Gelmas tossed me a hunk of meat, and I promptly got grease on my new clothes. Gelmas looked away, pursing his lips, and Detter smiled in the background.

That night I lay looking up; the sky arched empty of life above me. I had always liked to watch the little wisps of spirit plasma chasing each other in the heavens, appearing and disappearing, swirling and changing faint colors, but lle wasn't there for me that night. Maybe the night sky dance would never be there again. I wasn't sure I could sleep. The pathetic, horrible renegade mage lay rolled in a blanket on his side, with a sleep spell on him, both hands nestled under his battered head. Detter and Gelmas, to my foolish surprise, were lying indistinctly intertwined, in intent mutual motion, over at the edge of the circle of light from the fire. Well, at least somebody was getting something out of the situation. I turned over on my face, listened to the solitary dry sounds of wind and leaf, and eventually went to sleep.

CHAPTER TWELVE

In Which I Don't
Please the Master

When I caught up with him, I'd been eagerly examining every wayfarer I passed for three solid days, shading my eyes to peer at figures barely visible in the distance, even turning around to look behind in case I'd missed Kaihan somehow. The road west of the forest was a well-traveled one, and Amlik was getting nervous at my constant twisting and turning. Maybe Gelmas' spell had been intended only to take me far away, not to find Kaihan.

Then I came upon my quarry.

I was even with Kaihan before I recognized him. He smiled with all his teeth at me. There was no recognition behind those flat black eyes, only limitless greed. He darted suddenly at Amlik's head, grabbing for the reins, and as I pulled the startled horse away, he ran after, planning I don't know what. Once I was out of reach, though, he stood blinking at me, and I circled around him while he followed me with his eyes like a trapped and dangerous bear. He had a feral grin on his face. He looked healthy but somehow goblinlike, shrunken.

"Kaihan," I said cautiously, but he sprinted toward me suddenly, and I wheeled the horse and cantered away. He chased me for a moment, then stood in the middle of the road, his chest heaving, his face somehow flattened and animallike.

I reined up and said, "Master Kaihan," entreatingly; he took another step toward me; I backed the horse away and he stopped; when I halted, he moved again. We repeated the dance for a while, until I felt like a beast trainer with a large untamed tiger, or like the taunting Lady Fair in the Knife Dance. It was pathetic and frightening, and he never answered me.

Finally, he gave up, lost interest, and sat down in the middle of the road, looking like a broken machine. I drank from my waterskin, then threw it to him. He was thirsty, but it took too long for him to unplug it; his hands were as nimble as ever but he wasn't quite sure of the concept. When he had done drinking, he let the skin fall to the ground, and the rest of the contents dribbled out, making a small circle of mud on the road. He sat and stared at me, his black eyes bright and empty, and I stared back, feeling just as empty.

Though when in full possession of his powers he'd infuriated and disturbed me, now, staring at this husk, I found I'd suffered a loss much bigger than I could have imagined. What had I hoped to find? Someone who would make it all better, someone like Simon's long-lost father who'd tell me what to do? This was as bad as when I found the Adepts had taken my name from me, and just as puzzling. I couldn't put words to what I felt, but it was painful.

Eventually, he rose and kept walking, leaving the waterskin lying shriveled in the dirt. I followed the slim, shabby figure, hoping to wear him out or wait until he fell asleep. Other people on the road, seeing him approach, seemed to understand something was wrong with him and kept carefully away. He was staying alive by no obvious means, for he didn't seem to have the sense to eat. His time in Asterman's Wood had taken his mind away, perhaps for good. Gelmas had said that persuading Council to organize a rescue expedition for the lost mages would take a while, so I was Kaihan's guardian for the time being, and must figure out what to do.

Toward the end of the day, he sat abruptly down by the side of the road, rubbed his face, lay down, and curled up into a ball. I sat and watched him for a time until I was sure he was going to sleep, then retreated farther down the road to make my own camp. I turned it over in my mind, and decided to try sneaking up on him in his sleep. That way, I might bind him and take him back to Sassevin, where presumably the Council might consent to care for him. I didn't feel afraid at the prospect, more mournful, like I did at butchering time back home when last year's lambs were this year's mutton and the King was due to die. It wasn't as if we were going to kill Kaihan, I told myself firmly, just keep him from hurting himself.

When it was dark and the birds were finally quiet, I cautiously rose to my feet and started back down the road with my rope slung around my shoulders. The stars were blocked out by cloud, and there were no dwellings nearby, so I could barely see in the ller-bereft murk of the night. Once I nearly turned my ankle, and twice I strayed noisily off the road into thick underbrush, flailing and staggering. If my quarry were in command of his normal mind, he would have been long gone by the time I reached him. Instead, by the sound of his quiet snoring when I came near, he slept peacefully.

Taking a long breath, I readied the rope in my shaking hands, crept forward silently. Then I stepped full on one of his legs, tripped extravagantly, and fell on top of him. There was a roar of rage, wordless and furious, from Kaihan's throat, and a strangled grunt from me. I frantically untangled myself from the rope and from the man and tried to roll away, but a hand caught me, and I found myself in the middle of a random maelstrom of limbs and blows. Strong hands gripped and shook me, and I screamed, "Please, no, Kaihan." They relaxed slightly at the unexpected sound of my voice and I ripped myself free, feeling the fingernails tear my skin as I pulled. I crawled away as fast as I could. It almost wasn't fast enough, for something nearly caught my foot before I got free. My plan obviously had defects.

I heard scuffling noises off to my left, Kaihan casting about for his attacker, and I turned myself around, trying to find the road by sound. It was motherless dark and I had lost my rope. Then the scuffling ceased, and a deep voice, slightly slurred, sent a muddy wave of shock through my viscera. "Who it is?" Kaihan said, "Who it is? Who?" I took a step forward involuntarily, feeling my throat close. It was horrible to know he could speak after all. The scuffling sounded again, nearer, and suddenly a hand brushed my ankle and grabbed at me. I leaped with a yelp, and ran in the other direction, finding the road by accident with my face when I tripped in the ditch.

In the distance, the deep voice said again, "Who is?" I limped back up the road over the rise to my camp, while I heard the occasional question fade into the distance. It sounded like Kaihan was staying put, sending his garbled queries randomly into the darkness.

I finally found my blankets by the dim coals of my banked campfire. I sat shivering, and swallowing to keep from crying, for a long time. Kaihan was mixed in my head with the image of the Father-God, aggressive, angry, foolish, out of control, terribly sad, and utterly foreign to me. That we'd needed to resort to the hostile dance on the road, the hard struggle in the dark, made me want to throw up. I didn't like the mindless animal he'd become; I was angry that the self-aware, amused, restrained man had been swallowed up as if he had never existed. I didn't think I would have made a very good Kalten after all, if I was so easily disconcerted, but I knew that by now. I didn't make a very good anything, I thought, laid myself down to sleep, and passed imperceptibly into a true dream, in forced and garish colors.

Kaihan, Detter, Gelmas, and I were sitting on the ground with our backs to each other, triply guarding the rabbit-cheeked boy, who stood in our midst. My arms were pulled almost straight back in their sockets, my hands in the boy's hands, and so also were Detter's and Kaihan's. I noticed now other mages, their arms extended behind them, backed up to our seated knot and took their places between us, the renegade mage taking each offered hand and adding it to his grasp, which kept getting harsher and stronger and tighter on my own fingers. He grew taller, and the ring of seated mages surrounding him expanded and began to circle around him like a human maypole with human ribbons, until we were all flying in a circle around him, our arms stretched almost past bearing, and getting longer and longer.

We began to enter the clear blue sky as if it were a sea, swinging through blueness and dipping up, surfacing only to breathe. The blue became thicker and harder, and our spinning bodies battered through it. It glowed, glared blue, and I realized it was no longer the innocent sky, but the blue spirit-fire of the Enforcers, filled with knives and needles, ripping, tearing, burning. One by one, more mages joined the ring, falling in and dissolving into the wheel, and then more came, merchants and sailors and elderly ladies, until there were thousands, hundreds of thousands.

Suddenly Kaihan, still beside me, began to slip away from the wheel. I screamed, the first sound of the dream, and as his arms lost their grip, I somehow hooked my legs around him, holding him safe but dangling, twisting, spinning in the air. While he clung to my waist with desperate hands, his extended body tore a gaping hole through the blue fire, sliced it into fluttering shreds. He looked up at me with his black eyes, calm as ever and smiling, and I said to him as if we were not reeling and spinning madly through space, "I will not let you go this time." My legs began to slip, and the boy's hands tightened on mine brutally until I passed out of the dream with the pain. It was a harsh, fragmented dream, like someone shouting up the stairs.

When I got up in the morning, I felt like the gold-grain finder on harvest day, excited and anxious. I never knew how a true dream would affect me, and I couldn't interpret this one, but it made me feel good. I broke my fast, and went to find Kaihan. He was sitting still where we'd struggled the night before, with his arms around his knees, warily waiting for his assailant to return. There was an ugly scrape on his face, and his shirt was torn, but something else seemed different about him.

As I cautiously approached him, he spoke first. "I have nothing left worth stealing. You are wasting your time." He could speak clearly now. One layer of his mind had healed, though his memory had not returned. Perhaps the fight of the night before had hastened his recovery.

"I'm not a thief," I said. "You've been ill. I'm trying to take you home."

He was bitterly amused. "Do you often attack sick people in the dark? I assure you, if I had not been completely healthy, I could not have resisted you so well last night. Whatever it is you want of me, I do not have it. I beg you to leave me alone."

I grinned at him. "No. I'm not letting you out of my sight." He stood, offended and impatient, and started walking west again. I nudged Amlik after him, feeling like a disobedient younger sister trailing after her big brother. Kaihan even walked in a different way than the day before. Then, he had been an aggressive animal; today, he was without question a man, though not the man I knew. I didn't like this particular man much better than the animal he'd been, though I was less sorry for him now.

The next day, Kaihan, growing more articulate and more irritated by the hour, tried everything he could think of to lose me. He threw stones, ran off the road, shouted at me, tried to enlist the aid of passersby, attempted to frighten the horse, and made speeches. I listened to the speeches, avoided the stones, and ignored the rest. At night I offered him some food and a blanket, which he first refused and then took ungraciously when I left them in the road. I withdrew a good way and set up my own camp, but half an hour later, as I sat hugging my knees and missing my Voices, he stepped into the firelight with the blanket rolled under his arm.

"Since I cannot lose you, I will use you," he said, and slept near the warmth of the fire that night.

The next morning I woke early, before he did. Kaihan was neatly wrapped in his borrowed blanket, his hands tucked up under his chin, an exquisitely drawn picture. The sideways morning light caught one sculptured ear and then spilled over his cheekbone, but the rest of his face was shadowed, the sparse feathers of his lashes, the hard flared nose, the wide firm mouth no more relaxed and no less aware in sleep than it was when he was awake. As I lay there, my head propped on my elbow, allowed for the first time to stare at him unhindered, I realized guiltily that I thought him beautiful, that I had thought him beautiful when I was dragged in to see him in his study at school, and every time I'd encountered him after.

I didn't know precisely why I felt guilty about it. After all, in this world I was free to admire whatever man I wanted. Why couldn't I look at the Master if it gave me pleasure? But it was an embarrassed pleasure, nonetheless.

Of course, to the Lisane, the child who'd been raised to be a public oracle, queen, and breeder, even his apparent age was ancient to me, let alone the centuries he claimed. If I had been installed the year before, my partners for the next twenty years would all have been young men, boys in their early twenties, the only age idealistic enough to sacrifice itself for one year's glory. So the forty or fifty years Kaihan appeared to own seemed terribly old, and the two hundred or more he claimed was unimaginable.

Yet it was undeniable that I had been overwhelmed by his presence every time we met. I was fascinated by him, he passed through my thoughts constantly, and yet I denied him. Well, here I was lying on the hard ground, having followed him into the wilderness on a wild chance and the whim of my Voices to find him, and there he was, asleep and mindless as an infant instead of the old, hard, powerful lord he was. Now that I knew how I felt, I wanted to get up and leave him now before I could make myself a bigger fool than I already was, but I dared not leave him until he had recovered.

I stole one more self-indulgent look at him, running my eyes up the long line of his legs under the blanket, the elegant curve of his rib cage, over the raised shoulder, and ran smack into the cold gaze of his now open eyes. He had woken up while I was mooning over him.

"I see I cannot escape your attentions, Lisane," he said flatly, and I froze at the change in his voice and face. "I take it you came after me, after I told you not to?" He had changed again in the night. He was no longer the irritated, amnesiac, middle-aged man being harried for no reason by a juvenile vigilante. Now he was the Master again, and the frigid blaze in his eyes reduced my musings of the moment before to a stupid fantasy.

"You didn't come back," I said. It already sounded lame enough to me; the powerful leader of mages hadn't returned to let me know he was all right, so I'd taken it on myself to chase after him into the countryside.

"What vagrant brainstorm made you decide to herd me back like a stolen sheep?" Kaihan continued. "Didn't you have anything more valuable to do with your time than to waste it playing catch-up after one useless old man among many? You would have better used your energy attending to your own business, not in an uninvited, dragged-out, inept rescue of one solitary captive. What did you hope to prove? I expected better of you."

"Oh, you're welcome, I'm sure, you rat-faced, bug-headed, sister-splitting tree frog," I said venomously, shoving my hair out of my face, kicking my blankets aside, and standing up. I stamped past him, resisted kicking him in the side, and grabbed Amlik's bridle.

"If you felt you had to tag along after me, you could at least have cast a spell to keep me from wandering, or have you forsworn the use of magic even when it would be ordinary common sense?"

"You sound just like Gelmas," I said, throwing Amlik's saddle over him. "Is that part of the requirement for being a Wizard?" I was so angry my head hurt, and my mind was incoherent. I didn't feel like explaining anything to such a wrongheaded lout. I wanted to leave. He was obviously back to his old pigheaded self. He didn't need me. I could leave now if I wanted to. I bent over, cinched Amlik's belly-strap, and started to loose his tether.

From behind, Kaihan grabbed me, turned me around, and said, "Don't you run from me. Are you a complete idiot? What possessed you to do such a stupid thing?" His face was inches from mine, and I hated every arrogant scrap of it.

I kicked his shins as hard as I could. He exclaimed in anger, but he didn't let me go, so I screamed at him, "Yes. I'm a complete idiot. I should have left you there. Let go of me, you worthless old bag of wind." At that, he did let go of me, his eyes burning. I turned and vaulted up on Amlik, then realized I hadn't finished untethering him. Kaihan contemptuously loosed the line, tossed the end back up to me, stood back, and let me go. I rode away, back in the direction of Sassevin, without my pack or my blanket, knowing I'd been a fool all along. When I got out of range, I put my head on Amlik's stolid neck and began weeping in great gulping sobs, angry, shamed, and devastated. I didn't want to live on the same planet as that horrible man. I began, for the first time since I'd landed on this world, to wonder if I might make myself another ship to leave it. Then I remembered I had no more magic. I kept riding.

In the late afternoon, grim and growing tired, thirsty, hungry, having long since regretted my flight, I was still riding. Amlin tossed his massive head from time to time, annoyed and sweaty, poor mutt. It wasn't his fault. I leaned forward and rubbed his coarse and glossy forelock and rested my head a moment on his neck. His sweat-stained hide smelled like sea air and shoe leather. As soon as he felt my weight on his neck, he stopped walking and dropped his head to search for grass, almost tipping me over. Just as I had pulled myself together and decided to keep going, someone cleared his throat not two paces away, and I jerked up my head to see Kaihan standing there. I looked wildly around but found no sign of another horse; he must have enchanted his feet to come so far, so fast.

"I am sorry," he said. "May I apologize for my behavior this morning?" He looked as if he found me, and the entire situation, funny. I was stern and still by an effort of will, though my belly was hollow and I knew my eyes must be purple.

"No harm done. I lost my temper, too," I said, meaning it to sound gracious and forgiving. It sounded sad and silly instead.

"You certainly did," he said, and laughed unexpectedly, his face creasing up in startled warmth. I couldn't bear it, and must have looked as dismayed as I felt, for he took a step backward and put his hands behind him. "May I accompany you?" he asked politely. "I think our paths lie together."

I wretchedly nodded my head, and shook Amlik's reins to stir him forward again, but Kaihan stopped me. "Perhaps you should rest awhile," he said. "You have ridden far. Let me help you down." I let the reins slip from my fingers, and Kaihan helped me from my horse, help I didn't want but needed, and then settled me under a tree while he went to catch dinner. He behaved impeccably, like a well-trained servant, which made me feel even more the fool.

I leaned my back against the tree and looked up. The sky was barely visible through the unfolded leaves; early summer had welled up and flowed over the country while I was charging around saving people who shouted at me and thought me funny. The air was almost warm, and smelled of the white flowers that come just at the break of summer, all dusty pollen and heart of honey. I took out my comb from the pack Kaihan had graciously restored to me, tugged my tangled hair straight, and rebraided my hair tightly. If nothing else, at least my hair would be under my control. I rummaged for my mirror, and regarded my face intently. It was even grubbier than usual, thinner, and very sulky, but the eyes were liquid green, the skin was clear, and the hair was neat, black, and shiny. Somewhat reassured, I started to put it back and was startled to find Kaihan watching me.

He said only, "Would you care to eat?" and offered me his arm. I didn't want to take it, but I did. I was never going to be able to stand being near the man. His voice sliced through air like a knife through a grape, his figure cut a fluid, subtle silhouette, and even in a stained peasant shirt with a scrape on his face he looked as commanding as he had when he sat on the black throne.

As we sat down to eat, I looked through the corner of my eyes at him, at the corded neck, at the wafer-thin gap between his shirt's open neck and the firm skin of his chest, and thought, if you were anyone else in the world, I'd know exactly what to do with you, but you are Master Kaihan, and I'm lost.

After the sun set, I sat staring in the fire, trying not to think. Kaihan had said nothing more to me. A wind in the distance sighed, and I turned my head to one side to look into the night. As my eyes adjusted to the dark, I realized with surprise that the world had begun to be alive in my eyes again. In and of each leaf, each trunk, each weed, and the air itself, lle was glowing, swirling, and living dimly. "I can see," I said softly. "I can see again."

"You were blind?" said Kaihan, looking up under his brows at me. He had been staring at his hands for half an hour.

I opened my mouth and found there was nothing I could say. I didn't want him to know what I'd done for him. He would only get angrier. "It's nothing," I mumbled. He looked back at his hands again.

"I was very rude to you this morning, and I had no right," he said painfully, as if the admission embarrassed him. Mother and Father, what a lovely voice.

"You apologized already. I said to forget it."

"I'm afraid I must ask you. How was I freed? You did free me, did you not, or was someone else responsible?"

"I did it," I said, grudgingly.

"How did you do it?" he asked. "Were the others there freed as well, or was I the only one?"

"The others are all free, but they're scattered across the hills. If you're worried about the renegade, I sent him back to Sassevin with Gelmas and Detter."

"It was Gelmas who aided you?" he said quickly, looking relieved but puzzled. "He is the last I should have expected. What did you do to make him help you?"

"He didn't do anything at all until afterward," I said hotly, still burning with the injustice of it. "That idiot Detter insisted on running away with me to annoy Gelmas, and Gelmas chased after us to bring him back. Neither one of them was any help, and Detter even managed to get himself caught in the spell as well." I stopped, reminding myself suddenly that I was not going to explain myself.

"Then how *did* you do it, lady mage?" he asked insistently. "I am counted the most Powerful Wizard in the world, and my strongest shield spell wilted against that enchantment in an instant. I was taken as if I had no defenses at all."

"Then maybe you're not the most Powerful in the world after all," I said snidely, and regretted it in an instant. "No, I'm sorry, I didn't mean that. It had nothing to do with Power at all—in fact, just the opposite." Then I shut my jaw. I'd gone too far, I could see. The black eyes glittered at me angrily, a dawning realization arriving.

"What did you do, woman? What did you do to yourself?" The veneer of politeness had vanished. He was about to start lecturing me again, I could tell.

"You have no right to speak that way to me," I said. "I did what I had to do, and it's done. Take it as it is."

He drew breath to speak, and then paused, looked instead at his hands, and bitterly said, "I have gone to absurd lengths to ensure you a place in the fellowship of mages, at great risk to my own reputation, I might add, and you have rewarded my efforts by systematically sabotaging yourself. You have maimed yourself in some way, haven't you?"

"Whatever you have done for me, or done to me, I am not your property," I hissed at him. "I'd be better off if I had stayed in the forest starving—at least I wouldn't be jerked from disaster to calamity by your endless plots and plans. I didn't maim myself, if you must know. I just took spelldamp." My admission seemed to leave him unmoved. He sat like a statue, still staring down at his hands.

"It seems to be wearing off now," I finished lamely. He didn't answer. I turned back to the night and watched what blurry traces of spirit I could make out, fuming.

It was so reassuring to see ller again, even if my not-sight was still blurry and faint, that it took me a while to realize that what I saw of ller was agitated, frenzied. I was beginning to hear something, too. What I thought the wind was the foggy howling of many spirit voices. I strained my mind's ears, tried to make out the distant statements, and when lle realized I was trying to reach ller, I was suddenly drowned in ller.

It was like the day Gelmas had bound me, but this time the song was aimed directly at me. Lle knew exactly where I was, and was trying to sing, or more precisely shout, in my ear. I could almost make out words, thoughts, ideas. There was something about return, recapitulation; something about danger—I tried and tried to make it out, but it wasn't working. Kaihan was standing, saying, "Do you need help?" and I held my hand up sharply for silence. Lle wailed about me, swirling and swinging in loops. I was supposed to do something, supposed to finish something, I didn't know what.

"Ye essertver, lle benk, ye essertver," I pleaded, and abruptly found myself awake in the midst of a true dream. I was a hundred miles tall, and I stood straddle-legged above Sassevin looking down through the world to the other side. High above the mountains at the center of the Lesser Shore, there was a hole, a blackness, an absence, circling the world toward me and descending. It was a cancer on the world. It would consume everything, kill everything. All life was dying already. Fear was rising like hot air all about me, dancing and shaking, saying Death, Death, Pain, and I said all right, all right, let me go, let me go, I understand. The dream dissolved in a spiral around me and I found myself staring into Kaihan's concerned face.

"Whose spell was that?" he asked, and I answered, "Nobody's. Free the horse, we'll have to leave him behind. We're going back to Sassevin now. The Enforcers are landing on this world, and their ship is killing the magic." I started kicking dirt over the campfire as Kaihan ran to untether Amlik. When he returned, I grabbed his hand. Without any warning, a force that felt like all the ectoplasm in the world formed a canted whirlpool with us at the center, sucking us up into the cringing sky so fast my skin sagged. We shot southeast toward Sassevin as if flung from a sling.

CHAPTER THIRTEEN

In Which I Don't
Know What I'm Doing

Kaihan looked exhilarated, his body arching like a diver's, his mouth half-open and his glittering inlaid eyes staring into infinity. I couldn't stand looking at him, so I mostly watched the convulsing stripes of luminiferous ether that were acting in concert to shove us home, and listened to the chaotic roar of the wind, thinking worriedly about something odd.

I had just had a true dream. Of that there was no doubt. But I'd been shoved into it by a frightened thunderstorm of spirit-fire trying to tell me something. I'd always thought my dreams were direct extensions of myself to the future, aided by that part of the Goddess that lived in me, and filtered through my limited human mind. But this was more like a crude message from another part of the present, and Ile had been as terrified as if Ile were a person being tortured, instead of the bland, serene, sacrificial servitor of the gods. What was going on?

What if my dreams were instructions instead of visions, planted in my mind by the spirit-fire? I had understood that the Beast was revealed in his Room by magic, but what if he were made of magic too? Who was making whom do what here? Where were the Mother and Father in all this, or were they somewhere else entirely, paying no attention at all?

Finally I decided that whatever the spirit-fire was doing, I had never been treated badly by Iler, and I would do anything I could to protect this world from the Enforcers. Maybe later on I could sort things out.

We landed in Sassevin just before dawn, outside the building that housed the Beast's Room, and I remembered he had told me, "Remember we are bound here when the time comes." I guessed the time had come. The instant my foot touched the ground I headed for the nondescript door at a run. Kaihan staggered and fell, but as I put my hand on the door, he grabbed me and said, "What are you planning?"

"Magic is alive, and afraid, and must be free to fight," I said. "I'd undo every bound spell you mages have set since the beginning of the world if I had time, but I'll settle for the biggest one." He didn't move.

I said urgently, "This is the end of your world either way. Do you choose to sacrifice and start over, or be destroyed still clinging to your old life?" I didn't want to have to force him.

Kaihan said, "If you are sure those are the only options, then loose the Beast, for he is no longer really needed." I opened the door, and raced past the drowsing door-mage, who lifted his head wearily. Behind me, Kaihan spoke a word and the outside door fell off its hinges. The door-mage started to his feet, shouting at Kaihan.

As I reached the ebony doors, they flung open of themselves, ripping free of the jamb, and behind them the brass doors followed. It was as if magic needed only my intention to work of llerself, as if I were only along to serve as hands and will to ller desire and energy. With both sets of doors open at once, the Room was as bright as the heart of the sun, a seething, molten, essential Mind. I didn't dare stop, but plunged through to open the far doors as well. The essence of the captive Beast flayed, scalded, scraped me, turned me inside out so that the raw surfaces were lifted to the scorching heat, but when my rush carried me to the door, and it opened, I burst forth into the exit hall unmarked but without my neckrings.

The same jade-ringed Magician was there as when I came through before, asleep on a bench but awakening and rolling up to stare half-awake at me. The door shattered soundlessly into fragments, and the unbearable glare flowed out, liquid crystal, quivering flame.

I kicked the Magician off his impromptu pallet, screaming, "Run! Get out of here, fool!" He backed away, slipping and stumbling, calling "Help! Help!" as I ran past him. Outside, Kaihan was standing there watching the disintegration, the melting of his fellowship's heart and center, as if warming himself by a fire. The substance of the Beast was swelling out of the building, bowing and bending the walls.

Kaihan said, "Where now?"

Two dreams had told me to look to the puppet-master, so I said, "The renegade who captured you in the forest. I hope he's still with Gelmas." Kaihan turned and ran, and I followed. Behind us, I heard a screeching tearing sound and a loud crack, and I knew the low building that had housed the Beast was broken. Debris clattered down all over us, and streams, gouts, cataracts of ller shot past and through us, ravening, craving, clutching, but not touching us.

We pounded into Seven Snakes, past the provisioners' wagons and the mage-servants on their way into work. It was still barely dawn. I was gasping for my breath, my legs felt leaden, and sweat was burning my eyes, but Kaihan raced ahead, his legs pumping smoothly like pistons. We entered the tiny garden square at the center of the mages' enclosed quarter, and Kaihan flung himself through Gelmas' white front door, the door slamming back against the wall like thunder. I came in behind him, and stood half bent over, my chest on fire, wheezing and gasping, as he shouted in a voice like a gong, "Gelmas! I have won the wager! Gelmas!"

I wheezed, "What?" and half stood up, panting still.

Gelmas was coming down the stairs, settling his robe about his scarecrow frame. His white hair stood half on end. Waspishly he said, "Never mind that, Kaihan, some wretch has loosed the Beast," as if Kaihan's crack-of-doom reappearance among the living were entirely to be expected.

I gasped breath in, and wheezed at him, "Gelmas, where's that renegade? Do you still have him?" He spared me a glance, then jerked his head toward the top of the staircase. Detter was coming down, followed by my quarry, who paused and paled when he saw me again. He was still wan and foolish-looking, with a multicolored bangle of a mage-ring about his neck. What was I going to do with him? How could I persuade him to help? The house was filling up with a seething flood of ller, swirling and lapping about my thighs and crawling up the stairs.

Kaihan said, "The Beast is gone, Gelmas, but I have won the wager. There *is* life behind the skies and it is coming to kill us *now*." He sounded almost happy. Detter noticed his charge was dawdling, grasped him by the ear, and dragged him briskly forward.

Gelmas stopped, fastened the neck-catch of his robe, and said peevishly, "Where's your evidence, man?"

I said to Kaihan, "We've got to figure out a way to make that pasty outlaw geek up there link mages together without all of us going insane."

Kaihan said, "What?" in surprise and Detter said, "What?" in outrage. Gelmas just scowled, and said, "Who, Salki here? He's as close to useless as the tail on a pig. What are you talking about?"

"He can link mages together and somehow combine their Power and their minds. If we can get him to understand what we need and keep him from straying, we can join together—"

Detter, leaning at me and snarling, "Lise, you're such a fool!" must have inadvertently twisted Salki's ear further, for the new-minted Magician squealed in pain. Kaihan loped up the stairs past Gelmas and grasped the puppet-master by the shoulders, shaking him free of Detter.

The seething slurry of ller grew up over them like vines as Kaihan said gently to Salki, "Remember the forest and the palace?"

The young man nodded, smiling in relieved recognition, saying confidingly, "You were with me there." I could barely see them through the tangle of magic.

Gelmas said, "Will someone tell me what is happening?"

The walls were shifting and changing, slithering with spirit-fire jittering up and down around us. My Voices were yammering over the pounding of my heart. Kaihan said to Salki, "I can be with you again, and others as well—"

Detter said, "No!"

Salki nodded, placidly, trusting Kaihan, who said, "We need a larger space." They calmly proceeded down the stairs together, oblivious of the riot of power thrusting at them impotently, and walked out the front door.

"We don't have any time," I said to their backs, but they kept walking. The air, the ground, the buildings around us surged with elemental plasm, bright, hot, purposeful. We were the focus of a lens of magic. All the power in the world was forcing llerself into this tiny wedge of land.

I dithered, half-blinded, behind the two, saying, "Hurry, hurry, holy Mother, hurry," but they didn't move any faster, just walked to the square red granite building and up the wide ceremonial steps. The high rectangular door opened into a wide hall full of stone benches with a raised podium at one end. The room was bloated with magic, but Kaihan sat Salki gently down, took the young mage's head between his hands, and spoke to him in a low voice, Salki nodding earnestly all the time. I was dancing with impatience and fear, though I was deathly afraid of being swallowed up by Salki's spell. We all might end up like those ghostly people in the dark room, permanently lost in the pathetic mage's cage of a waking dream, but I remembered the tearing blue death of the Enforcers and how my mother had died. Kaihan linked one hand with Salki's, and jerked his head at me to join them. Gelmas, dragging Detter, joined the chain, to my surprise.

"Look to her for guidance," said Kaihan to Salki. "She will know. Remember to look to her." The rabbit-cheeked boy nodded one more time, looking at me doubtfully. He wasn't going to do any such thing.

It wasn't until everything was well under way that I realized something changed at that moment. At the time, it seemed per-

fectly reasonable to think of myself as five small animals running around in one human-shaped skin. Salki was the head,
Kaihan was a hand, Gelmas was another hand, Detter was a
foot, and I was the other foot. I said, "Wait a minute, wait a
minute," and squirted up the leg, while Salki ran in circles in
the skull trying to find the way out. We tangled, squeaking and
gasping, and Salki rolled and tumbled down the neck, while I
stood on my hind legs and peered out through the eyes.

I looked down at our body. The skin, whatever reality it
stood for, billowed and rippled like an unfilled hot-air balloon
in a high wind, with squirming lumps pushing out where my
partners were. We obviously needed more. This body was too
empty otherwise. I said so to Salki, and he said, "We're coming." Now I saw we were indeed. A clot of twenty or so half-
dressed mages were running to the central square, to alert the
senior Wizards that calamity had befallen the Beast. As they
entered, they came within the reach of the spectral grasp of the
body, and were gathered in, cursing and protesting for only a
moment. Suddenly I wasn't sure who the Lisane was or where
the Lisane ended.

We'd felt clumsy and hungry before. Now we began to feel
a wash of well-being as we filled out our form. It felt so good
to be whole that we almost forgot what we were doing in the
general glow. Somewhere in the mix of our mind, a ghost of
Gelmas' sardonic, acid thoughts sent out irritating sparks of
discontent, and we turned back to our task.

I turned our eyes outward, and scanned the city. There were
still more mages sleeping in the sparsely settled quarter. It was,
after all, still well before the time that normal people pried a
gummy eyelid open. Our hands reached out. Kaihan and Gelmas teased the sleepers imperceptibly in, and the feeling of
well-being flowed through us, a drugged bliss. No wonder Kaihan had been mindless when he left this meld. It must have
been like leaving the womb.

The feeling of joy as we all joined together was indescrib-
able, better than sex or a good meal, better even than thinking

a new thought. We could spend years this way, exploring. . . . I shook our head ponderously, to wake ourselves up. Every time we added more mages to our body, the euphoria nearly overwhelmed us. Some of the squirming souls that made up the whole tried to drift further into intoxication, but the rest of us struggled and screeched, shoving them into place, I thought, like a fat woman adjusting her breasts. That particular mental image was unfortunate, for it struck most of us as funny and we sniggered distractedly for a few minutes.

This wasn't working well. I shook the head again, feeling like a mouse at the reins of a rubbish cart full of rats, and plunged farther out into the world to gather more stuffing for the body. The more mages that melted into us, the more difficult it became to stay focused. It shouldn't have surprised me so; I already knew that the mages preferred argument, speculation, and dissension to action of any sort. I called out anxiously. I wasn't sure anymore where Kaihan and Gelmas were. The metaphorical hands of the imaginary body continued to harvest new minds. Suddenly I found Kaihan and Gelmas again, and acid Detter joined us snarling at Salki.

We were locked together in the center now, and the Lisane's eyes opened for a moment to see that the original five people still sat relaxed in the chamber, while others walked casually in and sat down, or paced back and forth, looking abstracted. She shut her eyes again, reassured to see they hadn't actually all dissolved together.

We, I, our body, our self, stood up gradually until we straddled Sassevin completely like the giant of my dreams. We were staggering, lurching, arms and legs elongating and shrinking, wobbling and sobbing. There were too many bright ideas winking into existence every moment to remember what we were supposed to be doing. I understood why Salki's fantasy palace had so many rooms, all so different. I purely hated mages, and shook impotent fists at them all, while our imaginary arms still stretched out toward the horizon to touch and seduce more minds. It was going to fail.

Then, outside the limits of the city, an annoyed woman was dragged into the bond. "Mages!" she said, exasperated. "Always fiddling with things they should leave alone!" Then she realized what was going on, and in an instant our luck changed. She set down her pestle and mortar, wiped her hands on her smock, and concentrated. Suddenly, we began to grow exponentially. Every village and hamlet outside of Sassevin had its herb-wife, and every herb-wife stilled her hands and joined in with us, generally with something acid to say about mages. I finally realized what herb-wives were. The mages protesting and resisting, our body shimmered and jelled into something firmer, and a terrible practicality washed over the lurching giant.

We finally remembered to look up at the sky, and saw an absurd globe spiraling half the world away, a swollen ball of leaden ugliness, shoving itself with grudging labor and sharp blue knives through the clouds. The coarse orange skin of the ship was broken at senseless intervals by hatches, portholes, access bays, and patches where the skin had worn away and been replaced by other material. All around the ship, dead waves of blue fire chopped the ller-filled air into rotting fragments that drifted and swirled like paper ash after a fire. The ship of the Enforcers was moving toward us, carrying my people and wielding death.

We could hear ller crying, sobbing, as lle died. Lle was dying in enormous clots, murdered by the movement of the ship. Hastily, with a lurch and a desperate grab, we flung our arms over the whole world, reaching for every Talent revealed and hidden on the planet, and found our body-skin stuffed like a sausage to bursting. There was only one ringed mage for every ten Talents we found. Somewhere in the part of me that still existed, I laughed in delight. No wonder there were so few mages. Council's Finders found only the incorrigible children they were meant to find; the herb-wives took the others and raised them right, teaching them to leave magic well alone. They were smiths and weavers, mothers and fathers, laboring farmers and greasy tinkers. I had fallen in with the dwindling criminal set—and Kaihan said acerbically, "Where you belonged"—when Simon took me to the school.

Still swaying slightly, we stood over Sassevin, dwarfing the mountains to the north, feeling clumsy, satiated, and bewildered. The Enforcer ship had almost reached us, was just above the air. From a warm corner somewhere, we found the strength and structure to straighten up, and there, just outside the atmosphere, the ungainly, wretched ship spun weightily, beginning to make an arc downward. The Enforcers were coming right at us, and I hadn't the least idea of how to stop them.

The end that aimed toward us, I saw, held the drive, the thing that cut with knives. It was like an axle, keeping still while all else around it revolved, but it dragged the rest of the ship with it. In the center of that axle, a dark translucent bulge stuck out like a dead cow's eye with a cracked pimple on it. That was the place where the people had marched out when they landed. I wondered if the brutish crew was staring out of that eye, bored as ever, and if twelve thousand Mennenkalts still milled mournfully in the swollen cells of the ship or if they'd been exchanged for some other set of victims. All around the ship, deadly razors of blue essence crackled, like fissures in the skin of the universe. We reached out one hand tentatively to touch the ship, but with a shrieking blast of pain, twenty of us died in the touching. The ship didn't even swerve. How could anything with a soul use such a terrible force merely to move from star to star?

Windmilling our arms, we managed to maintain our balance, and, once steadied, looked around us for answers. We saw that in addition to the magic that made up the fabric of our body, there were worms, trailers, clouds of magic coiled over and around us like snakes, and more swimming to us from everywhere, even from the guts of the planet and from the airless void above us.

We shouted, most of us wondering what we were saying, "Bel genteren, lle sesselfer, lle palkertes, lle sesselsechern," and the magic wound llerself into strands, into ropes, into a cable with a tiny loop at the end, just the right size for a human body.

The Lisane stood up suddenly, took a step forward, and started to rise up into the air. Kaihan opened his eyes, and leaping up, grabbed her feet before she got out of reach, yanking her down harshly. She tumbled with a thud to the floor, mewing and gasping in pain. Kaihan turned casually and flung himself into the air like a bird, passing up and out of the building.

One of us physically put himself into the loop, which tightened gently around his waist. The Enforcer ship revolved slowly down toward us, like a ball thrown from a long way away, spiraling in excruciating slow motion. We grabbed the multicolored, coruscating cable of ller that coiled in the air around us, pulled one immense arm back, and put all our strength into a whip-stroke that flicked the cable, with the man in the loop, straight at the starred crack in the eye at the center of the ship. Just as lle reached the ship, lle braked just enough for the man it held to fling himself unharmed at the crack, the iris hatch that led to the drive. The end of the cable itself flamed, shattered, and died under the blades of blue that, dead and mindless, flailed about the ship.

The man, who knew what all of us could know about the ship, efficiently worked the outside control of the hatch and slipped inside. We couldn't see him anymore, because we couldn't see past the skin of the ship. We stared up at the abomination. We were waiting, an imaginary giant with hands upraised, an invisible skin with thousands of souls pulsing inside it, poised for final action or for death. The Enforcer transport still continued on its implacable arc, spinning closer and closer. It seemed the ship would splash through us like a rock through still water. We could track its trajectory, a hard clean line coming straight at us.

Then the blue went away. The ship began to fall freely,

governed only by momentum and gravity, the still center suddenly revolving with the rest of it in an ungainly wobble that slewed the ship like a slowing top. Small struggling figures of men hurtled out of the central hatch, losing height and tumbling end over end. One of them was one of us.

Half of the captives aboard the ship suddenly became part of our union. They were indeed Mennenkalts, some sputtering about heresy and some just glad to be doing something, Jenneservet commenting sharply while lending a hand. We reached out one long, strong hand and grasped the powerless ship, guiding it gently in a powered fall to hilly land north of Sassevin.

Almost all our attention was on the ship, except for one shrieking, dancing, gibbering Lisane that caused us, as an afterthought, to reach out the other hand and catch the falling man in our cushioned palm. Most of us cared not at all for the individual minds that had come together to form our corporate self. Even the herb-wives were swept along into the grandeur of it all, and the rest had long since sunk beneath the surface. But the Lisane, screaming solitary in the center of the brain, wakened another mind, and Gelmas' voice, harsh and weary as a crow's, was added to the tiny dissonance.

The fallen man was still held in one immense cloud-hand. He looked around him for a moment, then ran to the edge and leaped off. Instead of falling, now he glided gently, down to the squat building far below him. We forgot his existence, forgot to bring him back in with us, engaged as we were in a desperate argument with ourself. Most of us wanted to continue our mass identity, intoxicated with the surge and flow of intention and agreement that animated us, but a very few were struggling against the tide, an angry herb-wife or two, a knife-sharpener, Detter drawling sarcastically.

Kaihan limped in the door of the hall and looked around. Every mage within walking distance had come into the chamber and was milling about among the benches. Salki, smiling, serene, stood in the midst of his enthralled subjects. The Lisane, Detter, and Gelmas were each surrounded by silent guards of mages, who moved only enough to keep them separate from Salki. Kaihan stepped into the room and began worming his way through the crowd. As he did, the Lisane opened her eyes with a tangible effort. Moving as if seeing double, extending her hands in front of her, she wriggled between two guards, then fell to all fours to scuttle away from them as they pursued her. Kaihan and the Lisane got to Salki together, the Lisane grabbing the boy by the legs and Kaihan grasping his shoulders, shouting into his ecstatic face. The other mages were plucking and pulling at them, their eyes still closed, like crabs at a carcass. Then Salki threw back his head in anguish and opened his eyes, flinging out his arms as if throwing something away.

I was on my aching knees as if praying, holding Salki's knees and staring up at Kaihan, when everything shrank back to normal. There was an appalled silence all around us. Several mages, finding themselves in the chamber with only the most tenuous and improbable memories of how they had gotten there, dashed for the door in panic. The others straightened and looked around, bewildered.

Kaihan, after imprisonment, insanity, pursuit, magical flight, destruction of the Beast, sabotage of the ship, and free fall from a crippled spaceship, was finally showing his age. His skin was flaccid, pale. He stood with eyes closed, breathing heavily, trembling, his shoulders slumped and sweat soaking darkly through his clothing. I didn't care. I wasn't sorry for him.

I said, "So you decided to play the hero again, did you?" His eyes jerked open, but he was too exhausted to move. "You decided it was all right for you to toss your life away doing something you didn't know how to do, just because you saw me doing it first? Blast your wrinkled hide, do you think you're expendable, fool? If you want to kill yourself again, kindly do it when nobody is depending on you."

Detter giggled crazily. "She'll kill you if you try to kill yourself again, Kaihan. You're warned." Gelmas casually smacked him across the face. The blond angel struck back at him like a snake, and the old man knocked him to the floor.

Kaihan was still staring at me, panting, exhausted, when the rest of the befuddled mages discovered a woman's presence in what was, apparently, Council Hall. The group had found something to focus their outrage on, and I was grabbed and flung down the steps outside, adding some juicy bruises to what was already going to be a major grape harvest. I dragged myself upright, limped to the little garden in the center of the square, and sat down on a bench. Inside the red hall voices began to rise. I figured the mages would be busy arguing for hours before they even got around to finding out what had happened, much less start thinking about what they were going to do with twelve thousand foreigners and a handful of dreary Enforcers. Not that it mattered, for they weren't nearly as important as they thought they were. Between the herb-wives, the Mennenkalts, and wayward ller, everything would probably be settled long before the mages finished shouting.

I heard footsteps. Gelmas swept up beside me and paused for a moment, his hand on the back of the bench. I was surprised he wasn't in there arguing. "Very impressive display," he said in his harsh, crowlike voice. "I hope Kaihan is properly humbled." My face reddened, and I looked down. "Who are the people held captive on that sky-ship? They seemed very strange."

"They're my people," I said. "I was on that ship myself once."

"If they're all like you, we will have serious trouble."

I shook my head. "They're not like me. I don't even know what they're really like." I sighed and shivered.

"I am going to get properly dressed and have breakfast," he said. "When you are finished moping, come tell me what we will do about these people of yours." He stalked back into the white house, his robe flapping about him. His white hair still stood on end, I noticed. Tell him what to do about my people? Moping? Senile bastard. To gehenna with them all. My feet hurt. I took off my shoes and wriggled my toes in the turf.

Somebody else's feet intruded into my field of vision. I looked up involuntarily, and Kaihan was standing there with his hands on his hips, looking at me. I squinted back at him, for the sun was shining in my eyes. "What am I to do about you?" he asked sadly.

"Why don't you just leave me alone?" I said wearily.

"If that is your wish," he said. His voice was too quiet.

I stared up at him. "It matters to you."

He walked away from me. I got hastily up and jogged after him, shouting, "Wait!" He kept walking, and started up the low smooth steps of the black building before I could grab his arm. He shook it off impatiently and strode through the open doors, as I said wretchedly, "Kaihan, please," and Detter laughed behind me. I whirled, saw the impeccable creature leaning against the side of the bench we'd just left, his face shining with pleasure.

"The ingratitude of it," he said softly. "Poor little Lisane. But you're going after the wrong man, you know. I've heard he had his troublesome parts removed a long time ago. You'd find it very frustrating."

It was finally enough. Detter had finally won. I stood white-faced, speechless with rage. His eyes widened when he realized his victory, and as I bore down on him with my fists clenched he straightened up and laughed again, amazed. I swung wildly at his belly and he grabbed my arm. I hit him in the neck with my other hand and he grabbed that arm too, and held me easily away from him, smiling merrily and holding his sleek head cocked back from my struggles. I twisted and kicked against him frantically, but he was stronger than I and held me still. I finally stopped, my face twisted in a grimace and flooded with angry tears.

"Your nose is running," he said calmly. "You're not very good at this, Lisane." Then he looked past me in surprise as a pair of stronger hands grasped and pulled me away from him. I struggled to pull free from my new assailant, who said imperiously in a voice I could feel in my bones, "If you ever touch her again, I will flay you myself."

I learned something new right then—Detter was actually afraid of at least one person in the world, for he said hastily, "She struck me first, my lord," and took one step backward.

"Is this true?" said Kaihan sternly to me like a schoolmaster.

"Yes, and if you take your hands off me I'll do it again, you flatulent old goat," I said breathlessly, but Kaihan didn't let me go.

Instead, he said to me, "Have you no pride at all, to scuffle in the gutter with every little pig who wanders by?"

I screamed at the top of my voice, wrenched free with a strength that surprised me, and stood between the two of them, panting, my fists balled, looking back and forth at them both. Then I stormed at Kaihan, who stood with his hands on his hips again, and I shoved him in the chest with the heels of my hands. He rocked, and looked disgusted, but didn't do anything, so I shoved him again. He stumbled back slightly, not resisting, looking down his nose at me like an owl. I shoved him again, started to laugh like a madwoman, and buried my face in his neck with my arms flung around him.

He snorted, his abdomen shook convulsively against me, and he started to laugh himself. Fiercely he wrapped his arms around me and rocked me back and forth, saying helplessly, "I am too old for this."

I mumbled into the neck of his shirt. He stopped moving.

"What did you say?"

I gripped him tighter and turned my head to one side to speak more clearly. "I said I hate you. I hate you, I hate you, I hate you." He freed one hand, and gently turned my head up toward his. The fathomless black eyes, with the humorous creases fanning from the corners, were only inches away from my tearstained face. I felt surrounded, enclosed, consumed by his embrace, and an exuberant and vulgar Voice chortled that Detter had been quite wrong.

"Lisane, what would you have me do?" he whispered.

I told him. Kaihan bent a little, sighing, and those lips found mine.

Detter said from somewhere, "Do you still need an audience for this performance, or can I go now?" I don't know whether he left then or later.

DEL REY® ONLINE!

The Del Rey Internet Newsletter...

A monthly electronic publication, posted on the Internet, GEnie, CompuServe, BIX, various BBSs, and the Panix gopher (gopher.panix.com). It features hype-free descriptions of books that are new in the stores, a list of our upcoming books, special announcements, a signing/reading/convention-attendance schedule for Del Rey authors, "In Depth" essays in which professionals in the field (authors, artists, designers, salespeople, etc.) talk about their jobs in science fiction, a question-and-answer section, behind-the-scenes looks at sf publishing, and more!

Internet information source!

A lot of Del Rey material is available to the Internet on our Web site and on a gopher server: all back issues and the current issue of the Del Rey Internet Newsletter, sample chapters of upcoming or current books (readable or downloadable for free), submission requirements, mail-order information, and much more. We will be adding more items of all sorts (mostly new DRINs and sample chapters) regularly. The Web site is http://www.randomhouse.com/delrey/ and the address of the gopher is gopher.panix.com

Why? We at Del Rey realize that the networks are the medium of the future. That's where you'll find us promoting our books, socializing with others in the sf field, and—most important—making contact and sharing information with sf readers.

Online editorial presence: Many of the Del Rey editors are online, on the Internet, GEnie, CompuServe, America Online, and Delphi. There is a Del Rey topic on GEnie and a Del Rey folder on America Online.

Our official e-mail address for Del Rey Books is delrey@randomhouse.com (though it sometimes takes us a while to answer).